WILDFLOWERS FROM WINTER

WILDFLOWERS FROM WINTER

A Novel

KATIE GANSHERT

WATERBROOK
PRESS

WILDFLOWERS FROM WINTER
PUBLISHED BY WATERBROOK PRESS
12265 Oracle Boulevard, Suite 200
Colorado Springs, Colorado 80921

Scriptures quotations are taken from the Holy Bible, New International Version®, NIV®. Copyright © 1973, 1978, 1984 by Biblica Inc.™ Used by permission of Zondervan. All rights reserved worldwide. www.zondervan.com.

The characters and events in this book are fictional, and any resemblance to actual persons or events is coincidental.

ISBN 978-0-307-73038-1
ISBN 978-0-307-73039-8 (electronic)

Published in the United States by WaterBrook Multnomah, an imprint of the Crown Publishing Group, a division of Random House Inc., New York.

WATERBROOK and its deer colophon are registered trademarks of Random House Inc.

Printed in the United States of America
2012—First Edition

10 9 8 7 6 5 4 3 2 1

For Ryan, my cute delivery guy turned husband.

Who knew what God had in store for us
when you delivered that first package?

Prologue

The summer I turned twelve, I tried to kill myself. At least that's what the lifeguard told the paramedics and the paramedics told the doctors and the doctors told my mother. I don't deny I swam to the bottom of the public swimming pool. I don't even deny I decided to stay there. I only defend my motives. My decision was much less about escaping this world and much more about joining another.

I think that should count for something.

When I regained consciousness, I opened my eyes to a pair of blurry faces. My mother with her perpetually pinched eyebrows, raking her teeth over swollen lips. And Grandpa Dan—with my father's face, only twenty years older. His callused grip pressed through the shoulder of my hospital gown, anchoring my body to a reality I didn't want to face, awakening my senses until I noticed stiff sheets rubbing against my toes, beeping monitors, the smell of antiseptic, and a man I didn't recognize.

He man studied me over a pair of bifocals and clicked his pen against a clipboard, jotting mysterious notes whenever I talked, or sighed, or breathed funny. His name was Dr. Nowels and he had a mustache the exact same shade as the dead mouse I found behind our trailer home the previous Easter.

After I was released from the hospital, my mom insisted I sit with him for an hour every Tuesday after school. I tried to convince her that I didn't need to see a shrink. That she was wasting her money. Or actually, Uncle Phil's money. But I sort of lost all credibility after the swimming pool fiasco.

At the start of each session, Dr. Nowels would lean back in his chair, cross one lanky leg over the other, and tap his pen against the bottom of his chin. "How do you feel today, Bethany?"

I would search for something creative to say. Something that might make his pen scratch in to a frenzy across his paper. But nothing ever came. So instead, I stared at the same spot I always stared at. His hair. Not for a single minute did I believe it was real. Throughout the entire sixty minutes, while he asked questions, I pictured walking over, grabbing a fistful and giving it a yank. I was dying to see what Dr. Nowels looked like bald.

Every time I told my mom this she'd bite her lip and ask me not to use that word—dying. Why not? I always thought it was appropriate.

Ten minutes before our time was up, Dr. Nowels would ask the same question he always asked. "Are you ready to talk about why you did it, Bethany?" It drove me nuts, the way he finished all his questions with my name.

"I don't know why, Dr. Nowels," I'd say, trying my best to imitate the annoying cadence of his voice. Sometimes he would look at me as if I'd said something profound and start scribbling while I narrowed my eyes one last time at his hairline. If it really was his hairline.

And so our sessions went. For an entire year.

Never once did I get to see Dr. Nowels without his toupee. Never once did he share what he wrote about me during all those hours. And never once did I explain why I did it.

One

Maybe it was the angle or the proximity, but Bethany Quinn had never felt so tempted to give Jeff McKinley's hairpiece a good nudge. At the very least, an innocuous brush with her elbow. It didn't help that he was waving a powdered doughnut over the sketches she had worked on for the past week, leaving a sugary dust behind. She gripped the back of his chair and looked over his shoulder. "What don't you like about them?"

He gestured with the doughnut, sliding his free fingers across one of her sketches where she'd drawn the floating ceiling tray. "It's a little elaborate."

She let go of his chair and straightened. "So?"

"I was under the impression this particular client was looking for something more...practical."

"They never said *practical*. They said *cheap*."

"Same thing."

"It's not a warehouse, Jeff. We're renovating one of downtown Chicago's most popular ballrooms. Fancy doesn't have to be expensive."

"If you want it to look good, it does." He set down the rest of the doughnut and folded his hands behind his neck. His hairline shifted higher up his forehead. "How much time before we meet with them?"

Bethany's back pocket buzzed. "We scheduled the meeting for three," she said, pulling out her cell phone. Her mother's number lit up the screen.

She furrowed her brow. Why in the world would her mother be calling at ten o'clock on a Monday? Mom knew better than to bother her at work. Bethany sent the call to voice mail, her mind rabbit-trailing to her brother David.

"Let's see what else we can come up with before then. It'd be best to give them several options to choose from, don't you think?"

Jeff's words floated in her ear, but thoughts of her brother bounced around inside her head and made it impossible to concentrate. David left for Afghanistan three weeks ago. And now her mother was calling.

"We're in no position to lose clients right now. With all this talk about downsizing, that wouldn't bode well for any of us."

Bethany nodded.

"Hey, you okay?"

"Yeah. I just… I have to take this call." Her knees wobbled as she grabbed the sketches and made the short trek to her workstation. She set them on her desk and spotted the flashing red blinker of her office phone. When the caller ID showed her mother's number, Bethany shut her eyes and sent a hopeful thought into the cosmos.

Please don't let this be about David…

She didn't believe in a loving God who listened to prayer, but sometimes she caught herself bargaining with the Universe—sort of like a bribe, only she didn't have anything to offer. She dialed voice mail and waited until Mom's worried voice filled her ear. "Bethany, it's your mother. Call me please."

Bethany pulled the phone away from her ear and glared at the receiver. That was it? No details? No hint of why she called? No, *Hey, Bethany, don't worry. This isn't about your brother*?

The ambiguity of the message tightened the muscles in Bethany's shoulders. Her mother's brevity left her with no other option but to call back. She picked up the office phone, dialed Mom's number, and fiddled with the lid on her half-empty Starbucks macchiato. The cup tipped, spilling lukewarm liquid over the mahogany desktop and soaked her sketches.

Sucking in a sharp breath, she righted the cup and swiped up her work. She tore a clump of tissue from the box near her computer and dabbed at the sheets. It was no use. The spilled coffee had turned the pristine white pages into a mottled stack of brown sogginess.

"Bethany? Is that you?"

Bethany grabbed the phone with both hands. "Mom? Why'd you call? Is it David?"

"Are you at work?"

"Where else would I be?"

"It's just that it's Monday and I didn't think—"

"Mom, tell me what's wrong. Is it David?"

A brief pause. "Oh, no. Your brother's fine."

Bethany's tension deflated. She sank onto her chair and pinched the bridge of her nose. She hated this. Worrying about her brother. Freaking out every time her phone rang. How was she supposed to cope with it for an entire year?

"It's not David. It's Robin."

Pieces of memory stirred at the sound of that name, rousing from a ten-year hibernation. Why in the world was Mom calling her at work about Robin?

"Did you hear what I said?"

"I heard you."

"Don't you want to know what's wrong?"

The question poked her stomach. Say yes, and spend the next thirty minutes listening to Mom's hysterics. Say no, and sound like a royal jerk. She didn't have time for the first, or energy for the second, so she picked up a pen and toyed with the bloated puddle creeping toward her pencil cup, the short-lived relief over David melting into a dull ache in the center of her forehead.

Silence stretched between the phone lines.

She gazed at the blueprints on her drafting board. Her boss needed specs for the River Oaks project on his desk by four o'clock, fake-haired Jeff McKinnley wanted to brainstorm "practical" ideas for the downtown ballroom, and Mom wouldn't give up until Bethany let her spill whatever news she had about Robin

"She was your best friend."

Was. Past tense.

"Every time I see her, she asks about you. If you like Chicago. How your job is going. If you're happy…"

"Of course I'm happy." The words came out too fast. Almost defensive. Bethany rubbed circles in to her throbbing temples and let a drawn-out sigh escort the inescapable question. "What's the matter with Robin?"

A throat cleared loudly behind her. She swiveled around and found her boss, his mouth curved into a frown. She hung up the phone and stood, heat creeping into her ears. Mom's news would have to wait. "Is everything okay?"

"Brainstorming session for First State at ten. Did you forget?"

Her stomach twisted. Mom's cryptic phone call had jarred her out of focus. "No, of course not. I was just on the phone with…" She fingered the blueprints on her drafting board. "Marketing about River Oaks."

Martin grunted, eying the mess on her desk.

An uncomfortable laugh bubbled past Bethany's lips. She stepped in front of him and fished a file from one of her desk drawers. "I drew up some ideas last week," she said, motioning toward the hallway. "I'm right behind you."

When she stepped into the conference room, she smoothed the front of her skirt and pushed the phone call from her conscience. Whatever problems Robin faced, she'd have to face them alone. Bethany didn't see how she could help. Robin's troubles didn't concern her. Not anymore.

Her hands shook as she unwrapped a stick of bubble-mint gum and shoved it in her mouth. She crumpled the wrapper and leaned against the hood of her Audi, ruminating over her mother's second phone call. For once Mom hadn't been exaggerating. Bethany exhaled and watched her frozen breath escape like mist into the night sky.

Cold pricked her ears as she tapped her foot against the blacktop of the Walgreens parking lot and traced the outline of the sympathy card tucked inside the small white paper bag. "Thinking of You" emblazoned the cover in a large, looping font. Stark white painted the inside. A symbol of what her friendship with Robin had become. What had she been thinking, buying it? What could she possibly write that might take up so much space when there was nothing to say?

She pulled her keys from her purse and climbed into her car. Maybe she would go to Dominic's, and when he came home from work she could unleash her guilt. Maybe she could purge the thoughts rolling through her head and regain some equilibrium. She started the engine, pulled on to the street, and forced herself to focus on the news analyst discussing the struggling economy on her XM radio.

Thirty minutes later, Bethany walked in the door of Dominic's apartment to lights and the aroma of Chinese takeout. Slipping off her heels, she found him hunched over the dining table in pajama pants and glasses, surrounded by a pile of papers, a half-eaten carton of General Tso's next to one arm, and a box of tissue next to the other.

She set her purse on the table by the door. "Are you sick?"

He started to answer but coughed instead. When the fit released him, he plucked a tissue from the box and blew his nose. "No, but Patrick sent me home anyway." Dominic peered at her across the living room. "You're done with work already?"

She glanced at the wall clock. It was half past seven. "I had a productive day." This, of course, was a lie. But how would Dominic understand her obliterated concentration when she couldn't explain it to herself?

She shuffled to the dining room, eased into one of the chairs, and reached for the white carton while he slid a thick manila folder from his briefcase and added it to the overflowing pile on the table.

"I wouldn't eat that." He stifled two sharp coughs in the crook of his elbow, and without looking up from his papers, jerked his head toward the refrigerator. "I got you Lo Mein. Chopsticks are on the counter."

Her stomach rumbled in gratitude. She heated her dinner in the microwave, returned to the dining room, and started eating while Dominic shuffled through the stacks of papers in front of him. Around the fifth or sixth bite, Bethany dropped her chopsticks and opened the fortune cookie.

Something you lost will soon turn up.

She rolled up the white slip and huffed.

Dominic ignored her.

"What are you working on?" she asked.

"Contracts."

"What kind of contracts?" She picked several cookie crumbs off the placemat and folded them in her napkin. When he didn't answer, she fidgeted in her seat. "Dom?"

"What?" The single syllable snapped across the table.

Bethany raised her eyebrows and pressed her lips together.

He took off his glasses and ran his hand down the stubble on his chin. "C'mon, Bethany, I'm up to my ears."

So much for unburdening her soul.

She snatched up his carton and pushed away from the table, the legs of her chair scraping against the hardwood floor.

Dominic groaned.

She stalked to the kitchen and dumped all the leftovers. Maybe she should go home. Sleep in her own bed for once and reconsider the long talk she and Dominic had over Thanksgiving—about moving in together once her lease expired at the end of the year. Why would she move in with him when he treated her like nothing more than a nuisance?

She closed the trash compactor and rinsed off a plate in the sink. If only memories could be as easily erased. If only a little water could wash them down the drain. If only she could send the stupid card and let this Robin thing go. She reached for a towel just as a pair of strong arms wrapped around her waist.

She stiffened.

He let go. "C'mon, Bethy, don't be mad."

The way he said her name loosened some of the tightness in her chest.

"I'm swamped at work and I feel horrible. I hate being sick."

She rolled her eyes. "I thought you weren't."

"I don't want to be." He took the plate from her and put it in the dishwasher. "You know how it is."

She bunched the towel in her hand. Maybe now, with his work in another room, he would listen. "You know Robin Price?"

His forehead knotted.

"Robin from Peaks? She sends Christmas cards every year? Birthday and Easter cards too?" Something uncomfortable fidgeted inside her. Why hadn't she ever responded? Sure, things had changed—Robin had changed—but was it really that hard to send a card?

"You know I'm no good at keeping track of that stuff."

"She was my best friend growing up. We were practically inseparable."

He grabbed a tissue from the box on the counter and blew his nose.

"I guess her husband had some sort of aneurism and now he's in a coma." She waited for a response, but the glassed-over look in his eyes told her she waited in vain. She crossed her arms and raised her eyebrows at him.

"I don't remember you talking about her."

"We haven't been close for a long time."

He grabbed a wine glass from the counter and nudged her away from the sink. "So why are you so upset?"

"I don't know." She picked at the corner of the marbled countertop. "I sort of feel like I should go see her. Maybe take some time off work and go back to Peaks for a few days."

Dominic's hands stopped moving beneath the water. "Go back to Peaks?" He turned and looked at her. "I thought you hated Peaks."

She laughed at the understatement.

"Why don't you just send her a card or something?"

"I was going to. But all the cards are just…I don't know. None of them were right."

"So let me get this straight." He shut off the water and flicked the glass. Droplets sprayed the side of the sink. "You're going to take an entire week off work, go back to a place you hate, just to spend some time with a woman who's no longer your friend?" He took the towel and dried his hands. "I'm sorry, Beth. I don't get it."

Frustration stirred. She needed him to understand. Because until he understood the magnitude of her childhood friendship with Robin, his attempts to dissuade her from returning to Peaks wouldn't cut it. And she needed to be dissuaded. "What if you heard Shawn was going through a hard time? Wouldn't you feel compelled to do a little more than send a card?"

Dominic dipped his chin and looked at her from the tops of his eyes. "Shawn's my brother."

"I know. And Robin was like my sister. That's how close we were."

"If you were that close, then why don't you keep in touch?"

"It's complicated."

He stared for a moment, his nose as red as Rudolph's, then lifted his shoulder. "I mean, hey, if it's something you think you need to do, don't let me stop you. You can go to Peaks if you want."

She blinked, dumbfounded. Is that what Dominic thought this was about? Getting *permission*?

"So listen, I need to get this work done before I call it a night. You should stay though." He kissed her cheek and escaped to the dining room.

She stared after him, one hand on the countertop, the other dangling by her side until her ringing phone interrupted the thoughts swirling through her mind. She padded to the front door and reached inside her purse. For the third time in one day her mother's number lit the screen. Bethany groaned. What more could Mom possibly have to say about Robin?

The screen went black.

She passed her phone from palm to palm, wondering if it would actually be about David this time, and dialed voice mail. If it was another ambiguous message, she might pull her hair and scream.

"Bethany, I know we just talked. And I hate to bother you. But I heard something this evening and thought I should tell you."

The usual stain of worry in Mom's voice had lifted, as if she'd doused her words in Clorox and scrubbed them clean. Bethany's heart quieted. This wasn't about David.

"Dan was admitted to the hospital the other night. I guess he had a heart attack. He's apparently doing fine. He's going home in a couple days, so there's really nothing to worry about. I just thought you'd want to know."

Grandpa Dan? When was the last time she'd talked to Grandpa Dan? She rewound time, thinking back several months, when she called to wish him a happy birthday. Hearing his voice always brought back a slew of memories. Feeding the calves, watching him and his cousin Ray pitch hay in the barn, listening while he taught her how to groom, saddle, and ride a horse. Every time she talked to him on the phone, an inexplicable feeling of homesickness would sweep over her—like a cloud passing in front of the sun. Now he was in the hospital, and that same unfamiliar feeling stole through her body. It didn't make any sense. How could she be homesick for a place she hated?

She plopped onto the leather sofa and rested her elbows on her knees. She had her reasons for avoiding Mom and Robin. She had her reasons for shunning Peaks. But Grandpa Dan? She couldn't shut him out of her life.

Bethany powered her phone off and rested back on the cushions, desperate to leave behind this headache of a day. But as hard as she tried, her brain would not rest. The idea of going to Peaks returned, stronger this time. She couldn't ignore it. Just like she couldn't ignore Robin or her grandfather. For whatever reason, Peaks wanted her back.

Three questions scrolled through her mind like sleep-repellent ticker tape, keeping her awake well past midnight. Would she go back? Could she live with herself if she didn't?

Could she live with herself if she did?

Two

Plowed fields, once rich with hay and corn, lay covered in patches of white, nodding off for a long winter's nap. The beginning of December always brought a sense of lethargy to the countryside. Bethany yawned as the two-lane highway undulated before her, an occasional barn or silo breaking up the monotony in brief but consistent intervals. Whenever she passed one of those solitary structures, with nothing but a pair of leafless oaks to keep it company, a lonesome feeling would nudge up against her. A feeling she had known well as a child.

She shook away the encroaching memories, steered her car through a sharp bend in the road, and spotted a chipped barn where three Shetlands had their heads bent low over a trough. It was the Masons' old farm. And although the horses had changed, the milestone hadn't. She was five minutes from Peaks.

She took a long, slow breath. One week. She could handle one week. Seven days to fulfill her obligations and get back to life in Chicago. Embracing the pep talk, she bent her head toward one shoulder, then the other, a poor attempt to release the stiffness that had accumulated during her three-hour drive into farm country.

Peaks' water tower emerged over the top of an abandoned barn. Her right foot shifted from the gas to the brake as she approached a familiar

four-way stop—the one with Jorner's General Store on the corner. The sight
of that old store sitting behind Peaks' unchanged population sign stroked
pieces of her soul that had lain dormant over the past ten years. The fatherless, trailer-park Bethany of her past threatened to resurface. She tightened
her grip on the steering wheel and pushed that girl back down. That wasn't
who she was anymore.

Bethany turned off the main road. Gravel pinged against the belly of
her car as Dan's farmhouse peeked from behind a large machine shed. A
glance in her rearview mirror showed two unfamiliar border collies trotting
alongside her rear tires. She shifted in her seat. The place was like an un-
aged photograph. She hadn't laid eyes on it in ten years, yet it looked so
much the same. Black shutters against white siding, floral curtains visible
through second-story windows, the rocking chair sitting vigil on a wrap-
around porch. Even the tire swing Dan put up for her and David still hung
from a bough of the elm tree out front. While time had its way with everything else, this farm had somehow escaped its snare.

The only change was the vehicles parked in the driveway. A black Ford
Ranger sat in the spot where Dan's rusted-out pickup used to be, and next
to it was a dirty Bronco decked with a bug-splattered grill. It hummed and
hissed as though the owner had turned it off only a moment ago.

Unease settled in her stomach. When she'd called Dan yesterday he
hadn't mentioned anything about visitors. She'd hoped it would be just her
and Dan at the farmhouse while she stayed in Peaks. She had no desire to
catch up with old acquaintances.

The dogs followed as she rolled her suitcase over the uneven ground.
She stepped onto the porch, wiped her hands on her jeans one at a time, and
raised her fist. Before she could knock, the door flew open and a man filled
the doorway, looking over his shoulder toward something inside.

Bethany's muscles jerked like a giant hiccup. Her hands flew out in case he lunged outside without seeing her.

The man turned his head and took a quick step back.

"Who are you?" They spoke at the same time, the deepness of his voice drowning out the surprise in hers.

He glanced down at her luggage, then back at her. Scruff covered the entirety of his chin and darkness circled beneath his eyes. The man looked like he could use three weeks of solid sleep followed by a long nap, and he still might not escape the exhaustion haunting his face. Blinking away her distraction, she stuck out her hand. "I'm Bethany. Dan's granddaughter."

His eyes flickered, then cleared into a curious amusement that bordered on impolite. "So you really exist. How about that."

She straightened her spine and moved to take back her hand, but he swaddled her palm with a callused grip. "Who are you?" she asked.

"I'm Evan. I run the farm."

The name sounded familiar. Dan must have mentioned him in one of their conversations, but she couldn't remember.

He crossed his arms and leaned against the doorframe. "Dan talks a lot about you and your brother. But ever since I started working here, I've never seen a trace of either of you."

"David's in Afghanistan."

"And you're in Chicago. Making it big as an architect."

She leaned back on her heels to put some distance between them. She didn't like this stranger knowing things about her when she knew nothing about him. She didn't like his tone either.

"What brings you back to Peaks?" he asked.

"Dan had a heart attack."

He scratched his chin and studied her, like he wasn't sure he believed her.

"It's cold out, you know."

He swept his hand toward the foyer. "By all means, come on in."

"Thanks for your permission," she mumbled, tugging at her suitcase.

"It's killing him."

She stopped. "His heart?"

"No." He reached out to help her, only she didn't relinquish her hold. She hadn't asked for his help. Despite her refusal to let go, he moved the suitcase over the threshold with one easy lift. "Resting. He doesn't like the doctor's orders. Yesterday I caught him trying to carry the cattle corn buckets, and those things aren't light."

"Do the doctors think he'll make a full recovery?"

"He's seventy-five. He has high blood pressure and even higher cholesterol."

"The farm's kept him active, hasn't it?"

"The farm's also fed him meat and potatoes every day of his life since he was a kid. Not so great for a person's arteries." Evan must have sensed she was going to jump in and say something, because before she could get the words out, he held up his hands. "Don't get worried. Dan just has to rest and cut back on the bacon, that's all. The doctors say he might live twenty more years."

He also might not. But Bethany swallowed the words.

"And he's well taken care of here. So if this"—he twirled his hand in the air—"newfound sense of obligation you're feeling is throwing a kink in your plans, you can go back to Chicago guilt free."

Her mouth dropped open, but before she could bring shape to her thoughts, Evan stepped out onto the porch and tipped his head. "It's been a pleasure."

He gave a sharp whistle. The two border collies emerged from behind the house and joined him as he walked down the driveway. He didn't get in either of the vehicles. Instead, he headed toward the paddock, and on his way, thumped the hood of her Audi.

"Nice wheels," he called over his shoulder.

She didn't miss the laughter in his voice.

The stairs creaked beneath Bethany's feet. Whenever she crept up that twisted stairwell as a child, she imagined walking to a secret lair, where something magical awaited. She and David would climb the stairs and hide in a cubbyhole in her grandpa's closet. They'd crouch in the corner and decorate the cobwebbed walls with bright, dancing circles from their flashlights. As an adult, she felt that same sense of anticipation. Only this time she knew nothing magical awaited her on the second story.

Just Grandpa Dan.

Her throat closed tight as she tiptoed down the narrow hallway, past the peeling,

rose-patterned wallpaper, and peeked through the crack in his doorway. Dan lie in bed, leaning on some pillows, flipping through muted television channels. Silver had crept up his temples and painted his once brown hair a shiny gray. Weak sunlight outlined his profile revealing the same prominent nose, the same cleft chin, the same wide forehead she remembered as a kid. It was the sight of his arm that made her suck in a silent breath. Once strong and tanned, it now hung deflated and pale, lax instead of taut.

She rapped her knuckle against the doorframe. The sound must have caught his attention because he turned away from the TV. His eyes flickered, cleared, then blinked several times. He gave his head a shake, as if she were nothing more than an apparition. Then his face crinkled into a grin—one that reached all the way up into his hairline.

"Bethany."

It was just her name. Nothing more. But a flood of unspoken emotion rested behind those three syllables. Joy. Love. Relief. Invitation. All the anxiety swirling inside her chest—fears that ten years of neglect would sour their reunion—morphed into the overwhelming urgency to sit next to him, to place her hand over the steady thrumming of his heartbeat. Assurance that he was alive and well. She hurried to his side, took his hand, and inhaled the familiar scent of tobacco and mint.

Home.

He squeezed her hand. "It's really you."

"It's really me," she said.

She admired him for an extended moment, taking in all the things changed and unchanged. Although new wrinkles adorned his pale features, he was still her Grandpa Dan.

"How's Chicago treating you?"

"Wonderful." The automated response stuck in her throat. Was it really wonderful? She had become an architect to design museums and hotels and skyscrapers. She hadn't become one to make run-down facilities less run-down. She shook away the pessimism. She was only twenty-eight. With more time and hard work, she'd get there. "How are you feeling? Do the doctors—"

Dan waved his hand. "I'm fine. Healthy as a horse. If it weren't for Evan, I'd be out there right now, fixing my tractor."

"Grandpa." She dipped her chin. "You had a heart attack."

He brought the palm of his hand to rest over his chest. "This heart's just fine. God was getting my attention, is all. Wanted to remind me not to take things for granted."

"I'm not sure I agree with his method of attention-getting."

Dan chuckled. "So is that why you came back? To check up on me?"

"I wanted to see you. Take care of you for a few days."

"I love you for that, Bethany. I really do. But I don't need taking care of." He patted her hand. "You can stay as long as you like. As a guest, though. Not as my nurse."

"I didn't take a week off work to sit around and be a burden. I can clean. Or keep you company while you're cooped up in this bed." She almost laughed at the concerned lines rippling across his forehead—like she was the one who had a heart attack instead of him. "Plus, it'll give me an excuse to slow down." And figure out how to approach Robin.

"I won't argue with you there. But the last thing I need is another person around here mollycoddling me. Evan does enough of it."

"Well, Evan won't have to worry about that anymore. He can leave it up to me. It'll give him more time to spend at home. With his family."

Dan frowned. "Bethany, this *is* his home."

"What do you mean?"

"Evan's lived here for the past five years."

Three

Bethany pulled the quilt over her head and turned toward the wall, away from the shafts of sunlight filtering through the blinds. She hadn't gone to bed until late. Very late. Earlier in the evening, Evan had cooked dinner. After the awkward meal, she'd spent her time with Dan, sitting in the worn-out recliner next to his bed, first talking, then watching black and white sitcoms he'd recorded over the years. *I Love Lucy. Leave it to Beaver. The Andy Griffith Show.* When Evan had fished the box of tapes from the cellar, it was the only thing that convinced her grandfather to stay in bed for the evening.

Although he fell asleep early, Bethany stayed curled up in the chair, staring at the screen, letting her mind take a much needed respite from its constant motion; until early turned to late, and late turned to the depths of night, when she could no longer resist the bed she lay in now. If Evan thought she was weird for watching five *Andy Griffith* episodes in a row, she really didn't care.

She brought the covers to her shoulders and stretched. The kind of stretch that arched her back and brought her toes over the edge of the bed. She wanted to stay there, in that room. Outside was Peaks and everything that came with it. Her mother. Small town gossip. Her looming visit with Robin. Inside was comfort. Peace. A calming familiarity.

A faint tapping filtered through the bedroom walls, creeping through the peaceful aura she'd cultivated upon waking. Bethany yawned and burrowed beneath the quilt. She let the heavy fabric encapsulate her in darkness and pretended she hadn't heard the noise. But the knocking grew louder. More insistent. She snaked her arm toward her cell phone and peeked at the time. 10:00.

She swung her feet over the side of the bed, curled her toes against the cold floor, and rummaged through her suitcase, taking out a cashmere sweater and her favorite pair of Calvin Klein's. She dressed, pulled her hair back into a neat ponytail, and rinsed her face and mouth before tiptoeing down the steps. By the time she reached the door, the knocks had grown desperate. Wrapping one arm across her waist, she grabbed the handle and pulled.

Bethany hadn't seen her mother in two years, and suddenly there she stood. On Grandpa Dan's front porch of all places. The color drained from Mom's face. Her hand fluttered to her hat, her throat, then rested awkwardly by her side. "So it's true. You're in town."

A groan took shape deep inside Bethany's chest, but she clamped her mouth to prevent the sound from escaping. She hadn't been in town for twenty-four hours, and somehow Mom already knew she was here. And why should this surprise her? Perhaps ten years elsewhere had clouded her memory, but this was Peaks. There would be no hiding.

"When were you going to tell me you were in town?"

Bethany kept her hand on the doorknob. "How did you know I was here?"

"Evan told me. Why aren't you staying at home?"

"Evan? How do you know Evan?"

"He's my mechanic."

Bethany pointed to the floor. "I thought he worked here, on Dan's farm."

"He also fixes cars. Mine wouldn't start this morning, so he jump-started it for me." Mom leaned forward, like she wanted to hug Bethany but wasn't sure how to approach it. So instead, she bit her lip, her chin dimpling in several places. "He told me you were in town."

"Mom, really, don't take this so personally. Coming here was a last-minute decision. I was just about to call you when you knocked on the door."

"So why don't you come home and stay with me?"

Bethany would rather live with Dr. Nowels and his ridiculous toupee. She may have lived there for nine years but that trailer had never been her home. "Because there's more room here. And I want to take care of Dan."

"He's a grown man, Bethany. He can take care of himself."

"He had a heart attack."

"That's because he's never eaten a healthy meal a day in his life. It's not your job to take care of him now that he's suffering the consequences of his behavior."

Bethany narrowed her eyes. "Did you steal those words straight from Pastor Fenton, or did you come up with that on your own?"

"I don't know what you're talking about."

"The 'consequences of his behavior'? Are you listening to yourself?"

"Dan's body is a temple for the Lord and all he ever eats is bacon and dough—"

"How would you know? You've barely spoken with him since I was nine."

Mom's spine stretched out in slow motion until she stood at least an inch taller. "I hardly think his eating habits have changed over the years."

"So Dan's just getting what he deserves? Like father, like son, is that it?"

"Your father was a good man."

Bethany tilted her head back and laughed, zapping all traces of pigmentation from her mother's face. "Absence really does make the heart grow fonder."

"I loved your father."

"You can keep saying that, but it's not going to change anything."

Mom twisted her hat. "What happened to him was not my fault."

"Of course not. It was *his* fault, remember? He was suffering from the *consequences of his behavior*." She put air quotes around her mother's convenient phrase. "Did you and Fenton ever figure out what he did wrong?"

"Pastor Fenton was trying to help. That's all he's ever wanted to do."

The edges of Bethany's vision blurred. "Trying to help?"

"You don't see it because your grandfather poisoned you against him."

Her temper snapped. This was exactly why she left. Exactly why she couldn't handle her mother. She would not stand in Dan's foyer—in the house that should have been her father's—and listen to Mom defend the man whose lies had torn apart her family. She reached for the door and yanked it open. "Thanks for stopping by. But I can't talk to you about this, Mom. I never have."

※

A headache gathered in Bethany's temples as she scrubbed the dish, working hard to scrape off the crusted oatmeal stuck to the sides of the bowl. No amount of scouring would wash away her mother's words. She paused and looked out the kitchen window. Evan's Bronco pulled down the long drive and parked next to her car. When he entered, she kept her back to him and focused on the hot water splashing against the bowl.

"Morning." His one-word greeting sounded gruff, like he needed to clear his throat.

She shut off the water and set her hands on either side of the sink.

"Good morning." As soon as she gathered the nerve, she'd turn around and teach him a lesson in minding his own business. He had no right telling her mother she was in town.

He stomped around behind her, his boots squeaking on the linoleum, his keys hitting the counter. The refrigerator door opened and shut, something cracked open, and by the time Bethany spun around, Evan had tracked a trail of soggy snow through the kitchen she'd just cleaned.

She followed the mess into the living room where he sat with his head in his hands, a can of Pepsi in front of him on the coffee table.

"Why did you tell my mother I was in town?"

He ran his fingers through thick hair but didn't respond.

"Did you hear me?"

He looked up from his hands, startled, as if seeing her for the first time. Somehow, his bloodshot eyes were worse today than they had yesterday. "What?"

The anger she'd nursed since kicking her mother off Dan's porch lost some of its steam. Did this guy have a drinking problem? "I wanted to know why you told my mom I was in town."

He leaned into the cushion and ran both hands down his face.

She stared, waiting, two seconds away from tapping her foot. And the longer she waited, the more time she had to replay the conversation with her mother. About Dan. Her father. Pastor Fenton. If a person wanted to believe in God, fine. But the minute they used those beliefs to attack someone Bethany loved was the minute it stopped being okay. Her anger returned, in need of a target, and Evan just sat there, ignoring her. Like he had no intention of responding.

"Are you going to answer my question?"

"I mentioned your name because you're her daughter. I thought Ruth knew you were in town. And it was something to talk about. By the time I realized my mistake, it was too late." He studied at her for a stretched-out moment. "It's pretty normal to tell your parents when you come in town, you know."

"My relationship with my mother is none of your business. You shouldn't have said anything." She grabbed a coaster from the end table and placed it under Evan's pop can, more to escape his glowering stare than any real concern about ruining the coffee table. She didn't know why he was glowering. She wasn't the one who'd done something wrong here. She snatched the afghan from the corner of the couch and shook it out. "She was upset this morning, and because of you, I had to deal with her."

"Wow." The springs in the couch squeaked.

"Excuse me?" She turned around and startled. Evan stood behind her—much too close—and underneath all that stubble, his face was ridiculously symmetrical.

"So sorry to inconvenience you," he said.

Her pulse fluttered against her neck. She took a step back and covered the silly reaction with her hand.

"I have a lot on my mind." It seemed like he wanted to say something more, like he might elaborate on whatever it was she didn't understand or was supposedly doing wrong, but before he could, the front door opened and a gust of cold air swept through the room.

Dan wiped the slush and mud onto the welcome mat on the porch, saw at the pair of them, and smiled.

"Where've you been?" Bethany's question came out harsher than she'd intended.

"Fixing the tractor." He stepped inside, rubbing his hands together. "It's chillier than I thought out there. Going to be a long winter, I think." He looked from Bethany to Evan, his smile stretching wider. "You two getting better acquainted?"

If that's what he wanted to call it.

Dan came over and sat in the recliner, groaning as he sunk into the cushion. "Thanks to you two, I'm as stiff as a board. This old body isn't meant to stay indoors."

Neither of them responded.

"Any news?" Dan addressed his question to Evan.

Evan returned to the couch, leaving Bethany stranded in the middle of the living room. If she wanted to sit, the only spot available was next to him. She took the seat and brought the bundled afghan onto her lap, her stiff posture identical to her mother's. Back straight. Fingers digging into the tops of her thighs. Only this wasn't church. This used to be her haven. And Evan's presence was throwing everything out of whack.

He shook his head. "Still the same."

Dan's face fell.

She searched for an excuse to get up and leave, so they could talk crops or cattle or whatever farm stuff they were discussing.

"Evan here sure knows an awful lot about you, Bethany."

The comment snagged her attention.

Dan dug into his back pocket, pulled out a can of snuff, and started to pack it with the tap of his finger. "I told him all kinds of stories about you and Robin. The trouble the pair of you used to get into out here on the farm whenever you came to visit."

Bethany crinkled her forehead. Why would Dan tell Evan silly stories about her and Robin? Why would Evan care?

Dan's mouth pulled down at the corners. "So Micah's not doing any better?" Micah. Robin's husband. Only Dan didn't direct the question at her. Bethany whipped her head around and stared at the man next to her.

"I just got back from the hospital." Evan's voice rattled. He cleared it and shook his head. "Robin doesn't want to believe what the doctors are saying."

She looked from one man to the other, her mind scrambling to put the pieces together.

"Are you sure the doctors are right? Isn't there a chance?" Dan asked.

Evan stared at the carpet. "They wanted to give it some time at first. I think the doctors were hoping he'd pass on his own." He drew in a long breath and let it back out. "His heart might be beating, but Micah's gone. The only thing keeping him alive is the ventilator. We're just waiting for Robin to make the decision. To send him home."

Confusion bubbled up inside Bethany's throat. "How do you know Robin?"

"Micah and Evan are brothers," Dan said. "Didn't he tell you?"

The room lurched. Puzzle pieces clicked together. Evan stared back at her, and she finally understood the cloaked animosity hiding in his eyes. Thanks to Dan, Evan knew she and Robin had been best friends. And thanks to her, Evan knew she hadn't asked about Robin or her husband once since her arrival.

Guilt and shame rippled through her. Robin's husband was in the hospital, supposedly not going to recover, and she was getting bent out of shape about an argument with her mother. She almost bit her lip. Almost. But she refused to turn into Mom at a time like this.

"We're going over to see her this evening. Her dad left this morning. He had to get back to Ohio. So this is her first night alone."

Bethany grabbed onto the armrest of the sofa and forced herself to think clearly. As much as her stomach twisted at the thought of seeing Robin again, she would have to visit her eventually. Sure, she came back to Peaks for Dan. But she came back for Robin too. Evan presented her with the perfect opportunity. "If you don't mind, I'd like to come with you," she said.

His head snapped up. "What?"

"I want to come with you when you go visit her."

"You're kidding."

"That wouldn't be a very funny joke."

His eyes narrowed. "Why do you want to see Robin? You haven't spoken in years."

The incredulous look on his face sparked something inside her chest. "One of the reasons I'm back is *because* of Robin."

"Give me a break. You came back because of *you*."

His accusation hit too close for comfort. "You don't know anything about me."

"I know enough."

She jutted her chin.

Dan came to the edge of his recliner, trailing bits of chaw onto the carpet.

Evan clamped his hands over his knees. "Look. Robin doesn't need to deal with you or your little high school reunion right now. Not on top of everything else."

"She won't have to *deal* with me. I came to offer my condolences. She was my best friend—"

"So where have you been for the past ten years?"

His question stole all her air.

"I'm sure my brother's collapse and Dan's heart attack put a real crimp in your plans—"

Dan stood and held out his hands. "Now, just stop right there. The both of you." He stepped forward. "Evan, I know you're exhausted and upset about your brother. But I won't have you two fighting like this in my living room."

Evan melted into the couch, his shoulders slumped, and examined Bethany with tired eyes. "Can't you take care of Dan for the week and leave it at that?"

His posture doused the fire raging in her chest, calming it to smoldering embers. Evan and Micah were brothers. How would she feel if the person in the hospital was David? She shuddered at the thought—at the very real possibility.

Still, she came back to Peaks to offer her sympathy. She wasn't going to get this far just to turn around and send Robin the card she bought last week. Evan might not trust her motives, but that didn't mean he had the right to tell her what to do. "I have to visit her. If you don't want me to come with you tonight, then I'll find another time."

He leaned his head back against the cushions and stared at the ceiling. By the time he looked at her, his face was stretched and white. "I guess there's nothing I can do then."

She met his stare. "I guess not."

Four

Evan swung the ax, taking all his frustration out on the hunk of ice covering the water tank. With the heater busted, the cattle couldn't drink. So he chopped away, hoping his aching muscles might distract him from his grief. He wound up and took another swing. The frozen block cracked and broke away. If only his pain would do the same.

He dragged his gloved hand across his forehead, wiping at the sweat beading above his brow. Searching for something else to swing at, he found a stack of logs next to the machinery shed and began splitting wood, trying hard to block out the image of his brother, a warm corpse surrounded by tubes and beeping monitors. And the image of Robin, knees tucked to her body as she sat watching Micah's chest rise and fall with superficial life.

Gripping the handle, he raised the ax over his head and brought it down with all his might. The log splintered and popped apart. He was angry—the same kind of angry he felt in high school after a car accident stole the life of his friend. He could feel the familiar emotion expanding inside him now, poking around for an outlet. Only this time he was twelve years wiser.

And this wiser version of himself understood death was like winter. Micah had better things waiting for him. An eternity of spring—new life. Evan knew all this in his head. His heart, however, was having a harder time with things. Life without one of his brothers didn't make any sense. He swung the ax into the chopping block. The sharpened blade stuck in the wood.

He needed to put a blanket over Storm, Dan's old mare, and get cleaned up before he went to Robin's. As he walked toward the paddock, his mind wandered to Dan's granddaughter, who apparently, would be accompanying him.

Yesterday, Bethany stood on the front porch like a piece of glass pretending to be steel, hiding behind a designer coat and an expensive car. At first glance it was impossible to dislike something so unknowingly fragile, but his amusement turned sour over the course of the evening.

She hadn't asked about Robin or his brother. Not once.

He walked into the horse barn, frozen dirt and hay crunching beneath his boots, and stopped. Bethany stood inside, lost somewhere in Dan's oversized parka, her chestnut hair pulled back from her face, her brown eyes wide, as if she'd been caught with a gun in her hand instead of a horse brush.

She brought the brush down to her side. "Sorry."

"For what?"

Faint patches of red stained her cheeks. She tucked her bottom lip beneath her teeth but released it just as suddenly, like she'd made some sort of mistake. Like biting her lip was a completely inappropriate thing to do.

He cocked his head. Bethany didn't strike him as the type who'd venture out in the cold to brush a horse. Come to think of it, Bethany didn't strike him as the type who'd venture out in any weather to brush a horse. He came closer and patted Storm's shoulder. "This gal likes the attention, I'm sure."

She stepped back just a little. "I used to ride her when I was a girl."

Evan tried to picture it, but he had a hard time.

"You look like you don't believe me," she said.

"It's not easy to imagine."

"Why not?"

He glanced at her brand-name boots. "You don't strike me as the farm-girl type."

"I'm not." She picked at the bristles, took another subtle step backward—the tiniest of shifts—and scanned the rafters, the strangest look passing across her face. Something soft and nostalgic. "At least not anymore."

He wondered what she might be thinking, but before he could ask, the look disappeared. "What time are we going to Robin's?" she asked.

"In an hour."

"I can follow you over."

"And get your car dirty?"

Her eyes flashed.

He scolded himself for his rudeness. Whatever Bethany's history with Dan and Robin, he had no right to make her his scapegoat. She wasn't the one he was angry with. Not really. He walked into the tack room, grabbed one of the heavy blankets off a shelf, and draped it over Storm's back. "We're both going to the same place. There's no reason we can't drive together."

She studied the ground, as if an excuse hid somewhere in the straw by Storm's feet. When it was obvious she couldn't find it, she ran her manicured hand down the length of the horse's neck and left the barn.

Evan squinted after her, his muscles no longer knotted with anger.

Bethany reached for the door of Evan's Bronco, only he beat her to it. He swung it open and swept his hand toward the inside, as if she wasn't capable of pulling on a handle and letting herself into his car. She climbed onto the passenger seat, her shoe knocking into a crushed Pepsi can. Cold vinyl rubbed against her palms, then the underside of her thighs, as she scooted in to place and brought the seat belt across her chest.

Evan's door slammed shut. As soon as he started the car, music blasted from the speakers—an awful twang that scraped against her eardrums. She clenched her fingers and pressed her hands into her lap, frowning at the silver cross dangling from his rearview mirror.

"What? You don't like Kenny Chesney?"

"Bleeding hearts and sexy tractors? No thank you."

Evan leaned over, kept his left hand on the wheel and used the other to fish something from beneath his seat. His hand reappeared holding a bulky CD case. He plunked it on her lap. "You pick something then."

She blinked at the gift. Somehow she doubted she'd find anything that interested her.

"I promise they won't bite."

Scowling, she flipped open the case and rummaged through the CD jackets. By the time she reached the end, he was driving on a black-topped road, the gravel no longer pinging up against the car, her initial suspicions confirmed. "They're all country."

"So?"

"I don't like country."

He jabbed the eject button and flipped his Kenny Chesney CD onto the case.

Silence filled the cab of the car. She pivoted in her seat and stared at the darkening landscape blurring past her window. Dirty gray snow drifts covering muted brown fields. Why would anybody choose to live here? She fingered the case on her lap.

Robin had.

And now, after ten years, all that separated her from her former best friend was a short drive in Evan's Bronco. She'd tagged along, determined to check this task off her to-do list, but now, bouncing in his passenger seat, about to face Robin, a cross dangling in front of her face… The irony was hard to miss.

She set the CD case on the floor while Evan pulled to a stop and turned on to Peaks' thoroughfare—a two-lane road that knew nothing of stoplights. After her long absence, she expected something to look different. Perhaps a new restaurant or updated storefronts. But no. Nothing had changed. The same, multi-colored Christmas lights wrapped around the same frost-bitten trees growing up on both sides of the same boring street. Even the gaudy, light-up Santa waving from the lawn of Arton's Jewelry Store was the same. The town wallowed in its sameness. Yet Bethany couldn't be more different. Neither could her relationship with Robin.

She fiddled with the window button on her armrest and the question she should have asked a long time ago tumbled from her lips. "How's Robin doing?"

"Not good."

The sudden desire to know everything, as if these morsels of information might arm her with the right words, welled up inside her. "You told Dan there's no chance Micah would recover."

"It's been a week. Nothing's changed."

"And now you want Robin to take him off the ventilator?"

A muscle in Evan's jaw pulsed. "He'd want to go home."

"That's the second time you've said that. What do you mean, 'go home'?"

"Heaven."

She huffed.

"You don't believe in heaven?"

"If I believed in heaven, then I'd have to believe in hell." She crossed her arms to ward off the chill. "I'd rather pass."

Oncoming headlights spilled inside the car, bringing Evan's face out of shadow. He looked over at her, his eyes probing in a way that made her squirm.

"Sorry. I wasn't trying to offend you," Bethany said.

"No offense taken."

"No?"

"It's a valid concern. You're not the only one to struggle with it."

She studied his profile, trying to catch him in the lie, but his expression held nothing but honesty. The whole exchange tied her thoughts in to knots. Threw her off balance. She scrambled to regain her equilibrium, while Evan pulled down a cul-de-sac lined with two-story brick houses surrounded by manicured lawns. He stopped in front of one that was no different than the others and turned off the ignition.

They were here? Already?

Bethany squeezed the tops of her knees and closed her eyes, refusing to let panic swallow her. She could do this. A hug. A pat on the back. An empty promise to be there if Robin needed her, then melt into the background while Evan and his family held Robin's hand. By tomorrow morning this would all be behind her.

Despite her internal pep talk, a shiver started at the base of her spine and took hold of her jaw. Her teeth chattered, tapping an indiscernible SOS that wouldn't stop.

"Are you all right?"

A layer of sweat broke out over Bethany's palms. She was really here. Not more than thirty feet from Robin's front stoop. She tried to swallow, but the muscles in her throat wouldn't cooperate.

Evan was talking. The muffled sound of his voice found her ears, but she couldn't make out any of his words. What if this was a horrible mistake? What if Robin slammed the door in her face? What if she couldn't think of anything to say? She inhaled, grasping at the composure seeping out her pores, and searched for the professional Bethany. The one who made goals and accomplished them. Because that's all this was. Something to accomplish so she could go back to Chicago with no more distractions. Sure, she felt terrible for Robin, but there wasn't anything she could do. So she'd perform the social niceties. A hug. A pat. And then she'd get out of there.

In and out.

The muffled sound of Evan's voice stopped. He reached for his door handle. The motion sent her paralyzed synapses into fast forward. She unclasped her seatbelt and hopped out before he had the chance to open the door for her again. With her chin tucked to her chest and hands shoved deep inside her coat pockets, she hurried to the front door, a cruel wind whipping strands of hair around her face. Evan climbed the stoop and knocked while Bethany's heart bruised her chest.

The porch light flicked on. She blinked against the flood of brightness. A chain rattled from the other side. The door opened. Evan wrapped Robin in a hug and stepped to the side, no longer a barricade between them.

Robin's fingertips flew to her mouth. Her eyes widened.

And Bethany's plan? Her goal to get in and get out? Vanished. Disappearing amongst the million unsaid words exchanged in the brief seconds of Robin's confusion. And behind the confusion? Pain. A haunting sorrow that filled her eyes. Bethany's heart twisted, then rent down the seam. Her friend—her soul mate for so many years—looked like nothing more than a heap of grief, her haunted eyes two hollowed-out pits of despair.

Robin closed her mouth. Her chin gave the smallest of quivers. Her shoulders twitched, then heaved. Evan held up his hand, as if to grab her elbow, but Bethany stepped past him, past her hesitancy, and reached Robin before he had the chance. And as Robin crumpled beneath the weight of her tears, Bethany gathered up the broken pieces of her friend's worn-out soul and pressed them against her body.

Five

Robin couldn't have come into my life at a better time.

The thing about living in Peaks, Iowa, population 1,539, according to the green sign on Jorner's corner, is that people talk. And anything remotely out of the ordinary drove the citizens of Peaks in to a gossiping frenzy. When I decided to swim to the bottom of that pool, there were worse repercussions than watching Dr. Nowels scratch mysterious notes about me on his clipboard for sixty minutes each week.

My actions hurled me in to an unwanted spotlight. The whispers followed me around every street corner. I came to expect those not-so-discreet, over-the-shoulder glances whenever I passed by a mother, or a kid, or worst of all—an old lady. I say the worst because those were the ones who would follow up their glances with words. Like, "Hey, aren't you Bethany Quinn? How could you do that to your poor mother? Hasn't she been through enough?"

As if either of those last two questions could be answered.

Despite my infamy, it was a very lonely time. Debbie Carter, one of my classmates, turned thirteen in the fall, and me and Bobby Fenway were the only ones in our class not invited to her party. I could understand Bobby Fenway. He wiped snot on his shirtsleeves and blew spit bubbles as he sat in the back of the classroom. But me? Debbie had invited me to her twelfth birthday party. The one where her dad rented out a river boat for the day and hired a real-live band. I couldn't understand what had changed, other than the swimming pool fiasco.

My subconscious mind must have realized the significance of meeting Robin. Because the day we met became a snapshot I could forever pluck from my head and examine in detail. I remember everything about it.

Stepping outside our trailer, ice and rock crunched under my boots, and the frozen air turned the ends of my damp hair to icicles.

Mom was working to shove a bundle of dirty laundry into the back seat of our two-door, rusted-out Pinto. She paused only long enough to scold me. "Bethany Rachel Quinn, get inside! Your hair is wet." Mom waved her hand toward our trailer as if she could shoo me back in. "You'll catch pneumonia," she added, using her boot to try to push the bulky bag past the passenger seat. Even through the layers of thermal underwear, jeans, long-sleeved shirt, sweatshirt, winter coat, and scarf, my mother's frame was slight.

A stubborn leaf clung to the barren branches of the oak tree growing in our front yard. It fluttered several times, detached, and swirled off through gray sky. I looked at my mother and I found myself wondering. If the breeze swirled in just the right way, might it pick her up and blow her away too?

Ignoring her, I shoved my hands into the deepest recesses of my coat pockets and scurried toward her. It was Saturday. My brother David was over at a friend's house, leaving me alone. Trapped inside. A prisoner to the cold. Whatever errands my mother had to run, I wanted to go with her.

So I stepped beside her and assisted with the pushing. It was a big bag. And the front seats no longer folded forward like they were supposed to. With one last heave, we stuffed the laundry into the back seat.

My mother straightened, out of breath. "I thought I told you to get back inside."

I stood my ground as wind tousled frozen bits of hair around my face. The sight must have made my mother reconsider. Maybe she thought it was safer for me to jump into the warmed-up Pinto than run all the way back into the house. "Get in," she said, her teeth chattering.

We drove to the Laundromat first. Although neither of us talked, the drive over was far from quiet. I wouldn't have been surprised if the whole town could hear our car. The muffler had fallen off a week prior, and every time my mom started the engine, heat would bloom across my cheeks, creep down my neck, and flush toward my chest.

When we pulled in to the Laundromat parking lot and turned off the ignition, the roaring in my ears stopped, and I let out my breath.

I really hated our car.

By the time we removed the bag of laundry from the back seat, it had started to snow. Silent, white flakes that floated in place against a backdrop of gray. I stuck out my hand, collecting a few snowflakes on my mitten.

"Bethany." The voice broke through my trance. Mom stood in the doorway, the opened door propped against her back, the bundle of dirty clothes sitting at her feet. "Come on."

A warm whoosh of air greeted me as I stepped inside. I unzipped my coat, slipped off my mittens, and ran cold fingers through my hair, separating the frozen tangles. As I followed Mom toward the two rows of machines, my boots squeaked against the gray speckled linoleum. Peaks' Laundromat wasn't very big and hardly ever busy. It made me think we were the only ones in town without a washer and dryer.

But not today. I took a seat in one of the plastic chairs and spotted another mother-daughter duo in the opposite corner. They were strangers.

I wiggled my toes inside my boots. They tingled and burned as I studied the unfamiliar pair. The girl seemed to be around my age. Her dark hair hung like silk curtains on either side of porcelain skin. When she looked up from the book she was reading, the pale blueness of her eyes startled me. I would have looked away. It was a defense mechanism I'd developed since the summer. People stared, and as a reflex, I turned my cheek. But her smile was so instant and so genuine, that before I could catch myself, I was smiling too.

I strained my ears as she said something to her mother, whose hair was just as black and shiny, but the rumbling of dryers blocked out the girl's voice. Her mother nodded, and the girl walked toward me, the same smile lighting up her features.

My heart thudded against my rib cage. I wasn't good at conversation. Especially not with strangers. And most especially not with ones who resembled glass dolls. She was the type of girl Debbie Carter would kill to have at her party. By the time she reached my side of the Laundromat, my mother and I were staring like a couple of dumb fish.

"Hi," she said, sticking out her hand. "I'm Robin."

I mumbled my name and shook her hand.

"We just moved to town." She plopped down in the seat next to mine, placed her hands beneath her thighs, and moved her legs like two pendulums swinging in opposite directions. "It isn't very big, is it?"

I caught my mother spying. She looked over her shoulder at the pair of us, running her front teeth over her bottom lip, probing me onward with her eyes.

"Didn't you see the sign?" was all I could muster.

For some reason, Robin thought this was funny. Her laugh sounded like Tinker Bell. "My dad warned me it would be a big change. We moved from Chicago."

Her legs continued their swinging and I stared at her boots, very conscious of David's hand-me-downs adorning my feet.

"It was so crowded there and the traffic was nuts. It took us practically an hour to get to school each morning. I think living in Peaks will be a lot nicer."

I inspected at her face to catch the fib, but her expression held nothing but sincerity.

"What grade are you in?" she asked.

My mind started to thaw. I was slowly remembering what it was like to carry on a conversation with somebody who didn't hold a clipboard. "Seventh."

Robin's eyes danced. "Me too. I start school on Monday. I'm really nervous."

I wondered what a girl like Robin could possibly be nervous about. The kids in my grade would flock around her, probably fight over who could claim her as best friend. Come Monday, she'd learn the difference between the cool kids and the loser kids. Sadly, I belonged in the second category. Me and Bobby Fenway. She'd figure out soon enough that I wasn't best friend material. Girls like Debbie Carter or Daphne MacComb would invite her in to their club and explain everything.

During those twenty-five minutes, while our clothes spun in separate washers, we formed some sort of mysterious bond. She asked me questions, all kinds. And I answered them without sounding like too much of a weirdo. Our lives were polar opposites. My family was poor. Her family was rich. The only reason they were at the Laundromat was because they hadn't had time yet to buy a washer and dryer. In fact, her dad was doing some legal work for the local Alcoa plant by the river. The same place my mother worked—only not as a lawyer.

Robin was beautiful and eloquent. I was plain and awkward. She had a dad and a mom and a bulldog named Burger. My dad was dead and the only pets I had were the calves at my grandpa's farm. When the washers buzzed, and my mom finished stuffing our clothes into a single front-loading dryer, she plugged it with quarters, turned to me and said, "It's time to go run our errands now, Bethany."

I didn't want to go. Robin must have felt the same way because she brought her mother over and introduced her to mine. She pivoted on her heels and looked between the two mismatched women. "Do you think Bethy could stay here with us? We'll take good care of her. Won't we, Mom?"

It was the first time anybody had ever called me Bethy. It made my arms tingle in a funny, light sort of way.

"We would be happy to watch Bethany, Ruth." Robin's mom placed her manicured hands on Robin's shoulders. "My daughter's been worried about making friends. I'm so glad we caught you here at the Laundromat. I know this will make her first day of school so much easier."

That first day of school worried me. I didn't want it to come. On Monday, Robin would find out everything. My summer mistake. My friendless existence. I wanted more time with her before that. I gave Mom a pleading look. The worried expression on her face seemed to waver, and I smiled victoriously.

When Mom returned an hour later, with the laundry already folded, there was nothing else to do but leave. I had the sudden urge to hug Robin. For one glorious day, I'd found a friend. I knew everything would change soon. The girls would fight over her. The boys would show off. And Robin, no doubt, would forget all about our morning at the Laundromat.

It didn't quite happen like that. The first part did—the part about our classmates vying for her attention. The second part, however—the part about Robin forgetting all about me—never happened. For reasons I could never understand, Robin chose me. Not popular Debbie Carter, or athletic Daphne MacComb. For whatever reason, whether it was because she found me first, or took pity on me, or genuinely liked me, Robin chose me. And my life was never the same.

Six

Bethany held on to Robin until something shifted, exposing emotions she had long since buried. She scrambled to cover them up, to regain her bearings, but Robin's muffled cries mangled her concentration. The instinct to comfort and protect her old friend dug its heels in and declared war against her desire to pull away. And all Bethany could think, the only thought running through her scattered brain, was that she should have sent the card.

She forced herself to step away. To put some distance between her present and her past. Robin pressed her knuckles against her cheeks, rubbed over the darkness circling beneath her pale blue eyes, and blinked at Bethany as if she weren't real. "What are you doing here?"

Blood pooled in Bethany's hands, weighing them down with a heat that clashed against the frigid temperature. Robin had just asked the million dollar question. The question Bethany couldn't answer herself. "I— I wanted to…"

To what? Offer support? Get rid of this self-proposed obligation that fermented in her gut so she could move on with her life? She could feel Evan staring, as if he was just as curious to hear Bethany's answer as Robin. "I heard what happened."

Evan placed his hand beneath Robin's elbow and led her inside.

Bethany followed and shut the door. The sudden warmth stung her ears. She stood on the rug while Evan sat Robin down on the couch.

"I'll be right back," he said, and with no explanation, he slipped off his shoes and disappeared down the hall, leaving a hulking silence in his wake, standing in the center of the room like an uninvited dinner guest.

She took off her hat and eyed the unlit Christmas tree situated in front of a picture window. Two stockings dangled from the mantle of a darkened fireplace. Holly and red-velvet bows wrapped around the banister leading up the wide stairs. All of it worked together to paint a depressing picture—not one of holiday cheer but of mocking joy. The holidays were a horrible time for tragedy.

"You look the same," Robin finally said.

Bethany couldn't return the compliment, if that's what it was. Whether Robin had aged in the past week, or over the course of ten years, she didn't know, but her once luminous friend had lost all her sparkle.

"I can't believe it's been ten years." Robin's voice cracked on the last word.

Bethany pushed away her descending guilt, straightened her shoulders, and focused on doing what she'd come to do. "I'm sorry about your husband." The empty words sounded lame…certainly not enough.

"I don't know what to do. Especially now that…" Robin clasped her hands in her lap, fresh tears gathering in her eyes.

Bethany took a tentative step forward, but before Robin could continue, the front door opened. Four people slipped inside and shut out the cold. A tall gentleman with somber eyes. A young woman, with hair the color of Evan's swept in to a high ponytail. And an older couple—tan, considering the season—carrying a foil-covered dish. Bethany pressed herself against the wall as the foursome swooped down on Robin.

When the embracing ended, the older woman dabbed her eyes, turned toward Bethany, and held out a trembling hand. "I'm Loraine. Micah's mother."

"I'm Bethany Quinn…" Robin's friend? Was that even true anymore? Unlike Loraine, she had no identifier. No reason for being there, partaking in this family's grief.

"Robin talks about you sometimes. You two were friends?" Loraine dabbed at her eyes again and placed the dish on top of the coffee table.

Bethany looked at her old friend, sitting with arms wrapped around her shins, lost in a world of grief. "Yes, we were."

"I brought lasagna," Loraine said. "I know we don't feel like it. But we should eat."

Bethany tugged at the collar of her shirt, which suddenly felt too tight. "Could you please direct me to the restroom?"

The younger woman pointed past the living room. "It's just past the stairwell, on your left." She placed her hand on her chest. "I'm Amanda. Micah's sister."

Bethany forced a polite smile, then hurried from the room, scrambling for air. Surely some oxygen and distance would push away the crowd of emotions pressing against her. She rounded the corner to the sound of a flushing toilet and stopped.

The door opened and light swept across the carpet. Evan stepped into its spotlight and stared at her, his eyes puffy.

She stared back, unsure what to say.

"That's the first time I've seen her cry since Micah collapsed." His words floated toward the ceiling, eliciting a compassion Bethany couldn't afford to feel.

She pushed up her sleeves. Wondered if Robin had accidentally set her thermostat to ninety.

"Is my family here?"

She nodded.

Evan stepped past her and Bethany lunged into the bathroom as if clarity might be hiding behind the toilet.

When she came out, the family had gathered in the kitchen, plates of untouched lasagna set in front of them. Loraine spotted her in the doorway. "I prepared a plate for you," she said, motioning to the empty seat between Robin and Evan.

Bethany tried to smile her thanks, but the gesture felt much too stiff. She shouldn't have let Evan talk her in to driving together. If she had her own car, she could give Robin one last hug and excuse herself. She didn't belong here. But her car was at the farm. And they were all staring. So she sat in the empty spot as everyone around the table took hands and bowed their heads.

All the moisture in her mouth evaporated. They were going to thank God? Now? With Micah in the hospital, lying like a vegetable? Before she could put her hands in to her lap, Evan grabbed one and Robin took her other—fire and ice. Blood whooshed past her ears. She pressed her lips together while Evan's father finished the blessing.

He barely said his amen before Evan released her hand and reached for his water.

Silverware clinked.

Bethany forced herself to take a few bites.

Amanda pushed the steamy meal around her plate. "Is Gavin coming?"

"He's not feeling well," Loraine said.

Robin shoved her plate away, porcelain scraping against the wood table. She brought her hand over her stomach, like she might be sick, stood, swayed, then sat back down. Evan's family shifted forward.

Bethany wanted to tell them to back off. To give her some air.

"I'm sorry." Robin's voice cracked. She looked up from her plate and faced Loraine. "I'm sorry for putting you through this. I'll do it tomorrow. In the morning."

Loraine covered her mouth with one hand and squeezed Robin's with the other and melted in to her husband's waiting arms. Bethany studied Evan from the corner of her eye, but she couldn't read his expression. He was losing a brother, and she had no idea how he felt about it. All she knew was that if the man in that hospital bed were David, she'd be wrecked.

"Bethany."

Her skin prickled. Somehow, within the confines of her whispered name, Bethany knew what Robin wanted. Only she didn't want to give it. Coming over to Robin's house and offering condolences was one thing. Holding Robin's hand while she took her husband off life support was another.

"Can you come?" Robin's voice pitched and creaked—like the old staircase in Dan's farmhouse.

She wanted to tell Robin no. She wanted to tell her that too much had changed. It wasn't her place anymore. But the words fell away.

Dan greeted Bethany as soon as she stepped through the door of the farmhouse, and for whatever reason, he wore his coat. She took in his attire and raised her eyebrows, but any questions she had about his plans fizzled before they could reach her lips. She slumped her shoulders, purse dangling by her side like a fifty-pound dumbbell as Evan came inside behind her. Dan shrugged off his coat while Bethany shuffled to the recliner and plopped down. She rested her head against the worn cushion and stared at the dusty mantle over the fireplace. Why had she agreed to go to the hospital with Robin? What had she been thinking?

Their reunion had formed a string—however thin—encircling Bethany's heart and attaching to Robin's. Bethany didn't want that string. It tied her to Peaks. It tied her to everything she wanted to forget. She suddenly craved the coziness of her Chicago loft. A glass of the merlot Dominic bought for Thanksgiving. The smooth crisp feel of her arm sliding across paper as she sketched on the drafting board by her apartment window, the city pulsing beneath her.

Bethany sighed and kicked off her shoes. Despite their differences now, despite the distance between them, she could not dismiss the heart connection she and Robin had once shared. Robin had helped Bethany get through her Tuesday meetings with Dr. Nowels. Robin had helped her laugh off Pastor Fenton. Robin had convinced Bethany that everything he said, all the hogwash he spoon-fed her mother, was nothing but lies. She assured Bethany that her father was dead—not burning for eternity in a pit of fire.

Robin had made life clear. She'd helped Bethany draw a line—with them on one side and Pastor Fenton and everything he stood for on the other. Bethany always assumed that line had been carved in stone, not drawn in sand. But that was before Robin decided to stay in Peaks and attend St. Ambrose University. That was before Robin met Micah Price, a handsome junior in her psychology class, from a town not more than fifteen minutes away. That was before Robin sent Bethany the e-mail—the one about Christ and forgiveness and salvation.

When Bethany read it, the words peeled back the bandages covering her past, exposing wounds still raw to the touch—wounds she'd endured at the hands of people who talked about Jesus and salvation. Bethany's only friend, her biggest ally, her sole confidante—the only person she had ever told the entire truth to—had switched sides. Robin had hopped over to Fenton's. And their promises to remain best friends for life fell away. Those promises no longer mattered. Not when the rules had changed. Not when their lives were headed in such opposite directions.

Bethany inhaled a deep breath and held it captive. She would be there for Robin tomorrow—but that was it. That was as far as she would go. Bethany would hold her hand. She would help her say goodbye. She would spend some more time with Dan. And then she'd head straight back to Chicago. She opened her mouth and let her breath run away, her shoulders relaxing with its escape.

"Has Robin made a decision?" Dan asked, hanging his coat on a hook.

Bethany pulled her gaze from the mantle and peeked at Evan, still by the doorway.

"She asked us to come to the hospital tomorrow. To say goodbye," Evan said.

"How are you holding up?"

Evan shrugged.

Dan patted his shoulder and let his hand drop away. He flipped on the nine o'clock news and sank onto the sofa. Evan did the same. Bethany got up from the recliner and forced a yawn. She kissed Dan on the cheek and moved toward the stairs.

When she reached the first step, a familiar name sounded from the television, and her foot paused. She turned toward the screen. Pastor Fenton stared back at her, ready to speak in to a microphone held by a reporter.

"So tell us, what does Project MAC stand for?" the reporter asked, her gloved hand tucking strands of windblown hair behind her ear.

The duo stood in front of First Light, the church Bethany had been forced to attend as a child. Pastor Fenton stood next to the reporter, his chest broad, his posture straight. "Make A Change. It's a ministry I started to encourage the youth to reach out to the community and make a difference."

The sight of him on that television screen dragged Bethany in to her childhood. She tried to fight her way to the present, but Fenton's stare pinned her to the stiff wooden pew of First Light's sanctuary.

Bethany had loathed going to church on Sundays, especially after her incident at the swimming pool. Fenton would often find Bethany during the climax of his sermon, singling her out with a glare, as if she needed to listen harder than everyone else. When the service ended, Mom would stay behind. Which meant Bethany and David had to stay too.

Her fingernails would dig crescents in to her palms, dreading the moment when Fenton would approach their still forms sitting in the empty pews. During those moments, while he walked toward them, her muscles would turn into tightly wound coils, ready to spring at the slightest touch. Her mother must have known, because she never touched her.

Pastor Fenton would talk in urgent yet hushed tones two pews ahead while David folded the bulletin in to a paper airplane, and Bethany looked down at her worn-out Keds. When they finished, she'd follow Mom out the arched doorway while Pastor Fenton's stare trailed her down the aisle. Her mother tried and failed numerous times to convince Bethany to talk to him about what she had done. Whenever Bethany mustered up the courage to glance over her shoulder, the look on Pastor Fenton's face told her all she needed to know. He didn't want to talk to her any more than she wanted to talk to him.

"Oh, good grief." Dan's voice broke through her thoughts. She grabbed a hold of his words and pulled herself free from the memories. "What a load of horse manure."

Bethany returned her attention to the lit up television screen.

"We've heard about the free basketball camp, run by Peaks' star athletes, Hank and Joe Tipton," the reporter said. "We've also heard about the tutoring service started by some of Peaks' high school students. What other ways do you encourage the youth to make a change?"

Fenton smiled.

Bethany's hand squeezed the top of the banister.

"To be honest, the ministry has outgrown me. These kids are coming up with all sorts of things. From cleaning up trash by the Mississippi River to volunteering at the local Children's Hospital." His brown eyes sparkled. "The attendance at First Light has increased steadily ever since the ministry began. We're getting attendees from Albine and even some from across the river. People are curious. They want to know what we're all about."

The reporter tucked more hair behind her ear. "In a time of economic strife, I'm sure people appreciate a helping hand. It sounds like you're experiencing the after effects of the community's appreciation."

Fenton nodded. "We've seen the blessings God has poured out on our church since I started this ministry. It just goes to show, God will always bless the righteous."

"Thanks for your time Pastor Fenton." The reporter turned to address the camera, holding the microphone beneath her mouth. "The mayor of Peaks will be honoring Pastor Fenton for his service to the community at Peaks' annual New Year's Eve Ball. So if you'd like to meet the man behind the ministry, mark it on your calendars."

The screen panned to the newsroom, where two unfamiliar anchormen sat behind a desk. Bethany's eyes lost focus. Pastor Fenton's words swept through her body, uncovering memories she didn't want laid bare.

God will always bless the righteous.

Maybe his words sounded good, but the layers beneath them dripped with unsaid meaning. She'd witnessed the damage those words had inflicted on her father.

Bethany released her hold on the railing and slogged up the stairs. She knew a sign when she saw one. Peaks was honoring Pastor Fenton. The Universe wasn't just telling her to leave. It was using a bullhorn.

Seven

Robin Price clawed at the tissue in her lap, staring at the shreds of white dotting her jeans. Bethany shifted beside her while the organ procurement coordinator, a lady with a gray business suit and hair to match, ran down a list of questions. Questions about Micah. Robin gnawed on the inside of her cheek and didn't stop until something warm and metallic touched her taste buds.

"Does your husband have any tattoos?"

She shook her head.

"Any piercings?"

"No."

"Was he a drug user?"

She blinked.

The lady looked up from her script and frowned. "I'm sorry, Mrs. Price. These questions are part of the process."

Robin jerked her head—an attempt at *no*.

The woman gathered the papers in to a stack and tapped them against the table. The matter-of-factness of the moment made Robin flounder. That was it? They were finished? What about the other questions? The questions that had haunted her for the past week.

Like who was going to read the rest of the Grisham book on Micah's nightstand? The one earmarked on page eighty-three. Or what about his Bible? His New Year's resolution had been to read the entire thing in one year and the inked margins stopped somewhere in the middle of Acts, followed by stark white space that made her want to scream. Who would fix the leaky faucet in the kitchen, or clean out the boxes crammed in the rafters of their garage, or finish a dozen other projects Micah had started? What about their dream to open a café together?

She massaged her knotted throat with ice-cold fingers.

The woman slid the papers across the table and smiled, like Robin should be proud of herself—like she wasn't about to sign her husband's life away. "Your decision will change a dozen lives for the better."

But not her own. This decision wouldn't change her life for the better.

The woman pointed to the tabbed-off signature lines. "We just need you to sign."

Robin tried to focus on the sheet in front of her but couldn't make anything out except fuzzy black print. What if the doctors were wrong? What if there was a chance he would recover?

A chair creaked. "Robin?" Bethany said. "Are you okay?"

The lady leaned forward and held out the pen. According to her, people were waiting for Micah's organs right now. People whose lives would be saved, or improved, all because of Micah's death. Maybe knowing this should have offered comfort. Maybe it should have brought a sense of meaning to such a loss. Some sort of twisted silver lining. But it didn't. She wanted Micah's organs to stay with him. She wanted him to wake up and pull her to his side and whisper that he loved her, that he was sorry for putting her through this. Especially now.

She covered her stomach with her hand. Micah didn't know. Maybe if he knew, he'd wake up. The lady lifted the pen higher. Robin shifted away from the offensive offering.

Lord, I can't do this.

"Mrs. Price? I'm so sorry you have to go through this, but we need your signature if we're to move forward with the procedure."

The procedure? What they were about to do to her husband could hardly be called a procedure. She clamped her mouth shut, squeezed her eyes shut, and turned her face away, fighting off the dizziness swirling in her head. Without thinking, she pushed her chair from the table and stood. "I'm sorry." She clutched her hand to her chest and tried to suck in oxygen, but the thick air refused to comply. "I just need..."

Bethany placed her hand on Robin's elbow.

Robin swayed, then regained her balance before turning away from the gray-suited lady. She stumbled down the hall, past the waiting room filled with Micah's family, and slipped inside his room. She leaned against the wall, heart beating like a fast-paced concerto. She didn't look up until she heard someone move.

Dr. Markson's presence startled her. He stood over Micah's bedside with a file in his hand, and for one brief and frantic moment, she thought he'd turned off the machines before she had the chance to tell Micah the news. But the swooshing of the ventilator soothed her fear.

Dr. Markson moved to her side.

She looked from Micah to the doctor, and the words she wanted to say since they'd performed all those tests poured from her mouth. "How do you know?"

Technology was always advancing. Always improving. Was it really that unreasonable to think Micah might recover someday? "How do you know he won't wake up?"

Dr. Markson tucked the file under his arm.

"I was looking on the internet, and there are stories. Stories of people who woke up from comas months, even years later."

The doctor examined her kindly. "Micah's not in a coma, Robin."

She shook her head and took a good, long look at her husband. Three bags of fluid hung near his bed. Blue tubing ran from a large white machine and attached to his mouth.

A sob bubbled in her throat.

Wake up!

The words echoed through her. Micah didn't move.

"We've run every test there is to run."

She knew. She'd watched doctors shine lights in Micah's eyes and stick tongue depressors down his throat, all the while holding out for good news. But it never came. No corneal or gag reflex. She watched them inject radioactive isotopes in Micah's bloodstream to measure the blood flow in his brain. When the results came back, she'd demanded they do it over. Nothing changed the second time around.

"I wouldn't say this if I wasn't one hundred percent positive, but Micah's gone."

His words, though not the first time she'd heard them, stole her breath. "I need a moment."

Dr. Markson nodded and left the room.

As she approached Micah's bedside she recalled the first night of their honeymoon, when she'd touched his arm after he'd fallen asleep. He'd jumped up in bed, almost out of his skin, so fast that she screamed and swatted him for scaring her so thoroughly. Then they both laughed, and the sound of it chased away her fear.

Holding her breath, she reached out a tentative hand and touched his arm. But this time he didn't jump. He didn't open his eyes. He didn't do anything. "Micah." The warmth of his whispered name blew across her lips and floated away, just out of reach.

She squeezed his hand.

Nothing.

A tear gathered and rolled down her cheek.

Please Lord, bring him back.

It wasn't a hopeless prayer. Or a half-hearted one. She believed God could do it. She believed with every ounce of her being that God could give her Micah back if He wanted. The God of the universe—who had spoken the heavens and earth in to being—could surely breathe life into her husband's brain. It felt like such a simple request compared to the creation of the world.

Please Lord...

The bed creaked as she eased herself onto it. She took Micah's hand and placed it over her stomach. She leaned over his body and brought her lips to his forehead. The warmth touching her skin stirred her soul. He was alive and she was pregnant. After eighteen long months of trying, of negative pregnancy tests, of dashed hopes, their dream was finally coming true. Only Micah had collapsed before she could tell him the news. Once he knew, his eyes would open, and he'd look at her and he'd smile. She moved her lips across his scalp, the softness of his hair brushing against her chin.

"Micah." She kissed his temple. "Please wake up."

Nothing.

She stared at his closed eyes, willing them to open. Desperate to see that look of his—two parts intimate, one part mischievous, like he had a private joke just for her. She wanted to gaze into the depths of his hazel green eyes and see her love reflected there. She wanted him to open them and give her that thousand-watt smile he was so famous for.

She wove her fingers through his. "I have something to tell you."

Should she say the words? Was she ready? She took a deep breath. What if she said them and nothing changed? Then what? The organ procurement coordinator was down the hall, pen in hand, ready for her to sign. The surgeons were standing by, ready to fly Micah's organs in a dozen different directions. His family waited outside, preparing to say goodbye so they could begin the grieving process.

But what if they didn't have to grieve? What if she could run into the hallway and cry out that Micah was awake? Her chest swelled. Jesus brought Lazarus back to life. Was it really too much to ask Him to do the same for her husband?

She wove her fingers tighter, squeezing his large palm in her own. He would wake up. Their dreams—plans to have children, open a café, and grow old side-by-side—were fused together, welded into a whole that could not be separated. And with a positive pregnancy test and plans for the café down on paper, they were too close to their future for God to take it away now. She bent over and brought her face next to his. She shut her eyes and poured the words into his ear.

"Micah, I'm pregnant."

She imagined them working through his canal and snuggling deep inside his brain. She imagined them fixing whatever was broken. She took a breath. Then another. And another. Her heartbeat gathered momentum, picking up speed until the thunderous pounding drowned out the swooshing of the ventilator.

She opened one eye, then her other. His lids were still closed. His lax expression unchanged. She jiggled his hand.

Nothing.

She shook it harder.

Nothing.

"Wake up." She placed her hands on his shoulders and pressed them against the bed. "Didn't you hear me? I'm pregnant."

Her hand slapped his bicep.

His eyes stayed closed.

She grabbed his chin, as if he were a naughty child who'd said a bad word. His head lolled and his lips parted. The Micah she knew would jump at the news. He'd let out a whoop, grab his cell phone, and start calling everybody he knew. The Micah she knew wouldn't leave her to deal with a pregnancy on her own.

Something violent burst inside her, snapping all reason. She balled her fists and hit his chest. When he didn't respond, she pounded all the harder. She cursed Micah's name. She screamed for him to wake up until her throat burned.

When her rage was spent, she crumpled in to a ball at Micah's side and surrendered to the tears. Surrendered to the pain of lost dreams, an empty future, and a child who would never know its father. And after that, when there was nothing left but her hollowed-out soul, she stood from Micah's bed. She brushed her wet lips one last time against his. She pressed her palms against her swollen eyes. She smoothed her rumpled clothes. She walked down the hall. And she signed the papers.

Bethany stood in the hallway, trying to close her ears to Robin's lament, but it was like she was twelve years old all over again, overhearing Pastor Fenton and Mom talking about her father. As much as she wanted to plug her ears, she couldn't.

Frustration and helplessness swirled inside of her. How was her being there helping anything? Robin had Micah's family. And God. She did not need Bethany.

She stepped closer to the wall.

The waiting room, filled with Evan's family and a white-haired man who called himself Pastor Gray, blocked her exit. Evan sat with his head in his hands while his father wrapped his arm around Loraine. Evan's oldest brother, Bryan, paced the room. His wife Amy clutched her purse in her lap. Evan's youngest brother—whose name Bethany had forgotten—mimicked Evan's posture, only his shoulders shook, and Amanda wiped at a steady stream of tears leaking from her eyes.

The scene unfolding in front of Bethany brought her back to a time when it had been her family waiting for news, her father the one tied to life by a fragile set of tubes, her mother the one weeping. Bethany pushed the memories away and took a tentative step toward the elevator just as Robin emerged from Micah's room and drifted down the hall toward the room where the organ procurement coordinator had explained everything.

Within moments, the waiting room emptied, as some followed Robin and the others disappeared into Micah's room. Only Evan remained, his head still buried in his hands.

The elevator dinged.

Now was her chance. She'd done her duty. She'd comforted Robin. And as far as Dan—well, keeping him inside and quiet was a practice in futility. Her job in Peaks was over. It would be pointless to stay another few days. The elevator doors slid open and two men dressed in scrubs stepped out.

She needed to move toward them, but Evan's deflated posture pulled at something in her chest, and her feet took on a mind of their own. She walked toward Evan instead, her mind screaming its protest as she eased onto the edge of a nearby seat. Bethany reached out, her hand hovering above his shoulder blade, and stared at the cotton shirt outlining Evan's muscles.

She was not his mother. Rubbing his back would do little to offer comfort and much to add to her already frazzled nerves. So she moved her hands under her knees and pressed them against the chair.

Evan turned toward her, his upper body bent over his knees, his hazel eyes shadowed and strained. "How did you get through it?"

The scratched, whispered question raised gooseflesh on her arms. "Through what?"

"Losing your father."

What did Evan know about her father? How much had Dan told him? Did he think their losses somehow united them? That she would let the pain of losing a beloved family member gather them beneath the same umbrella of grief? She'd forced herself out from under that umbrella a long time ago. She had no connection to Evan. He was just a farmhand on her grandpa's farm.

But his eyes... They begged for an answer. They begged for comfort.

She touched his forearm. "Somehow, you just do."

He looked at her hand, at the spot she touched, his eyelashes dark and wet.

Bryan reemerged from Micah's room, Amy at his side, dabbing a tissue beneath her eyes. Bethany jerked her arm away.

Evan stood and disappeared inside the room. It was the strange desire to follow him, to grab on to his hand like Amy held on to her husband's, that brought her back to her senses. With Evan gone, and Bryan and Amy wrapped in a hug, she swung the strap of her purse over her shoulder and strode to the elevator, urging it open before anybody could catch her escaping.

The elevator dinged and the doors slid apart. She stepped inside and jabbed the button for the ground floor several times. She didn't exhale until she reached the parking lot. The tension in her shoulders leaked away with every step toward her car. The farther away she got from Peaks, the better.

Eight

Bethany inhaled the scent of Pine-Sol and freshly cleaned carpets and ran her fingertips over the mahogany surface of her desk. After her three-day leave, she had returned to work to a pile of memos, e-mails, and voice mails waiting for her. She plucked a file from her desk and scanned the printouts inside, tapping her pen against the manila folder.

The memory of Robin's face poked Bethany's conscience. She exhaled a deep breath, as if she could expel the memories of the last few days. Grief had wrapped Robin in such a hazy cocoon, she probably hadn't noticed Bethany's absence.

But what about Evan? He accused her of going to Peaks for selfish reasons, and she had done nothing but prove him right. The printouts rattled in her trembling hand. She straightened the corners of the papers crinkled in her grip and slipped them inside a folder. So what if he thought the worst of her? What did she care? They were nothing more than strangers—forced together by coincidence and location and mutual acquaintances. What he thought about her didn't matter.

She swiveled toward her computer and clicked on an unopened message from the architectural design department. When the e-mail popped up on her computer screen, she noticed Jeff McKinley's address carbon copied below her own. She squinted at the screen. Why would design include Jeff in an e-mail concerning the River Oaks account? Sure, they sometimes worked together since they were the only two architects in the renovation department, but Martin had specifically given this account to her, not Jeff. She skimmed the body of the e-mail, feeling out of the loop. She didn't like it.

She stood and rolled her shoulders. She would head down to design right now and crank out a 3-D rendering that would make Martin's head spin. She exited her workstation, strode down the hallway, and turned in to the lobby, her heels clicking against the granite tile. Parker Crane's receptionist sat behind a desk, bathed in a stream of sunlight pouring in from the high-paneled windows. She looked up at the echo of Bethany's footsteps and smiled as she marched toward the double doors leading to design and marketing. The elevator opened and Martin stepped out, carrying his black leather briefcase in one hand and a Starbucks Grande in the other.

"Bethany," he said, raising his eyebrows.

Her chest swelled with pride. Not many employees came back early from vacation. If that's what she wanted to call her trip to Peaks.

"You're back."

She pulled herself straighter. "I was eager to get going on the River Oaks project."

"This certainly is a surprise." Martin turned to the receptionist. "Could you page Rhonda for me and tell her Bethany is here?" He gave the top of the desk two firm taps with the bottom of his coffee cup and looked at Bethany. "If you don't mind, I'd like to speak with you in my office."

The 3-D rendering dropped from her radar. She fell behind him and followed, the clicking of her heels no longer keeping the upbeat tempo they'd found upon entering the lobby.

Martin held the door open for her and swept his hand toward a chair. "Please, have a seat."

As Bethany sat down, Rhonda came in and closed the door behind her.

Bethany clasped her hands in her lap and focused on keeping her posture straight, her face relaxed, her thoughts positive. This could be something good. Like a promotion. Or a bonus. There were plenty of reasons why Martin would call her into his office, and many of those reasons would involve their company HR rep. But the frown on Martin's face prevented her from jumping full throttle in to such optimistic thinking.

Her boss sat in his high-backed chair and leaned forward, folding his hands over the papers on his desk. "Bethany, over the past four years, you've been a wonderful employee for Parker Crane."

Bethany tried to smile, but whenever Martin started with a compliment, he liked to follow with bad news. "Did you get the memo about losing the First State account?"

She swallowed. "No. When?"

"On Monday afternoon. It was one of our biggest accounts. Losing that, along with Florenstine putting an indefinite freeze on their new spa line, really hit us hard."

Her forehead knotted. She looked from Rhonda to Martin. "The president of First State expressed interest in my ideas." She forced a calmness in her voice she didn't feel. "And Florenstine has nothing to do with renovations."

"Yes. I know."

"So why are you telling me this?"

"I know none of this is your fault. But Parker Crane is taking a big hit right now. I'm afraid our only option is downsizing."

Bethany clamped her hands around the armrests of her chair. "Your only option?"

"While you were gone, we had to let Anthony go."

Her mind whirled. Martin fired Anthony? She knew things were hinting toward this direction, but she'd only been gone three days. How could all this have transpired in such a short amount of time?

"Right now, with the economy the way it is, we can't afford to keep two renovation architects on staff. Our company policy states we keep our employees based on experience, and Jeff's been here longer. I'm sorry Bethany, but we have to let you go."

She tried to follow his words, but they jumbled together with dizzying speed. "Is this because I took time off?"

Martin gave his head an emphatic shake. "Of course not."

Rhonda began talking then. Bethany could see her lips moving. She heard bits and pieces here and there, snatches of words and phrases. Something about severance pay and health insurance. Then Martin's voice broke through.

"I have a lot of respect for you as a worker, Bethany. You have a talent that will get you right back on your feet again. I'm sure of it." He stood and moved toward the door.

She stayed in her seat, a pile of questions stuck in her throat. What about the past four years? What about the clients she had wooed with her vision and attention to detail? What about the bonuses and the promotions and the success she'd promised herself when she'd been hired at Parker Crane? Bethany took a deep breath and forced herself to concentrate. She would not panic. She would remain in control.

"Please let me know if there's anything I can do. I can write a letter of recommendation, if you'd like. Just have our receptionist make a note of it."

Bethany stood, her legs wobbling beneath her. She tried to find her voice, but Martin gave her a strained smile and scooted her out the door. That was it. They were done. She was done.

The entire time she cleared out her desk, the unfairness of the situation pressed against her. She had poured her heart and soul into Parker Crane for the past four years. She had worked long hours deep in to the night to ensure her work was of the highest quality. And now they were just going to throw some severance pay at her and toss her out the door?

As she filled her box with favorite pens, pictures of her and Dominic from various vacations, and other odds and ends she'd accumulated over the years, her resolve solidified. She wasn't a helpless girl anymore. It was time for her to take control of her life. And if she had to fight for her job, then that's exactly what she would do.

✵

Bethany stared at the wall clock, the small hand just shy of ten. Her foot tapped the floor, an attempt to keep her insides from crawling to the outside. This was late. Even for Dominic. She'd tried his cell phone a half dozen times throughout the day and never once had he answered. So she passed the time cleaning her loft, then cleaning Dominic's apartment, then scouring the internet, researching employee rights. When the door opened at quarter past, she sprang from her seat. "Where've you been?"

He set down his briefcase and gave her a peculiar look. "At work."

"Until ten?"

"I have an important case tomorrow."

"Didn't you get my messages?"

"You know I don't take personal calls at work." The clipped tone of his voice tweezed her nerve endings. What if she'd been injured? Or killed? Would he ignore the coroner's phone call too? He stepped closer and ran his hands up the length of her arms. "I'm glad you're here though."

He leaned in for a kiss.

She pulled away.

"What's wrong?"

She braced herself against the words. There was no easy way to say them. No matter how she strung them together, they would all came out the same. In the course of a day, she'd gone from success to failure, from focused to floundering, from architect to unemployed. "Martin let me go."

Dominic's hands fell to his sides. "What?"

Saying it once was enough. Did he really need her to say it again?

He brought his hand to the top of his head and fisted his hair. "Did he give you a reason?"

"Downsizing." Bethany practically spat the word. "But I have my doubts."

"You think he's lying?"

She wanted to say yes. Actually, she wanted to shout yes. But that wasn't the truth. The truth was there'd been whispers of downsizing ever since the summer. She just never imagined the downsizing might include her. Tears welled in her eyes, but she blinked them away. She would not be one of those distraught women who needed a hand to hold. Those women didn't think straight, and straight thinking was exactly what Bethany needed if she was going to move forward. "I want to fight this."

"Was anybody else laid off?"

"Anthony."

"And you still want to fight it?"

What she really wanted to do was peel the doubt off his forehead. Just once, for something so important, she needed his support, his confidence, maybe even some indignation on her behalf. "Yes, and I want you to help me."

Dominic held up his hands. "Whoa there, Bethany. I can definitely understand your frustration, babe, but you don't have a case. Not if they let Anthony go. And not if Martin can prove downsizing was necessary." He slipped the tie from around his neck. "Besides, I'm swamped. I can't take on another case right now. Especially one I won't win."

His words and the matter-of-fact way he delivered them slashed a fatal wound through her determination. The old helpless Bethany reared, bucking against the woman she had become. A woman who took control of her life. A woman who poured her heart into her work to ensure this very thing would never happen. How was she going to fight Parker Crane without Dominic's support? She opened her mouth to argue, but before she could get anything out, her cell phone vibrated in her pocket. She pressed it against her ear and barked an angry greeting into the mouthpiece.

"Bethany?"

The man's voice sounded familiar, like an impossible-to-place déjà-vu.

"It's Evan."

Warmth drained from her face. Evan? Why was he calling? In the milliseconds before she spoke, her mind whirred with a thousand possibilities, each one worse than the last. "Is everything okay?"

"I hate to tell you this." The sudden urge to hurl the phone across the room overwhelmed her, but before she could tear the device from her ear, Evan sighed into the receiver. "Dan had another heart attack."

Stillness enfolded her. A moment of nothing. A calmness that came and went before she could finish blinking. No. She didn't believe it. Getting let go from her job was enough for one day. Grandpa Dan having another heart attack could simply not happen.

"I think you should come back to Peaks." There was a pause. Another sigh. "He didn't make it."

Nine

I t's hard to pinpoint the exact moment my world went wobbly. Perhaps it was when Dad fell from the silo and his hands and legs decided not to work anymore. Or when I found him dead eight months later. Or when Mom decided she hated the farm and announced she was moving David and me away from the only home we ever knew.

I just know there reached a point where my nine-year-old self started walking lower to the ground, as if one more blow might knock me off planet Earth altogether. While eleven-year old David, all jutting angles and knobby knees, tried hard to comfort our mother, I spent that time trailing Grandpa Dan. Joining him out in the fields. Feeding the cattle. Brushing the horses. My grandpa had a sturdiness about him that made me feel less off-balanced.

Two weeks after I watched my dad's casket lower into the ground, two days before my mom moved us into a trailer park, I spent an entire day riding beside Grandpa in the combine, way up high above stalks of corn. We didn't say one single word to each other that whole time and something about the silence comforted me. By then we were both pretty sick of words. So there we rode, in the small cab of that giant machine, not saying a thing until he turned off the engine.

And even then we sat still in our seats, my feet dangling above the floor, watching the horizon turn to peach. Three days prior, Pastor Fenton showed up on Dan's front porch. Mom tried to invite the pastor inside, but my grandpa refused to let that man set one shiny shoe into our home.

I remember smiling about that. I remember feeling safe on the other side of my grandfather. Until Mom told me later that we were moving. That I needed to hurry up and pack my room so we could go away. I couldn't help wondering if Grandpa Dan shouldn't have let Pastor Fenton inside after all. If maybe that's why Mom was so adamant about moving us into a small trailer home when we could stay right where we were. At the farm.

Grandpa Dan sniffed.

The sound, after such a long stretch of silence, made me look over. Tears trickled down his face. It was the first time I'd ever seen him cry. He hadn't when my father had his accident. He hadn't when my father came home from the hospital and spent all those months learning how to eat and drink and live all over again. And he hadn't at the funeral. But now, there he sat, chopped corn surrounding us on all sides and sadness rolling down his weathered cheeks.

I reached over and placed my small hand over Grandpa's broad one. He turned up his palm, laced his fingers with mine, and held on like the world wobbled for him too. My throat became all tight and hot, and before I knew it, my cheeks were just as wet as his.

He reached over and scooped me into his lap like I weighed nothing at all. I leaned against his chest, rising and falling with each one of his breaths, wishing I could stay like that forever. But a question niggled into my brain. A question I'd been thinking on ever since Aunt Sharon dressed me in that black, itchy dress for Dad's funeral.

"Grandpa?" I asked.

"Hmm."

"Who's going to walk me down the aisle now that Daddy's gone?"

His chest expanded—nice and big—pushing me up. He turned me around to face him—his tears all dried. "What made you think of that?"

The question wasn't what a typical nine-year old might ask, I guess. But ever since I'd seen my other grandpa walk Aunt Sharon down a rose-covered aisle eight months ago, I'd been obsessed with weddings. I shrugged and stared down at my skinned knees.

Grandpa Dan placed his knuckles beneath my chin and lifted my face, his blue eyes filled with such steadiness that I snuggled further into his lap. "When the time comes, I'd be honored to walk you down the aisle."

Even though he kept my face tilted toward his, I managed to cast my eyes away. I wanted to hold on to Grandpa Dan's promise for the future. And I wanted to stay with him on the farm now. Everything I loved was being stripped from me. Too many things were changing. "Grandpa?"

"Hmmm?"

"Why can't we stay here and live with you?"

"Bethany," he said.

I looked up in to his eyes, and mine started burning all over again.

He stretched his callused palm flat against my cheek and curled strong fingers around the back of my neck. "You're welcome here anytime you want. This farm is just as much yours as it will ever be mine. And no matter where you live, that won't ever change."

Ten

Bethany hitched the strap of her purse over her shoulder and stared at the mortician hunched in front of her. Talk about solidifying a stereotype. Spending so much time amongst dead bodies had turned Floyd McCormis in to an eerie replica of his craftsmanship. When Bethany shook his hand, she imagined squeezing a refrigerated nectarine. She hid her grimace and spotted Evan, scrutinizing her from the opposite side of the table, looking in dire need of a hot shower, a thorough shave, and a good night's sleep.

She swung a bagged suit over the table and set her purse on the ground by her chair. "I bought a suit. For Dan. I wasn't sure if he had anything to wear." The plastic crinkled as she slid it closer to the mortician. "It's Ralph Lauren." A blush crept up her neck. Who cared if it was Ralph Lauren?

She slid to the edge of the seat and massaged the tops of her knees. "I'm not sure what we're supposed to discuss. I've never had to plan a funeral before." She resisted the urge to glance at Evan, who no doubt had just helped with Micah's.

"That's what I'm here for, Miss Quinn. All you have to do is answer some questions and I'll take care of the rest." Floyd's voice rattled when he spoke, like he needed to clear his throat.

A shiver scurried up her spine. She bent over and rummaged through her purse, pulling out files and papers and whatever else she'd been able to gather in such short notice. "I brought insurance papers, Dan's birth certificate, and a few other things—"

Floyd reached out and patted her hand. "All in good time, Miss Quinn."

She pulled away from him and rubbed warmth into her arms. Evan didn't speak. He didn't even move. He just sat there with all the world's grief gathered on his shoulders. She imagined scooping hers up and putting it there too.

"I have some standard questions I'd like to ask, if you wouldn't mind." Floyd picked up the list in front of him and clicked his pen. "Where would you like to hold the service? Our funeral home is available, or perhaps you have a church in mind."

"Here will be fine."

"Do you have a pastor or a priest you'd like to direct the service?"

"No."

"Yes." Evan leaned over the table. "The same pastor who spoke at my brother's funeral offered to speak at Dan's. His name is Pastor Gray." He motioned to Floyd's pen, like the old man should make a note of his suggestion.

Bethany leaned forward. "No pastor will be necessary. I spoke with one of my grandfather's cousins. He's prepared to give a eulogy."

"Dan would want there to be a pastor," Evan said.

"No, he wouldn't."

Evan's eyes glinted. "How would you know?"

"My grandfather wasn't religious." As far as she knew, he didn't even go to church.

"What does religion have to do with anything?"

Her mind sputtered, but she couldn't find a single word to throw at his question.

Evan turned to Floyd, who stared at the pair of them with his pen poised over the paper, mouth ajar. "If Dan's granddaughter doesn't want a pastor, that's fine. I'll be saying a prayer."

Floyd's pen didn't budge. He looked from Bethany to Evan, then back to Bethany again. "Is that okay with you, Miss Quinn?"

She folded her arms across her chest. "Fine." If it made Evan feel better, he could say his childish prayer. It's not like it would bring Dan back. No amount of praying, no amount of crying, would undo the truth. Her grandfather was dead.

Evan stared into the casket and took in Dan's appearance. Closed lids molded together as though made of candle wax, gray hair swept across his forehead, rough hands folded over a black suit. In the five years he'd known Dan, the man had never worn a suit. They should have buried him in a pair of grease-stained overalls and his Carhartt jacket, with a can of Copenhagen in his pocket.

He slid his hand across the pine and prepared himself to receive the line of guests waiting to say goodbye. The whole familiar scene picked at his overstretched emotions with the sharpness of a vulture's beak. First Micah. Now Dan. Only this time, instead of a broken widow standing by his side, he had Bethany.

It made him grit his teeth.

She offered no explanation for her sudden departure from the hospital, no apology for abandoning Robin, no excuses for missing Micah's funeral.

And now she was back, plowing her way through Dan's funeral arrangements like a combine. She treated the entire thing like a to-do list. If she had any emotions, she vaulted them behind steel-reinforced concrete.

"Your judgment is palpable," she whispered.

He jerked his head. "What are you talking about?"

"You think I'm horrible for forbidding a pastor."

Evan forced a smile and shook hands with a family shuffling through the line. "That's not true. I think you're horrible because of the way you left Robin last week."

Her posture went from stiff to full-blown rigor mortis. "I had to leave. I have a life in Chicago, you know."

"I didn't say *because* you left." He pushed the words between his teeth and forced himself to shake hands with another family shuffling through the line. "I said because of the *way* you left."

She shifted beside him.

"You could have told Robin you were leaving." Never mind the ridiculous notion that she could have said goodbye to him as well. One minute the woman was comforting him at the hospital. The next, she'd disappeared. He had no idea why it made him so angry.

The DeLuves stepped forward. They lived down the road from the farm and Mrs. DeLuve played pinochle with Dan on Sunday evenings down at Gurney's sports bar. She hobbled forward and reached out her arms in an attempt to hug Bethany. But Bethany stuck out her hand, stopping the old woman's gesture. This didn't thwart Mrs. DeLuve. The two ended up in an awkward side-hugging shoulder pat. When the old woman reached Evan, he welcomed her embrace to make up for Bethany's coldness.

"He was a fine man," Mrs. DeLuve said, dabbing her dewy eyes with the tissue she'd pulled from her purse. She turned to her husband. "Wasn't he a fine man?"

Mr. DeLuve gave a somber nod. "One of the finest."

The old man grasped his wife's elbow and moved her through the line. They paused in front of Dan's casket, bowed their heads, and crossed themselves. Their mirrored actions looked choreographed. Fifty years of marriage had turned them in to two parts of a whole, a right and a left hand, working together in perfect unison. Exactly what a marriage should be. Exactly what Micah and Robin's had been. Now Robin had to find a way to adjust to life without her right hand. After seven years, it was bound to be a long and heartbreaking process.

Evan cleared away the tightness in his throat and peered down the line of people, his mind giving no thought to the faces before him until he came across one that was much too familiar. Robin stood in line—sunken cheeks and swollen eyes—a postcard for grief. His eyes widened. She shouldn't be here. Not three days after Micah's funeral. This was too much. He took a step toward her, but Bethany let out the faintest of gasps and halted his movement.

He looked at her, but Bethany's eyes were glued to the lectern at the entryway, where the guest book rested. Just beyond that, he spotted Bethany's mother Ruth being escorted by Pastor Fenton, the Pastor of First Light.

When Pastor Fenton took Ruth's coat from her shoulders, the hardness in Bethany's eyes vanished, replaced by a vulnerability that parted her lips and stirred something foreign in the pit of Evan's stomach. By the time Ruth and her guest reached the front of the line, the rapid pulsation ticking in Bethany's neck made Evan wonder if she might faint from the sudden onset of arrhythmia. His own muscles tightened, and he didn't even know why.

"Bethany," Ruth reached out to touch her daughter's arm, but Bethany pulled away.

"What are you doing here?" she asked.

No hug. No greeting. No smile.

"The same reason everybody else is here, Bethany," Pastor Fenton said. "To pay our respects." He turned to Evan and stuck out his hand. "We're deeply sorry for your loss."

Evan took the offered hand and shook it. Fenton's grip was firm. Confident. For whatever reason, Dan had never liked this man. He wasn't the only one, either. People talked in town, and not everything Evan heard about First Light was good. But Bethany's reaction went much deeper than dislike.

She scorched Pastor Fenton with a stare that could wilt Evan's crops. Only the man did not wilt. He gave Bethany an indifferent smile, positioned his hand on the small of Ruth's back, and shuffled her past the casket.

Bethany's eyes fastened upon Fenton's hand. When they passed, and the Crammers stepped forward, she spun around, hair whipping about her shoulders, and stalked away. Evan stared after her, a million questions zinging through his head. What in the world had just happened?

Bethany zeroed in on the bathroom door, counting the steps until she reached her escape. Ten. She refused to look anywhere else. A few people might have smiled at her, and somebody patted her elbow, but she paid no attention. Seven more steps.

Her entire focus rested on the *Ladies* sign. She needed to escape, to get inside, so she could lock herself away and regain her frazzled composure. Five. She could not believe her mother had the nerve to come. And with *him.* She stepped around a gathering of people. And just before she slipped through the door—

"Bethany."

The sound froze her momentum. Her mother stood off to the left, her waif-like frame blending in with the wall, hands clasped together in front of her. "I know you don't want me here, but I had to come and pay my respects."

"Since when have you ever respected Dan?"

Her mother flinched. "Please. I don't want to fight."

Bethany ground her teeth, so sick of her mother's timidity. She hadn't always been this way. She used to have an ounce of backbone. "Why did you really come?"

Mom twisted her hands.

"To see for yourself he was dead? To make sure the last keeper of our shameful secret was no longer a threat?"

Mom's eyes zipped one way, then the other, as if searching for potential eavesdroppers. She dipped her chin and leaned in close. "I don't know what you're talking about, Bethany."

"Of course you do."

Mom's pupils dilated. She stared, as if unsure what to do with Bethany's odd string of accusations. Bethany couldn't blame her. After all, she never told her mother what she knew. People in Peaks speculated, but Mom did her best to squelch the rumors and hide the truth from Bethany and David.

A part of Bethany wanted to let Mom squirm over this new revelation—that she knew the truth. But the other part couldn't handle her mother's discomfort. She rolled her eyes. "Where's your *boyfriend*?"

"Don't be ridiculous. Pastor Fenton is not my boyfriend."

"Then why's he always with you? Why's he always touching you?"

Her mother blanched. "Why...that's just..." She put her hand to her throat. "He's just a very caring man."

"Yeah. That's it." Bethany twisted her neck to follow her mother's stare and found the man under discussion. He used his hands while he conversed and carried himself in a way that demanded attention. His magnetic presence reeled people in with a rusty hook. The same rusty hook that had snagged her parents. All of a sudden, Bethany felt sick. "Please, don't let me stop you from paying your respects." She stepped around her mother and swung open the door to the ladies' room.

Once inside, she moved to the sinks and placed her hands on the countertop, hating the way her poise unhinged at the sight of Pastor Fenton. She hadn't expected to see him. Especially not at Dan's funeral. Especially not with her mother. Mom's reverence for that man had always bordered on worship. Today had been no different. It reminded her of everything she wanted to forget.

Bethany stuck her hands beneath the faucet and splashed water on her cheeks. She pulled several paper towels from the dispenser, dried her face, and studied her reflection in the mirror. Her twelve-year-old self stared back. Knobby elbows, slumped shoulders, and brown hair curtaining a pair of eyes much too large for her thin face.

She blinked away the image away. She wasn't that helpless girl anymore. She wasn't an object of pity. She was a woman who'd risen above her circumstances and created a life most people in Peaks would envy. She straightened her shoulders and smoothed her blouse. She wasn't going to hide in the bathroom. Bethany was done hiding. She pulled her hair away from her face and repositioned her clip.

Just as she turned away from her reflection, a low-pitched moaning rumbled from one of the stalls. Bethany studied the space between floor and partitions, searching for a pair of feet. She found them at the very end just as another moan stabbed the air. Her heels clicked twice against the tile as she moved toward the stall.

Another moan, only fainter this time. She took another step and touched her fingertips to the cool surface of the door.

"Hello?" Her tentative greeting echoed against the tiled walls.

The shuffling on the other side stopped.

She leaned closer. "Are you okay in there?"

"Bethany? Is that you?"

"Robin?"

Another groan.

The hairs on the back of Bethany's neck prickled. "Robin, are you okay?"

No answer.

She eased the door open and found Robin, doubled over on the toilet, clutching her stomach, the white porcelain floor beneath her stained crimson. Alarm shot to the end of Bethany's fingertips. "What's wrong?"

Robin looked up, her pale face paralyzed with shock, as if she didn't know where she was or what was happening. "I think I'm having a miscarriage."

The room darkened, then came back in to sharp focus. Bethany wrapped her fingers over the top of the stall divider to still the swaying. A miscarriage? Robin was pregnant?

Bethany exited the bathroom, hurried into the lobby, and cut through the line of visitors, her motions set on automatic fast forward. Evan stood by the casket, shaking hands and receiving hugs. She rushed to his side and yanked his arm.

"Whoa, what is it?"

She whispered what she'd just seen in his ear and watched the color drain from his face. Without hesitating, he left his place by the casket and brushed through the crowd, pulling her behind him. He burst into the restroom where Robin wobbled in front of the sink and scooped her into his

arms like she was nothing more than a fragile rag doll. Not even a full minute later, they were in Bethany's car, Robin lying in the backseat, speeding
to the hospital. Bethany gripped the steering wheel, pleading with a God
she didn't believe existed.

Losing Micah was enough. Don't take her baby too.

Eleven

W hile there hadn't been an alarming amount of blood, it had been bright red. That, combined with the cramping, was enough to draw the nurse's concerned attention and call for a doctor. Bethany stood by, afraid to move or speak, gauging Robin's pain by her facial expressions. Right then, with closed eyes and a relaxed face, she suspected the cramps had subsided. If only she knew what to make of Robin's moving lips.

Was she praying?

"I can't do this." Robin's words came out as an almost-invisible whisper, disappearing as soon as they parted from her mouth.

Even though Bethany was the only other person in the room, she had a feeling Robin wasn't talking to her. So she kept quiet and tried to push away the images repeating in her mind: Evan sweeping Robin up in his arms, carrying her to the car with strong, sure strides.

If there was one thing Bethany prided herself in, it was her self-sufficiency. She didn't need a man to take care of her. She didn't need God to be her crutch. But now, with her nerves jumbled, she couldn't help but think how nice it would be to have somebody rescue her the way Evan had rescued Robin.

Batting away the disturbing thoughts, she placed her hand on Robin's

KATIE GANSHERT

shoulder. She would see Robin through this evening. She would bury her grandfather tomorrow morning. Then she would go back to Chicago and find another job—a better one. People liked to say perfection wasn't attainable, but she sure came close during her four years at Parker Crane.

"Last night I asked God why this was happening…" Robin looked down in to her lap. "I told God I didn't want this pregnancy." Her breath hitched. "Not without Micah."

The muscles in Bethany's chest knotted.

Robin buried her face in her hands. "I didn't mean it."

Bethany opened her mouth, attempting to form words—to find a way to reassure her friend that her brokenhearted request meant nothing, but anything she tried to say stuck to her tongue. So instead, she squeezed Robin's shoulder, feeling silly. Inadequate. Until the doctor entered the room. He sat in a swivel chair on the opposite side of Robin's inclined bed and asked her a quick series of questions. The nurse came in as he finished.

"Okay Robin, we're going to take you across the hall and do an internal sonogram. We'll search for a heartbeat and see if we can't find out what might have caused the bleeding."

Robin looked up from her lap. "You don't think I miscarried?"

Bethany closed her eyes against the hope straining her friend's voice.

"There are a number of things that can cause bleeding. It's not always indicative of a miscarriage. The good thing is that the bleeding has stopped."

"What about the cramping?"

"Many women experience cramping in the first trimester. Usually it's just the uterus expanding. However, since it was accompanied with bleeding, it does cause some concern."

Robin rested her head back and gazed at the speckled ceiling tiles. "Do you think my baby is alive?"

The doctor kept his face neutral, taking great care not to offer false hope or cause unnecessary concern. "The ultrasound will show us how the baby is doing." He patted Robin's knee and exited the room.

Bethany helped Robin to her feet and escorted her to the door. The doctor might not be concerned with Robin walking, but Bethany thought her old friend looked ready to collapse with grief and exhaustion. As soon as they came out into the hallway, Evan stood, his hair a mess. As if he'd run his fingers through it a thousand times in the last thirty minutes.

"They're going to do an ultrasound," Bethany said.

His eyes zipped to Robin, then to Bethany. "Is the baby...?"

Bethany gave her head a subtle shake. "They don't know."

Robin's fingernails dug into Bethany's skin. Evan grabbed Robin's opposite elbow and the three of them followed the doctor down the hall. When they reached the room, Evan let go and ran his hand back through his hair. "Do you want me to come in?"

"It's okay," Robin said. "Bethany's with me."

"I'll be out here praying."

Bethany exchanged a long glance with Evan, then ushered Robin into the small room with a table and an ultrasound machine. Robin changed in the bathroom, came out clutching a sheet around her bottom half, and lay down while Bethany stood in the corner, wishing she could switch places with Evan. What was she supposed to do—what was she supposed to say—if they couldn't find a baby?

"The technician will be here in just a minute," the doctor said. "I'll be back to speak with you afterward."

The ultrasound technician arrived almost as soon as the doctor left. She introduced herself, turned on the machine, had Robin place her feet into stirrups, and began working. Bethany stared at the computer, trying to pinpoint something that might pass as an embryo. Black and white blotches rippled across the screen. She couldn't make sense of any of it.

She swallowed and braced herself for the worst. She tried to think of something to say or do that might relieve Robin from her accumulating grief. But her mind was blank—a worthless cavern packed with fuzz. She looked from the screen to the technician, who furrowed her brows as she searched for some sign of life.

And that's when Bethany saw it. A blip on the screen. A tiny, white, flashing blotch. Her heart sputtered. She turned to the technician. The lady's eyebrows spread wide, stretching away the deep V that had creased her forehead. It was there. Bethany hadn't imagined it. A heartbeat. A precious, miniscule heartbeat.

Life.

"Do you see this right here?" The woman pointed her finger to the spot Bethany had noticed a second earlier.

Robin lifted her head and looked at the screen for the first time, as if she'd been too afraid to face whatever might not be there. When she saw the beating heart, a small gasp escaped her lips. "Is that…?"

The woman nodded, her expression melting in to a large grin. "Yep. The rate is 165. Very healthy. Very normal."

A sob bubbled from Robin's mouth, escaping before she moved her hand to cover it. Bethany blinked several times, unsettled by the burning in her eyes.

The technician showed them a blob of black and white haze, which she said was the placenta. She insisted it looked healthy and just the right size. She took several more measurements, clicking her mouse on the screen. "You're measuring about seven-and-a-half weeks. The computer has August 12th as your due date."

Robin gasped.

Bethany pulled her attention away from the screen. "What's wrong?"

"That's Micah's birthday."

The doctor asked Robin to stay overnight to rehydrate, which forced Bethany and Evan into the confines of her Audi. Unlike the comfortable silence Bethany shared with Dan, this silence crackled with tension. When they finally arrived home, she retreated to her bedroom, eager to put the craziness of the day behind her. But she lay in bed with eyes wide open, unable to escape the image of that heartbeat on the screen.

Or of Evan carrying Robin in his arms.

The farmhouse groaned with emptiness. The lonely sound seemed to empty her as well. Tomorrow, she would bury her grandfather. Never again would she sit next to Grandpa Dan and listen to the deep rumble of his voice. Never again would she look into the steady blueness of his eyes. For the past ten years, she'd taken for granted that he'd always be there—presumed he always would. But now he was gone. If she was going to make it through tomorrow with her composure intact, she needed a good night's rest.

Her eyes refused to stay closed.

Bethany kicked off the quilt and grabbed the coat hanging from one of the bedposts. Holding her breath, she tiptoed past Evan's bedroom and down the stairs, grimacing whenever a floorboard or step creaked beneath her weight. When she reached the foyer, she shoved her feet into her boots, put on the coat, wrapped herself in an extra blanket, and stepped into the night. Grayish black engulfed the sky. Invisible storm clouds.

She pulled the blanket tighter around her shoulders and marched across the frozen yard, out into the darkness of the field. If someone saw her now, marching alone across the farm at night in the middle of December, they might think her crazy. But she didn't care.

A creek ran through Dan's property. One Bethany spent many summers wading through with David, tying chunks of hotdogs to bits of string, luring crawdads up from the rocks. Toward the north end of the pasture, behind the barn, an incredibly large rock jutted out from the bank. It had always been one of her favorite places on the farm. Dan called it her thinking spot. Said everybody had one, and that rock was Bethany's.

She had the sudden urge to go there now.

Her eyes adjusted to the dark, and snow began to fall. Fat flakes clung to her hair and gathered like moondust over her shoulders. She stepped over a low string of barbed wire fencing and came to the bank of the stream. The frigid water flowed over rocks, making its way to the Mississippi River. Bethany wondered, as she approached, if the rock would look as big as it did when she was a child. She looked over the bank and yelped, cupping her hand over her mouth to squelch the sound.

Somebody was already there.

Evan turned, ear buds plugged in each ear. He pulled them out and stood. Clumps of dirt came loose from the embankment and plunked into the stream. "Bethany? What are you doing here?"

Bethany couldn't answer. She was too busy trying to catch her breath. When her heart resumed a semi-regular beat, she gaped at him through the darkness. "I could ask you the same thing."

"I needed a place to think." He brushed snow from his hair. "This is a good spot for it."

She took a few steps down the bank and joined him by the rock, unsure how she felt about her and Evan sharing the same thinking spot.

"So what are you doing here in the middle of the night?" He held out his hand and gathered falling snow on his glove. "Right before a snow storm?"

A hint of familiar music mixed with the frozen air. It wasn't the twang she'd expected. "Is that Bach?"

"Country's not the only thing I listen to."

"Huh." She stared at the creek, hypnotized by the snowflakes melting into the uneven stream of water. "I love Bach."

Robin was responsible for Bethany's affinity for classical music. The infatuation started in junior high, when the two of them would go to Robin's house after school, drink ice cold Snapple, and eat lemon bars while Robin's mom, Mrs. Delner, played the piano in the sunroom. She produced music so elegant and sophisticated that Bethany often pretended Mrs. Delner was her mother and that big, beautiful house was her home.

Evan sat on one edge of the rock and nodded to the spot beside him. "Are you going to sit?"

She wasn't sure she wanted to stay anymore. How was she supposed to gather her thoughts with a slightly hostile man sitting beside her? She was about to make her excuses and leave when Evan said something that made her stop.

"This spot reminds me of Dan."

The snow continued to fall. It was as if somebody had placed them in the center of a giant snow globe. Bethany pulled the blanket over her shoulder and sat on the edge of the boulder, as far away from Evan as she could get. But the distance was minimal and the warmth of his body beside her made her ultra aware of her own. She studied his profile. "Don't you ever sleep?"

He wound the cords of the ear buds around his iPod. "It's hard to come by these days," he said.

She understood. She had a hard time with it too.

Silence settled between them, but this time it wasn't as unnerving as it had been in the car. Something about the vastness of the night and the softness of the snow diffused the tension.

Bethany was first to speak. "I used to come here a lot when I was younger."

She could feel Evan look at her.

"In the spring and summer, the bank of this creek is covered in wild-flowers." When she was a kid, she used to lay in their scent and stare up at the wide expanse of the cloud-dotted sky, listening to the trickle of the stream and the cicadas in the trees.. "At least it used to be."

"It still is."

Bethany closed her eyes and pictured it—the purples, whites, and blues of Sweet William and Virginia bluebells. It seemed impossible, that something so beautiful could grow up from the cold, hard ground her boots rested on now. "I used to pick them and make bouquets for my mom."

"Well, this pasture will be flooded with them next year. We're supposed to have a brutal winter. Lots of snow."

"What does that have to do with wildflowers?"

"The snowier the winter, the more wildflowers you get in the spring."

"Really?" She stared at the barren land surrounding them, disappearing beneath a layer of white. "I didn't know that."

The snow fell faster. Thicker.

Bethany brought her knees up to her chest and wrapped the blanket around her shins. She rested her chin on her kneecap and let her eyelids sink with heaviness.

"You're wrong about Dan's faith, you know."

She stiffened. "I hope not." She tried hard to keep the bitterness in check, but some of it slid out with her words.

Evan stared at her for a bit longer than politeness warranted. She ignored him and focused her attention on the sound of trickling water.

"What's your story?" he asked.

"What do you mean?"

"Why are you so angry with God?"

"I'm not angry. I'm indifferent."

"Okay." He drew the word out, like he didn't believe her at all.

She tugged at the blanket again and glared through the darkness.

"Come on, Bethany. There has to be a reason you react the way you do."

"You wouldn't understand." The man hung a cross from his rearview mirror for crying out loud.

He chuckled.

"What?"

"It's just… I probably understand more than you think." He scuffed his boot against dirt and snow. "I wasn't always such an upstanding Christian, you know. I went through a time in my life when I was pretty ticked off."

Bethany arched her brow. "Somehow, it's not so hard to imagine."

His lips curved into a private grin—one that held a secret he wasn't about to share. Her stomach fluttered. He looked down at the ground and took his smile with him.

"So why were you angry?" she asked.

When he looked up, his grin was gone. "My best friend in high school died in a car accident my senior year." He picked up a pebble near his feet and flipped it around in his hand. He took a deep breath. And his fist tightened around the pebble. "I was driving."

Bethany's face softened.

"I was the good Christian kid, just like my parents raised me to be. I didn't drink. I was the designated driver—made the *right* choices. Except we got in a car accident anyway, and I had to bury my friend." He peered at her with that same intense look, the one that made her feel as if he could see past her skin and bones, right into her soul. "I was angry at God for a long time."

A few snowflakes caught on Bethany's eyelashes and she blinked them away. "You seem to be over it now."

"Thanks to Dan."

Bethany pressed her lips together.

"He might not have been a conventional Christian, Bethany, but your grandfather was a man of strong faith."

She wanted to shrug him off or change the subject. How had they ended up here anyway? "What's your point?"

Evan tossed the rock into the stream. "I'm sure Dan would have liked the chance to tell you the same thing he told me."

"Which is…what?"

"Even if we do everything right, things are still going to go wrong."

The words stuck. She tried to shake them off, like the snow accumulating over her blanket. But they wouldn't budge, and something about them broke her heart.

Maybe because they were Grandpa Dan's words, and she longed to hear him say them instead of Evan. Maybe because she'd done everything right at Parker Crane and lost her job anyway. Maybe because those words were so different from the message Pastor Fenton preached when she was a girl. Or maybe, just maybe, it was because those words might have saved her father's life.

Twelve

Through her sleep-induced haze, the idea of somebody working a drill in her room made sense. She turned her face in to the pillow, trying to block out the sound. Only when the drilling stopped, did the haze dissipate enough for Bethany to realize the noise had been her phone vibrating. She also remembered where she was and why she was there. Today she would bury her grandpa. And last night, she'd shared the oddest moment with Evan. She snuggled deeper into the bed and brought the sheets over her chin.

The drilling came back. She removed her hand from beneath the pillow, flopped her arm toward the vibrating until her hand made contact. Whoever called had left a message. She didn't recognize the number on her screen or the man's voice.

"This is Drew McCarty, Daniel Quinn's lawyer. I need to meet with you, David Quinn, and Evan Price about your grandfather's will."

She propped herself onto her elbows and swiped her bangs from her eyes.

"I thought it might be easiest if you and Evan could come to my office after the funeral. It's located in downtown Davenport."

She grabbed for her purse on the floor by the bed and rummaged for a pen. "Please give me a call." Her fingers found one just as he gave his phone number. With no paper to write on, she jotted the numbers on the back of her hand.

After the message ended, she escaped the warmth of the heavy quilt and brought her feet to the floor. A drafty chill swept across the bedroom. She wrapped her arms around her waist and crept to the window. A thick blanket of snow covered the countryside, already sullied by trails of boot tracks leading from the house to the shed, to the barn, and out in to the fields. Just seeing them all made her tired. Overhead, dark clouds rippled across the sky and stretched past the horizon. More snow was on its way.

Dreary weather for a dreary day.

She'd planned on driving back to Chicago as soon as the funeral ended, but now it sounded like she needed to make a detour first. As she dressed for the funeral, she couldn't help but wonder what Dan could have left her and David, other than a few savings bonds and some knickknacks to remember him by. What could be so complicated about his will that it couldn't be explained in a letter or a phone call? Dan had never been a wealthy man. The farm had been enough to provide food and shelter and the comforts of a middle-class life. He farmed the land because he loved it, not because it filled his coffers. And now, most likely, it would be sold to pay off the mortgage.

Bethany stifled a yawn as she made her way down to the kitchen. She grabbed the plastic bin of Folgers from one of the cupboards and scooped a few generous spoonfuls into the top of the coffee machine. Compared to her usual Espresso Macchiato from Starbucks, Folgers smelled like a cheap imitation of the real thing. She opened a cupboard and took out a John Deere mug just as footsteps and a sneeze sounded behind her.

She turned—and for a deluded second—expected to see Dan. She found Evan instead and did a quick double take before fumbling her mug into the sink. He looked up from fastening his cufflinks. She picked up the mug and scooped more coffee grounds into the filter, scolding her heart for having such a ridiculous reaction.

With black dress pants, a moss-colored button-up, and his face clean-shaven, he looked nothing like a farmer.

She dodged his gaze and flipped the coffeemaker's switch, so the brew would be ready before they had to leave. He'd dressed so casually for the visitation, she'd expected the same today.

"Good morning," he mumbled.

She snuck glances at him in the reflection of the microwave door as he shuffled around behind her. "Did you get any sleep?" she asked, forcing her voice to steady. The words Evan had spoken to her last night, and the way in which he had spoken them clung to her.

When she turned, he was standing much closer than she expected. The glass on the microwave should have read, "Objects are closer than they appear." She pressed her back against the counter and tried to ignore the dark ringlets of hair curling above his collar or the way the color of his shirt brought out the green in his eyes.

He reached over her to grab a mug. "Have you talked to Robin this morning?"

Bethany grabbed a dishcloth and started wiping a counter that was already clean. "She didn't answer her phone."

"Did Dan's lawyer call you?"

She stopped wiping. "Yeah. This morning."

He filled his mug with tap water, standing so close she could smell his aftershave. "You meeting with him later this afternoon?"

She nodded, trying to contain all the things that pounded against her skull. Losing her job. Dan dying. Running into Pastor Fenton. Robin's pregnancy. Her strange conversation with Evan last night. His closeness right now. They gathered together, eliciting a helplessness she loathed. She needed to get out of her head, regain her composure. Only she had a funeral to attend.

He took a slow drink and studied her over the rim, a suspicious look cast across his face.

She left the dishrag bunched atop the counter and abandoned her mug. The coffee would make itself. Without offering an explanation, she exited the kitchen.

"What?" Bethany fixed her eyes on Drew McCarty. She must not have heard him correctly.

He leaned over the conference table. "Dan left you the farm. All five hundred acres."

Her mouth dropped open. She expected a meager savings bond, and maybe—if her grandpa had been smart—a few IRAs. She did not expect a farm. She blinked several times to clear the fog that came with Drew McCarty's news. What in the world was she supposed to do with a farm? "He didn't give it to Evan?"

"He left Evan the farm equipment." Drew rustled through the papers and slid one from the stack. "It's right here. The combine, tractors, hay mower, et cetera, et cetera." He scanned the paper and picked up another.

Bethany craned her neck, trying to read the miniscule writing upside down from across the table, just in case this was a joke and what the paper really said was that Dan had given her the money in his savings and the old phonograph they used to play Christmas records on.

Drew peered at the paper. "He left Evan all of his beef cattle. As well as the farmhouse and the surrounding ten acres."

"What?" She didn't mean to sound like a broken record, but Dan left the farmhouse to Evan? She turned to the man beside her, who sat with his hands clamped around the armrests of his chair. "Why would he leave Evan the farmhouse but not the farm?"

If Dan was going to leave Evan with something, the farm made so much more sense. So why had he given Evan the farmhouse? Why wouldn't he leave that to her? She forced away the tightness in her stomach. She had no reason to feel betrayed, or jealous, if that's what she was feeling. Sure, maybe at one point she had loved that farmhouse. Maybe at one point she had yearned for it to be her home again. But that was when she didn't know any better. That was when all she had to compare it to was a worn-down hunk of metal plunked in the middle of a trailer park. Although her childhood eyes had seen the farmhouse as a mansion, filled with cubbyholes and crawl spaces, her adult self knew it was nothing but an old house in need of lots of repair. Not to mention, it was in Peaks. What did it matter to her who her grandfather left it to?

Drew steepled his fingers. "I had a very lengthy discussion about this with Dan several months ago. He was very clear about who he wanted to inherit what."

"Did Dan leave David anything?"

"He left your brother all his savings and the shares from his stocks. There's actually quite a bit. He was careful with his portfolio."

Bethany's thoughts chased after one another. She tried to isolate one thought long enough to follow its course, but at the present, she couldn't focus. She wanted to wake Dan up from the dead and ask him *why*. He never did anything without thinking long and hard about it. There had to be a reason he left her the farm. But all she could think was that it tied her to Peaks. Permanently. She didn't want to be tied to Peaks. Not even temporarily.

"What in the world am I supposed to do with a farm?"

Drew leaned back, crossed his ankle over his knee, and shrugged. "You could sell it."

Evan lurched in his seat. From the pained expression on his face, he appeared to be using immense restraint to keep whatever he wanted to say inside. She turned her attention to Drew and waited for him to elaborate.

"Land development has slowed down in the recession, but developers still seem to be buying around here. And from what I've heard, farmland is going for a good amount of money right now."

Drew's suggestion planted itself in her brain. The roots took and altered her thoughts, taking them in a direction she'd never considered before. Without thinking too much about it, she blurted, "How much could I get if I sold?"

Evan huffed. "You're not actually thinking about this."

Drew let out a low whistle. "Five, six thousand an acre."

Bethany did the calculation in her head. When she reached an answer, her eyes bulged. That couldn't be right. She ran the numbers through her mind one more time. Only she came up with the same figure. With six zeroes attached to the end. Two-and-a-half-million dollars? Was this a joke?

Evan's stare drilled holes through her skull, but the threat was nothing more than an echo of rumbling thunder in the distance.

"And because he left the farm to me, I'd get the money from the sale?"

Drew smiled. "Yes, that's usually how it works."

Bethany could have grabbed the lawyer's face and planted a wet kiss right in the middle of his forehead. Two-and-a-half-million dollars? She could do all number of things with two-and-a-half-million dollars.

The loud scrape of Evan's chair across the floor yanked her back to the moment. He turned his seat toward her, scarlet climbing up his neck and in to his face. "Do you really think Dan left you his farm so you would turn around and sell it?"

Bethany's composure faltered. She searched for some justification—something that might validate the possibilities swirling inside her head and combat Evan's outrage. "Dan knew I wanted to be one of the best architects in the Midwest. He was proud of me. This could be his way of helping me reach my goals."

Evan's mouth fell open.

Bethany's cheeks flamed. She looked away and pretended to care about the wreath hanging in the center of Drew's office window. Evan might think her selfish, but wasn't he being selfish as well? The only reason he wanted her to keep the farm was so that she wouldn't put him out of a job. Well, couldn't he find another farm? There were plenty of them to go around. She gripped the armrests of the chair and fixed her eyes on Drew. "Who would I talk to about selling?"

"So that's it? You've already made up your mind?"

Her grip tightened as she attempted to ignore the angry man beside her.

"A Realtor who specializes in selling farmland, I'd guess."

Evan stood, toppling the chair. Bethany couldn't help herself. She peeked at him. His eyes burned with an intensity that made her draw back.

"You and I both know Dan didn't give you that land so you could sell it. Dan didn't care about money. He cared about people. He cared about *you*. There's a reason he gave you the land. And it's not so you could make a profit and ride away on a pile of gold."

Bethany lifted her chin. Easy for Evan to say. He wanted the farm. She didn't. And even if what he said were true, she didn't have time to sit around and learn whatever lesson her grandfather might have wanted to teach her. She was an adult with goals. Dan would be happy to know he'd helped her accomplish them. She refused to allow Evan's words to water the guilty weeds sprouting inside her.

"Will selling be a problem when I don't own the house and the surrounding acres?"

"Could be." Drew tossed his pen on the table and shrugged. "I'm not sure. You'd have to ask the Realtor."

"Wow." Disgust saturated Evan's one-syllable word. "You sure do have a lot of respect for your grandfather." He strode to the door and stepped out into the hallway. "I'll leave you two to talk business."

The door slammed shut. Bethany jumped in her seat and looked across the table at Drew.

He twirled a pen around his thumb. "So what do you think?"

Thirteen

Bethany stepped outside Drew McCarty's office, an odd combination of excitement, guilt, and too much coffee coursing through her veins. Ever since Drew mentioned five to six thousand dollars an acre, her adrenal glands had kicked into overdrive. A dream ignited. If she sold Dan's farm, she could use the money to start her own firm. Fighting for her job at Parker Crane no longer mattered. Why go through the hassle of renovating an old job when she had the resources to build something completely new? Something completely exciting.

Bethany let out a shaky breath, unable to suppress a grin any longer. No more spending time improving worn-out buildings in order to earn the respect of her superiors. Not when she had the means to jump straight to the top of the ladder—president and CEO of her own firm. Untapped vision burst to the surface, tampered only by the niggling guilt Evan left in his wake.

The honest part of her knew his accusations were well-founded. Dan poured his heart and soul into the farm. After her dad's accident it was the only thing that kept her grandfather sane. The only thing that gave him purpose. He'd go out in the fields and stay there until dark and come back looking better than when he left. Once, when she asked him why, he told her he met with Jesus out there. She remembered thinking two things. 1) Jesus didn't live on a farm; and 2) how could the same Jesus turn her mother into a lump of fright but her grandfather into a man of peace? When she'd asked, Grandpa Dan said it wasn't Jesus who terrified her mother. He said it was Pastor Fenton. In Bethany's young mind, the two were interchangeable.

She pushed aside the memory of Evan's angry face before he slammed Drew's office door and refused to give credence to the guilt fermenting in her stomach. Evan thought she was dishonoring her grandfather. But Dan was dead. Period. There was nothing left to dishonor. She wasn't going to keep a farm and stifle a perfectly good dream for the sake of nostalgia. If Evan worried about being out of a job, that wasn't a problem, was it? He had a head start. Sixty cows and a machine shed full of farm equipment. He could rent some land. Maybe better land than they had now. Better hay. Bigger fields. Maybe in a year or two he'd actually thank her. Maybe by then he'd be able to buy his own farm.

Foregoing the elevator, she descended three flights to the ground floor and found a swirling mass of white outside the windows. When she opened the front door of the building, a strong gust of frosty air whipped her hair about her face and assaulted her bare hands. She tucked her chin to her chest, stuck her hands into her pockets, and stepped onto a fresh layer of snow—almost three inches deep. She began to run in the direction of her car and didn't stop until she spotted the red mass a few feet away.

She flung open the door and ducked inside. She started the engine, cranked up the heat, and reached for her snow brush to remove the buildup on her car windows. When her task was complete, she dropped onto her front seat and rubbed her hands together, peering out the windshield into a blinding cloud of white. How in the world was she supposed to drive to Chicago in this?

Once her hands were dry and somewhat thawed, she fished her cell from her purse and dialed Dominic's number. It was Sunday, so she was certain he would answer. She could tell him about her inheritance while he looked up the storm on the radar. Maybe his excitement would cut the thread of guilt trying to string its way around her heart.

Dominic answered on the third ring. "Hey. I was wondering when you'd call." His voice sounded higher than normal. "How'd the funeral go?"

"It was a funeral, Dom. How do you think?"

"Right." Papers shuffled in the background.

"I can't wait to get out of here."

"I'm not sure that'll happen today. Not with this crazy weather."

A gust of wind rocked her car. "It's snowing in Chicago too?"

"It started a few hours ago. It's pretty nasty."

"Could you check the radar for me? I want to come home," she ducked her head and squinted into the blur of whiteness, "but right now, I can barely see out my window."

Dominic laughed. "I don't need to check the radar. There are blizzard warnings spanning the entire Midwest. They're calling for twelve to fifteen inches and high winds. Half of Chicago's schools have already cancelled class for tomorrow. You're not going anywhere tonight."

"Twelve to fifteen ten inches?"

"Welcome to winter."

Bethany groaned.

Dominic shuffled more papers.

She wanted to tell him the good news in person, but she didn't think she could wait until the weather calmed. She needed to talk to somebody who'd be excited about this with her right now. Somebody who wouldn't react like Evan. She took a deep breath.

"So I have some pretty crazy news." They said the exact same thing at the exact same time. Bethany laughed. So did Dominic.

"You go first," he said.

"I just met with Dan's lawyer. He left me his farm." Bethany paused, waiting for his reaction. When he said nothing, she went on. "It's worth two point five million dollars."

"Wow, Bethany, that's great. Are you going to sell?"

Was she going to sell? What kind of question was that? "Well, I'm not keeping it. That's for sure. What would I do with a farm?"

No response. Nothing.

"I'm thinking about taking the money and starting my own architecture firm."

"Wow."

All kinds of hesitancy lingered behind his *wow*. "What does that mean, Dom?"

"Starting a business is a pretty big deal."

"So?"

"Well, no offense, but do you think you're ready for that?"

Her insides clamped tight. "I know plenty about architecture."

"I know that. But knowing about architecture and running your own firm are two completely different things. You were just laid off because one of Chicago's most reputable firms is struggling. That can't be a good sign, Bethany."

The tightness spread to her jaw. He was squashing her hope, stealing away her vision. Why, just for once, couldn't he be excited for her? "You don't think I should do it?"

"Is that what I said?"

"You just told me I know nothing about running my own firm. So basically, yeah."

"All I'm saying is, I think you should think about it. Don't jump into anything without looking at all your options."

"Please tell me you don't think keeping the farm is an option."

She could have wound the silence into a hundred spools of thread. And with each new spool, her heart beat faster. "What was your crazy news?" she asked.

"I got a job offer." His voice went all high again and the tone of it made her swallow. "As partner for a really great firm."

"Are you going to take it?"

"I'm accepting the offer tomorrow."

She ducked her head and peered out the windshield. She was trapped inside a giant snowball. "Dom, that's great."

"It's in Atlanta."

She blinked. "Atlanta?"

"I know. Crazy, right? I've never pictured myself living in Atlanta."

He didn't say *I never picture* us *living in Atlanta.* Any excitement that had taken shape moments ago in Drew McCarty's office, leaked right out of her. Her lease was up in less than two weeks. Her boyfriend was moving to Atlanta. And she no longer had a job. "When did you get the offer?"

"Last week."

"And you didn't think to talk to me about it?"

"You've had a lot going on. I didn't want to burden you with something else."

"So you just left me out of the decision? How is that any better?"

"C'mon, Bethany. What would there have been to talk about?"

"Dominic, just last month you asked how I felt about moving in with you." Sure, they entered the relationship with the understanding that their careers would come first. No strings attached, they'd both said. Bethany never wanted to become a needy girlfriend. But this? Dominic accepting a job several states away without saying anything to her?

"That's because your lease was coming up. I had no idea I was going to move."

"Well, my lease is still up." It was creeping past the middle of December. Her lease expired on the thirty-first. "What am I supposed to do?"

"Can't you renew it?"

She leaned her forehead against the steering wheel and closed her eyes. "I don't even know if I'll find a job in Chicago."

"You could room with Lisa for a while."

Bethany groaned. "I'm not rooming with Lisa." They might be friends, but Bethany could never live in those conditions—with cats and canvases and dirty cereal bowls lying about in every nook and cranny.

"What about your friend in Peaks? Robin something or other?"

Bethany rolled her forehead back and forth on the steering wheel. "No. No way."

"You have to figure out what to do with the farm, right? I'm willing to bet selling it won't be as easy and quick as you seem to think."

Especially when she didn't own the farmhouse. But she refused to share that tidbit with Dominic. He'd only make her feel worse. Start talking about all the legal problems that came attached to that minor caveat. "I don't want to stay in Peaks." The place elicited too many memories. Everywhere she turned, she ran into her past.

"You could come to Atlanta." He paused. Too long. "If you wanted."

"I'm not going to follow you to Atlanta." Her mother dropped out of college to follow her father and look where that landed her. Working third shift at an aluminum plant in a small, stifling town.

"So what does this mean?" His voice hummed in her ear.

Somehow, the swirling outside her car turned into swirling inside her body. And she had no idea what to do with it. "Look, Dom. You dump this on me while I'm stuck in a car in the middle of a blizzard. You're the one who made plans for Atlanta. Without me. So why don't *you* tell me what this means."

"C'mon, Bethany. The opportunity fell into my lap. It's not like I planned it."

She wanted to scream but kept her fury checked. "What is your plan, then?"

"I was thinking every other month one of us could fly to the other for a weekend. It might be sporadic at first. You know how it is starting at a new firm." His invitation didn't inspire confidence. "But I'm not ready to say we'll never see each other again."

Yet he was completely okay with seeing her once every other month. He cared about her only as much as she fit into his life. She thought she was okay with that. But maybe not. Bethany curled her fingers around the back of her neck, then combed them through her hair, unsure what to say. How to respond. She was being down-sized. First at her job. And now in her relationship.

Another gust of wind whistled against her windows. She closed her eyes and leaned her head back against her seat. Her life was being pulled out from under her. She'd lost her job. She'd lost her grandfather. She'd lost her boyfriend. She'd gained a farm. In the span of one week, everything tying her to Chicago had unraveled. And like a noose, Peaks had looped itself around her neck, determined to choke her dreams.

Fourteen

When I was eight, my best friend was a cow. I named her Mrs. Frisby after a widowed mouse in a chapter book my mom read to me each night before bed. That was back when Dad's hands and legs still worked, and he and Grandpa Dan had a whole barn full of dairy cows.

As spring break approached, my classmates would sit in the cafeteria eating peanut butter and jelly sandwiches, talking about their upcoming trips to Disney World or the Ozarks, or in Bobby Fenway's case, Graceland.

"Where are you going?" they'd ask.

"Nowhere," I'd say. "I'm staying on the farm."

They'd stop chewing, triangular sandwiches frozen in front of their lips, faces lengthening with visible pity. I'd smile back and shrug. The kids who lived in town might be able to go on vacations, but they didn't have a whole barn full of cows that needed milking twice a day. And I wouldn't have traded those cows for all the Disney trips in the world.

David felt differently.

He told Dad he wanted to go fishing in Canada. Some mysterious place called the Boundary Waters. Dad would remind David about our cows and how they'd get mastitis if nobody milked them. For some reason I pictured udders exploding like water balloons, while David grumbled and trudged off to the creek with his fishing pole.

Every day over spring break, I'd wake up with Dad at 4:30, and depending on the weather, ride the four-wheeler or the snowmobile with him to the cow barn. While Dad milked, I'd do my best to help, but mostly, I'd talk to Mrs. Frisby. She had intelligence in her great big eyes, a funny looking left ear, and a giant black patch the shape of Africa on her withers. One of the mornings, I noticed her eyes looked dull and her left ear sagged lower than usual. Even her Africa spot looked a bit off.

I turned to Dad. "What's wrong with Mrs. Frisby?" I asked.

"She's got pneumonia."

My already big eyes grew even bigger. She dropped her calf a few weeks before and ever since, she'd done some struggling. I'd taken to worrying about her like a regular mother hen. "What's pneumonia?"

"A sickness in her lungs. Like a cold with a cough. Only worse."

"Will she be okay?"

Dad glanced over his shoulder and smiled that special smile of his. Mom used to call it crooked. And devilish. My father was a very handsome man. I knew so just by looking, but also because I'd hear other ladies whispering and giggling about him in town.

"She'll be fine, honey. We have her on antibiotics."

So I sat with Mrs. Frisby, petting her head, talking to her about Mom's poor attempt at pie-making the night before, until Dad finished the milking and came over to join us. He stood next to me, tall and strong, and pet Mrs. Frisby's head.

"Dad?" I said.

"Yes?"

"When I grow up, I want to be a farmer."

"You do?"

"Yep."

His brown eyes twinkled. "I don't know. Farming's hard work. Might be easier if you choose something less demanding."

"But you're a farmer."

"I am." ·

"And I like getting up early."

"That's true." He moved his hand to Mrs. Frisby's Africa-shaped patch, gave her a firm pat, and eased onto a nearby stool. "Now, that brother of yours. I'm not so sure he inherited the early bird gene. I don't think he inherited the farming one either."

"That's because David's stupid."

"Hey, now."

I ducked my head, properly remorseful. "He says he wants to invent things and get rich off the royalties." I didn't know what that meant, but David said it so much I did a perfectly fine job parroting the words. "Not me. I'm going to marry a farmer and we're going to live right here, so I never have to leave you or Mrs. Frisby."

Dad put his large hand against his chest. "That warms my heart straight through."

"I'm not afraid of hard work," I said.

"No, you're not." He smiled again and his eyes crinkled in the corners. "I have no doubt you'll make a fine farmer one day, Bethany."

I set my small hand between Mrs. Frisby's eyes. "You promise she'll be okay?"

He put two fingers together in the air. "Scout's honor."

Five months later, Dad fell from the silo. And I stopped worrying about Mrs. Frisby.

Fifteen

E van threw open the door and stomped inside, shaking snow from his hair. He'd just returned from the barn, where he'd put Storm after retrieving her from the pasture. Their other mare had died last spring and this one was getting on in years. Too old to be out in the middle of a blizzard.

Tomorrow morning, he'd have to start hauling hay out to the cattle now that snow threw a thick cover over the stalk fields. Maybe he'd round up the herd and drive them into the nearby corral. From local banter and his trusty internet almanac, he'd planned for a brutal winter. He just hadn't expected it to hit so early in the season. He made a mental note to put chains on the tractor tires. Even though the snow started a few short hours ago, the drifts already reached past his knees. Getting hay out to his herd and keeping tabs on the water tanks would be a pain.

It might not be a pain much longer. Not if Bethany sells…

Losing Micah, Dan, and now the land he'd farmed and loved over the past five years milled his guts in to silage. The wind whistled past the window panes and slammed the kitchen door behind him. He shrugged off his coat and tossed it over the back of a chair.

He couldn't let some high and mighty country-girl-turned-city-slicker steal away Dan's land. Obviously, Bethany had fooled her grandfather. If Dan knew Bethany's plans—plans to sell and destroy the land he'd sweated over for more than fifty years of his life—he wouldn't have given her a single acre. Of that, Evan was sure.

Wet snow dripped from his flannel-lined jeans onto the floor as he leaned against the counter and surveyed the room. The ceiling sagged and the warped linoleum swelled and dipped in spots. It was an old house. But it was his. When Drew told him he'd inherited it this afternoon, a sudden possessiveness invaded him. Dan had loved this home. Evan would do no less. But his heart yearned for the farm.

Farming ran in his blood. Whenever he and his family visited Uncle Manny in Missouri, his siblings would plug their noses as they drove up the lane leading past the pig pens. But Evan would inhale deeply. His uncle said it smelled like money. To him, it smelled like the future—his future.

He'd spent many summers in Missouri, rising early to milk the cows, shoveling silage, and pitching hay while beads of sweat trickled down his brow. His uncle taught him how to drive a tractor when he was nine. The combine when he was fifteen. Driving such a powerful piece of machinery, suspended so high up above the corn fields, made him feel like he could reach up his hand and touch the floor of heaven.

Evan knew at a young age that he wanted to be a farmer. There was only one problem. One small hiccup to living out the dream he'd envisioned for himself. He was stuck in the middle of farm country with no land of his own.

He worked on his uncle's farm after college, but Manny had two sons following in his footsteps, and back then Evan caused trouble. The night he drank himself silly and wrecked one of the tractors was the night his uncle kicked him out for good. With nowhere to go, he swallowed his pride and headed home. To Iowa. A vagabond, a farmer without a farm, determined to fix enough cars and farm equipment until he could rent some acreage of his own.

But God had other plans.

Five years ago, Robin told him about Dan's farm and his need for help. Evan couldn't resist the opportunity. At the time, Bryan and Amy and his parents still lived in Iowa, and they liked to pester him about his faith, or lack thereof. Dan was different. He let Evan continue his long-standing wrestling match with God and patiently answered whatever questions Evan hurled his way. Until Evan grew tired of wrestling, and tired of his brokenness, and in the middle of Dan's cornfield, recommitted his life to Christ. It made his connection to this particular land that much stronger.

Recently he caught himself imagining what it might be like to expand. Buy more beef cattle. Maybe some hogs, too. He hadn't thought much about what might happen if Dan were no longer around. Never considered that Dan's heartless granddaughter might come along and steal his dreams out from under him.

Evan ran his hand down his chin. Too many things were changing, and God wasn't letting him sit down to grieve. He kept throwing tragedies in his path, one after the other, and all Evan could do was toss one aside, so his hands would be free to catch the next one to follow. Well, he wouldn't toss this aside. He'd hold on for all it was worth.

Outside the window, a white mess swirled. He couldn't see the land, but he could picture it. The paddock. The cow pastures and fields that curved around the farmhouse like one giant horseshoe. He hated seeing cornfield after cornfield disappear, swallowed up by the expanding upper-class housing developments suffocating rural Iowa. And now Bethany wanted to sell, concerned only by how many zeroes came attached to her profit. Dan and the farm had turned into a stepping stone. There had to be a way to convince her to reconsider.

Evan turned on the faucet and filled a cup. He gulped the cold liquid and set the glass on the counter. He was about to unlace his boots when he heard noise at the front door. He poked his head around the corner just as the door flew open. A gust of blustery wind swept through the house, and a dusting of snow blew across the wood floor.

He clomped into the living room, leaving behind a trail of slush. Bethany came into view, looking first at his boots, then at his face. She lugged her suitcase behind her and let it clatter to the ground. The storm slammed the door shut like an angry child.

"What are you doing?"

She righted her fallen luggage and moved her fingers through her hair, brushing away snowflakes, her expression cool. "I was hoping you'd let me sleep here."

He cocked his head. Was she serious? She'd probably already called a Realtor, had a queue of land developers lined up to survey the farm, and she had the nerve to come to her grandfather's—no *his* house—and ask to stay? "I thought you were going back to Chicago."

She made a sound—half sigh, half squeak—and pointed out the window. "In this?"

He closed his eyes and prayed for kindness. Because at the moment, he wasn't feeling very kind. She kicked off her shoes and pulled her luggage toward the staircase.

"Hold on a second."

"Please can we not do this right now? It's been a long day." She played tug-of-war with her suitcase as she tried to heave it up the steps. Her luggage probably weighed more than she did.

Out of habit, he moved to help, but stopped himself. She obviously didn't want it. So why give it? "Don't you think you should fill me in on your plans first, seeing as they have a pretty profound effect on my future?"

Her fingers curled around the banister.

"I guess all that attention you paid Dan finally paid off." He pushed the words between his teeth and glared at the woman standing on his staircase. "Do you want me to grab some wine, so we can toast to your newfound fortune?"

Her face paled. "I loved my grandfather."

"Of course you did. All the time you spent with him over these past five years, why would anyone doubt it?" His bubbling emotions got the best of him, spilling from his mouth without censor. "Two-and-a-half-million dollars. Is that the going rate for your love these days?"

Bethany tottered back on her heels, as if his words had slapped her across the face. When she steadied herself, her eyes narrowed into slits. "Think what you want. I loved Dan. With or without this stupid farm."

"You loved him so much that you're going to toss away his livelihood? You loved him so much that you're going to get rid of the gift he gave you?"

Her hand released its hold on the suitcase. It flopped, then slid down several stairs. "It's not a gift to *me*," she said, jerking her hand to her chest. "What am I supposed to do with a farm? What do you suggest I do? Buy a pair of overalls, some boots, and go muck out the barn? Is that what you want from me?"

"I want you to think longer than two seconds about what you're doing. The farm was a gift. A wonderful, amazing gift. Only you don't have the eyes or the patience to see it. You're not even going to look." He ran his hand through his hair and lowered his voice. "I want you to consider—just consider—that Dan might have left you his farm for a reason."

"I don't have time to sit around and wait to learn whatever lesson Dan might have wanted to teach me. I have a life in Chicago."

"I thought you weren't working at your firm anymore."

"How did you know that?"

"I heard you talking to your boyfriend on the phone the other day."

"How dare you? You had no right to—"

"How dare *me*?" He took two steps closer, his eyes bulging. "I've busted my butt on this farm for the past five years, working by Dan's side, being more of a grandkid to him than you ever were. And you come waltzing back to town and destroy the one thing he gives you? The one thing I've worked so—"

"Stop judging me!" Her voice cracked. She looked away and wiped her cheek. "I didn't ask for the farm."

A knife plunged into his gut. The only other time he'd made a girl cry was in fifth grade, and guilt ate at his insides for an entire day until he broke down in tears himself and sought his classmate's forgiveness. He might not like Bethany but he knew better than to treat her this way.

"You think this is easy for me?" Her voice faltered. "You don't know me. You don't know one single thing about me." She wiped her other cheek and grabbed for her suitcase. "I was stupid to come here."

Her tears wrung the anger right out of him. In Drew's office, she'd been nothing but business. But right then, shimmying her suitcase down the staircase, tears filling her doe-brown eyes, she looked like one strong wind might pick her up and blow her away. He wanted answers. He wanted to know her plans. But maybe tonight wasn't the best night. He took a deep breath and joined her on the steps. The closer he came, the harder she tugged at the suitcase, as if nothing could be more important than getting it back down the stairs before he could help. When he reached for her luggage, she looked up with watery eyes.

"What are you doing?"

Evan took the suitcase from her hand.

"I don't need your help."

He shook his head. Never before had he met a woman more determined to go through life without help. He picked up her luggage and stepped around her. She protested the entire way to the guest bedroom. He set the suitcase in the doorway. "You're welcome," he said.

A look of pure annoyance had replaced her tears. He wiped his palms against his thighs and left Bethany at the door. They could finish this conversation tomorrow. When the weather—and their nerves—weren't quite so tumultuous.

Bethany set the suitcase against the wall and plopped onto the bed. The rusted springs jostled her up and down. She brought her hands to her face and rubbed circles in her eyes. How could she burst into tears in front of Evan? She pressed her palms against her hot cheeks and let out a long breath. She was losing it.

Whenever Evan was around, she couldn't think straight. All his yo-yoing between anger and gentle made the man impossible to figure out. She flopped back against the mattress and stared at the textured ceiling.

She waited for her thoughts to calm, for her nerves to settle. She was out of the snowstorm now and away from Evan. But her mind refused to unwind, especially in light of what had just happened with Dominic. She tried to untangle her emotions, search for heartbreak or grief or a buried sadness. After three years together, she expected to find something. But her search came back empty. She could imagine it was just the thing Dr. Nowels would love to examine—her emptiness. She felt like if she probed this empty space where life with Dominic had been, she'd find something cold and callous and not at all tender. Perhaps it was better to focus on figuring out her uncertain future. She pressed her palm against her forehead.

Should she stay in Peaks? A town she'd spent the past ten year of her life ignoring? The prospect made her shudder. But what other option did she have? Sure, she could go back to Chicago for a few days until her lease expired, but then what? She'd be homeless and no closer to straightening out this mess with the farm—a mess she wanted straightened now, not in two weeks. She squeezed her eyes shut, attempting to block out her headache. And the irony. She'd spent ten years running from this place only to find she'd run in a giant circle. She was right back where she started.

In Peaks. With a zero dollar budget.

So where was she going to stay? Because she'd sleep on the streets before involving her mother. There was always Robin, but what right did Bethany have knocking on that door when she'd closed it herself ten years ago? She raked her fingers through her hair. Evan had made it quite clear he didn't want her to stay here. She was lucky he hadn't tossed her out in the snow already.

As much as it might gall her, this was his house now. He had every right to kick her out.

Bethany groaned. If she were him, she'd kick herself out. She was selling his dream, after all. But come on. Iowa was swimming in corn. Would it really matter if she sold one measly farm? With farm acreage surrounding them on every side, Evan could easily find another plot of land to work. And even if he couldn't, she didn't owe him anything. So he'd helped Dan over the past five years. She never asked him to. Just like she never asked Dan to give her the farm.

She sat up and leaned agains the headboard. Even if she could justify selling, could she really open her own firm? Dominic's comments nagged at her confidence, perverting her exciting plans into nothing but a big glob of self-doubt. What *did* she know about running her own business? Sure, it sounded like a great idea in theory, but would she be able to pull it off in practice? Especially in the midst of a struggling economy?

Maybe she needed to find a job with another firm. It would give her more time to shop the farm around, search for the best deals. Then, when the time came, she could invest the money until she had enough experience on the drafting board to venture out on her own. Maybe she needed to build her reputation, knowledge, and experience first, open her own firm second.

She rummaged through her suitcase for her toothbrush and peeked into the dark hallway. The last thing she needed was another encounter with Evan. Satisfied that the coast was clear, she crept down the hall and a floorboard creaked—right outside his room.

She cringed.

Part of her wanted to shout, "I'm out here, all right? So just stay in your room until I'm finished getting ready for bed." But she kept her mouth shut and closed herself in the bathroom.

Once inside, she studied the claw-footed tub, the porcelain not only stained with soap scum but with memories. One in particular. She shuddered. Now wasn't the time to think about the ghosts of her past—no matter how horrible. Now was the time to think about her future.

She turned on the faucet, splashed water on her cheeks, and stared into the mirror as she dried her face with a towel.

What's ahead, Bethany? You've always had everything planned out. If you can't open your own firm right now, what lies in the immediate future?

She could freelance while she tried to sell the farm. But waiting to apply for a new job with a firm could be dangerous. For all she knew, the farm could sit on the market for months, leaving her with an undesirable gap on her resume.

As she smothered her toothbrush in white paste, she decided to leave her options open, let the Universe have a say. She would begin searching for jobs, maybe take out an ad in some newspapers for interim freelance work and postpone looking for an apartment until she knew where she'd be working. She wasn't tied to Chicago. She could go anywhere. New York. Los Angeles. Maybe even out of the country. Like London, where her dreams to be an architect had solidified. And in the meantime, she would find a Realtor.

She rinsed out her mouth and hurried toward her room. Too lazy to change into pajamas, she slipped off her clothes, left them in a heap on the floor, and buried herself in bed.

As wind pushed against the house and snow danced outside her window, Bethany reached a decision. She would stay here through the holidays. She would use the two-week prison sentence to pull the pieces of her life together. By then, she'd either have a new job lined up or a land developer interested in the farm. Win-win either way.

Now all she had to do was tell Evan her plans and find a way to convince him to let her stay in his new home.

Sixteen

Bethany searched through the front closet and pulled out Dan's parka. She had to go find Evan and see if he'd be willing to let her stay a bit longer. He couldn't be too far. Not when the temperature hovered somewhere in the teens.

Earlier that morning she'd awakened to bright shafts of sunlight filtering through the crack between the blinds and the windowsill. The ray of sun bespoke of warmth and invitation, as if spring waited outside. But looks were deceiving. The temperature paid no attention to the sun. The air outside turned melting snow into knobby icicles hanging from the gutters.

She pressed her nose to the parka and inhaled the familiar scent of Dan's tobacco until her eyes burned and she had to blink several times to soothe the stinging. She slipped it on, zipped it up, shoved her feet into Dan's work boots, and clomped outside.

The snow came up to her knees, higher in some places. She made her trek easier by following Evan's footsteps, which led as far as the drive. From there, they crisscrossed in a number of different directions.

She brought her hand to her forehead to block the sun and squinted at her surroundings. He had to be around here somewhere. She revolved in a slow circle, peering toward the silo and grain bins, to the machine shed and back to the house. She repeated her 360 a second time and paused when the barn came into view. Maybe Evan was there, feeding Storm.

Giving herself a pep talk, she high-stepped through the drifts and headed toward the paddock. She'd made a fool out of herself last night. She refused to repeat such an offense today. She'd simply tell him her plans and be done with it. She would not get emotional.

As she neared her destination, a white pick-up turned in to the plowed lane and headed toward her. A gust of wind swept over the land and stirred up the snow. It blew against her face, and for a moment she could see nothing but white. Pulling up the collar of the parka, Bethany trudged the rest of the way to the barn.

As she approached, the low rumbling of a man's voice replaced the howling wind. "Evan?" She stepped inside, dusting the snow from her hair when the sound of Storm's blows filled the barn. Boots scuffled against the ground and Bethany looked up, her eyes adjusting to the change in light. Storm, Dan's chestnut mare, stood near a pile of snow and straw at the opposite side of the barn, where the double doors opened wide into the paddock. Bethany's sudden presence must have spooked the animal, because she backed up, her tail flicking. Evan held on to her halter and murmured something into her ear, as if trying to stop her from moving.

It worked. Storm stilled.

And something about that stillness heightened Bethany's senses. Storm's front right leg was cocked with her hoof just barely touching the ground. Something about it didn't look right. From her brief stint in 4-H she knew horses rested with a back leg cocked. But she'd never seen one stand quite like this, breathing so heavy and quick she could see its giant ribcage expand and contract.

Bethany took two steps closer, but Storm snorted and swished her tail. Evan held up his free hand for Bethany to stop and whispered more soothing words to the horse. And as if he could read Bethany's mind, Evan addressed her questions, his voice calm and even. "She slipped on the ice." He jerked his head toward a patch of ice that disappeared beneath the snow leading out into the field. "I'm pretty sure she broke her leg."

Somebody stepped behind Bethany—a middle-aged woman holding a black bag. She didn't bother introducing herself. Instead, she approached the injured animal. Storm didn't move. She just stared with pain-filled eyes that pierced Bethany's soul.

Horse eyes had always fascinated her. Two large walnuts colored with wisdom and expression. But Storm's eyes were different. As the mare watched the woman approach, her eyes looked lethargic, almost dead. Bethany wanted to go to the horse. She wanted to place her hand between those eyes and make them come to life, but she was afraid if she tried, her movement would only cause her more distress.

"Keep your hand on her neck, Evan. We don't want her to injure herself more by moving. That's a girl." The woman's voice came out like honey, smooth and inviting. "How did this happen?"

"I was out fixing one of the fence lines. Right there." Evan nodded toward the pasture. "Storm decided to come out and visit. Something must have spooked her because she startled and then she slipped on that patch of ice. She got up fast but hasn't been able to bear any weight on her leg." Evan stopped talking to the woman and whispered to Storm. So gentle. And while he did, the quickness of the horse's breathing slowed just a little.

The woman crouched and ran her hands up Storm's leg, stopping and applying pressure in various places. The horse didn't move until the vet's hands came about halfway up the leg. When she reached that spot, Storm shifted away. Evan moved with her. The vet examined the spot again, then scooted back and frowned.

"You were right." She stood. "She fractured her cannon bone."

Evan's head dropped.

Nobody said anything for a stretched-out moment, leaving the horse to wallow in her pain. Why wasn't the vet doing anything? So Storm had a broken bone. Instead of staring at her like she had just been diagnosed with a fatal disease, they should be preparing a splint or doing whatever needed to be done to fix the injury and relieve her pain.

Evan rubbed the mare's velvety neck, scratched her withers, then stroked her back—almost as if he was saying some sort of goodbye. After a few moments, he gave a discreet nod to the vet, who bent over and reached for something in her bag. When she pulled out two needles, Bethany closed the gap between them. "Do you give a horse some sort of narcotic when they're in a lot of pain?"

The horse startled at her fast approach. Evan spread his hands against Storm's neck and made a shushing sound. Nobody answered her question. "What are you doing?" she demanded.

"Bethany, I think you should leave."

The hairs on the back of her neck prickled. "Why?"

"We have to put her down."

Bethany swayed. "Put her down? But—but she's standing. She can't be hurt that bad."

"She can't put any weight on her front leg. If we keep her alive, not only would she be completely lame, she'd be in constant pain." As if to prove his point, he moved his hand from Storm's neck to her withers, where the animal's quick breathing was more pronounced.

"It's just a broken bone." Bethany turned to the vet, who flicked at the bubbles in the ominous needles. "Don't you know how to fix a leg?"

"A fractured cannon bone is too severe an injury to fix. Horses are hard to mend—especially old ones. It's best if we put her down."

"Best for whom? You and Evan?" Instead of taking the extra effort to care for the injury, they were just going to dispose of the entire animal? Her stomach flexed, then lurched. She pictured her dad in his wheelchair right after the accident, her grandfather spoon feeding him while her mother hid in a shadowed corner and stared. With what? Fear? Pain? Revulsion?

Bethany spun toward Evan. "You can't do this."

"She's almost thirty," he said. "She's not going to recover. She'd have no quality to her life."

His words smacked her in the face. Quality of life? Since when was he in charge of dictating the quality of life? Just because a person—or an animal—was injured, didn't mean they didn't deserve to live anymore.

"She's in pain, Bethany."

"I'm not allowing this. This is my farm." Bethany grasped for something to hold on to. Anything. Storm might belong to Evan, but maybe if she put enough authority behind her words, he wouldn't remember. "I want you to treat the injury." Her traitorous voice shook and pitched in an uneven tone.

Evan let out a frustrated sigh. "Leaving Storm alive is cruel. She's lived a long life. Putting her down is the humane thing to do."

Pastor Fenton's words echoed through her mind. *It's for the best, Ruth. This is a blessing in the long run.* She pushed his voice out of her head. She didn't have any grounds for argument, other than one. She clung to it with desperation. "It's my farm."

Evan's face pinched. Whatever he was about to say, she could tell he didn't want to say it. "She's my horse. Dan left me the animals, remember?" He nodded at the vet, then turned back to Bethany. "Please Bethany. I really think you should go."

She shook her head and backed away, unable to block out the image in front of her. Evan holding on to Storm's neck. The horse's labored breathing, her eyes dull and lifeless, each ear twisting from voice to voice, as if listening to their entire conversation. Did she know? Did she sense what the vet was about to do? Just as Bethany bumped into the barn wall, the vet brought one of the needles closer to Storm. Bethany clamped her hand over her mouth and ran out the door.

❧

Loud rustling filled the barn as Evan shook the tarp out in front of him. He draped it over Storm, took a long breath, and shut his eyes. How much death would he have to endure before the week ended? Putting down the horse in the wake of everything else was like jabbing a needle into an open wound.

He'd have to get the Bobcat out from the machine shed and dig a hole in the frozen ground. The sooner the better, especially with Bethany out and about. His mind revisited the look on her face—eyes more frantic than the injured horse's. She hadn't understood why they had to put Storm down. She'd looked at them like they were a pair of sadists. He needed to find her and explain. For whatever reason, he didn't like Bethany thinking him cruel.

On his way to the house he spotted her snow-covered car in the driveway, half-surprised she hadn't left yet. He'd expected her to pack her bags as soon as she knew the needles weren't pain medicine. How could a woman with seemingly no sentimentality throw such a fit over a horse?

He entered the dark kitchen through the side door and poked his head into the living room. Bethany sat on the couch, her back to Evan, so still he couldn't even detect the rise and fall of her breathing. He cleared his throat, but she didn't move. What was she doing, sitting in the living room like a statue? He walked around the couch, so he could see her face.

Her bloodshot eyes stared at the wall in front of her. He didn't understand it. She didn't cry for her grandfather or her brokenhearted best friend, but she cried for a horse? One that lived on a farm she didn't want? He cleared his throat again, just to make extra sure she knew he was there. Her eyes flickered.

"Are you okay?" he asked.

She didn't say anything at first. She just sat there until he became painfully aware of his hands. He let them hang by his sides, folded them behind his back, then settled on sticking them in his pockets.

"Why did you have to kill that horse, Evan?" It was the first time she'd addressed him by his name, and the way she said it pulled something tight in his chest.

He eased onto the couch, careful to stay on the opposite side. "Storm was thirty years old. She broke her cannon bone. She wasn't going to recover from that."

"Just because something isn't useful, it doesn't give you the right to kill it."

Somehow, he had a feeling they weren't talking about the horse anymore. He studied her profile, trying to figure out who they *were* talking about. A tear spilled over and raced down her cheek. She brushed it away and stole a furtive glance in his direction, as if checking to see if he'd caught her lapse. He pretended he hadn't.

"You sound just like *him*."

He shifted his weight, the couch protesting. "Who?"

"Pastor Fenton."

Evan's eyes widened. He didn't understand how putting a horse out of its misery made him sound like the pastor of First Light. "Explain to me what you're talking about."

She stood and hugged her waist and made like she was going to leave, but he grabbed her arm. "Bethany."

She tried to shrug him off. "Never mind. It doesn't matter."

"Obviously, it does." He didn't let go. Dan had never liked Pastor Fenton. Evan always assumed it was because he didn't agree with the man's preaching. But after Bethany's reaction to Fenton at the funeral, and now this, he wanted to know what role that pastor had played in Dan's family.

She pulled her arm from his grip and all traces of vulnerability vanished from her face. The detached professional Bethany was back, leaving him more than a little disoriented. "I came to find you to tell you my plans."

Everything in him sank. She was going to sell. She didn't even need to say anything out loud. It was written all over her face.

"I'm not sure what I'm going to do yet," she said.

His heart skipped over her words, cultivating a hope that came much too quick.

She must have noticed, because she hurried onward. "I mean, I'm going to sell. I just haven't worked out the details yet."

His hope fizzled.

She sat down in Dan's recliner. "I'm not going back to Chicago. At least not right away."

He leaned over his knees, heat gathering in his chest. Bethany was going to sell. She gave a whole one-night's thought to her decision.

"I was hoping you'd let me stay here while I worked out the details."

He looked up, sure he'd heard wrong. When it became obvious he hadn't, he pointed at the floor. "Here?"

"Where else am I supposed to stay?"

"I don't know. Your mom's?"

She gawked at him like he'd dropped a calf in the living room.

"Or Robin's? I don't care where you stay. It's just not going to be here."

She threw an irritated glance in his direction. "This used to be my house, you know."

"And I used to have a farm. I guess *used to* doesn't mean very much right now." He unzipped the top of his Carhartt and ran a finger beneath the collar of his flannel shirt. Maybe if he walked outside and lay in the snow, he'd cool down.

She eyed the Bible sitting in the center of the coffee table. "This is about your beliefs, isn't it?"

"Huh?"

"You won't let me stay because you're worried what people are going to think." She crossed her arms, her entire posture radiating accusation. "This is exactly the kind of thing that bugs me about you people."

"You people?"

"Yes. *You* people."

"Care to elaborate?"

She jiggled her leg. "Christians."

He looked from her bouncing foot to her thin face. "You do realize you've stopped making sense, don't you?"

She continued to glare.

"I don't want you here because I can't stand what you're going to do with the farm. If I have to sit around and watch you work out the details, I'm pretty sure I'll go insane."

Her eyes flashed.

"And if I'm being perfectly honest, I don't think you're a very nice person."

"What?" She jumped out of her seat. "*You* don't think *I'm* a nice person?"

"Not exactly. No."

"Who called who *horrible* at Dan's visitation? That's not a very nice thing to say. And you're the one who just put down a horse because of a broken bone."

"That was me being nice." He stood with her and enunciated each one of his next words, trying to drive the point into her thick skull. "Bethany, the horse was in pain."

She made a beeline for the staircase.

"Where are you going?"

"To pack my things," she said, stomping up the stairs. "I'd hate to be the one to drive you to insanity."

He followed after her. "Why are you upset? I'm not the one stealing someone's dreams here."

She stopped in front of her room. "I'm not trying to steal your dreams." Her bottom lip trembled when she spoke. She twisted the knob and pushed open the door. "Look, I'm tired. I'm over-emotional. I miss Dan…" If a tear fell, he didn't see it. But she brushed her cheek anyway.

The motion stabbed his chest. He wanted to tell her he missed Dan too. He wanted to tell her he missed him so much he couldn't sleep at night. And that fighting like this wasn't going to help either of them. But while he struggled to formulate the right words, she stepped inside her room. "I'll be out of here in fifteen minutes."

She closed the door before he could respond.

Seventeen

The rational part of Robin's brain knew better. But grief had obliterated her ability to think rationally. Grief was the royal flush in a hand of poker. It beat everything.

Nestling deeper inside the closet, she pulled at the sleeve of a dress shirt and brought it to her cheek, inhaling the scent of Acqua di Gio still clinging to the fabric. She brought her knees to her chest, placed her hand on the weathered Bible resting near her toes, found the wall with her back, and let the dangling clothes hide her. Light from their bedroom crawled across the carpeted floor, stopping just short of her slippers. For a moment, she wished she could melt into the shadow of Micah's clothes and disappear, but her hand moved to her abdomen and she pushed the thought away. This baby threw her grief into chaos.

Robin pulled the sleeve closer to her face and inhaled again. The scent whispered his name. *Micah...Micah...Micah...* She closed her eyes, leaned her head against the wall, and imagined him sitting beside her. They were underneath the willow tree—the one that grew over the pond near the bike path winding past her old home. The tree she and Bethany had spent an entire summer climbing and swinging. The tree they'd sat beneath after Robin's mother died their sophomore year in high school.

She'd brought Micah there once. The day before their wedding. Six years after her mother's death. They sat beneath the dangling branches of that tree, and she told him how much she still missed her mom, how much she missed not having her there, helping with the wedding plans. Micah called the place a canopy of grace. He said she didn't have to cry there. He said the branches wept for her. But now Micah was gone, and the same grief she'd felt after Mom died pierced her all over again. Only this was somehow sharper, and there was no Bethany to sit with under the tree.

A tear trickled down her cheek. She brought Micah's Bible to the tops of her knees and let it fall open. Even through the semidarkness, she could see his slanted, miniscule scrawl decorating the margins of Proverbs in different colored inks. As she flipped through the thin pages of that particular book, she couldn't find a single stretch of white.

Oh God…

She didn't know what else to pray. Where else to start. Her body had a puncture somewhere. Everything was leaking away, and she didn't know how to plug it up. She didn't even know how to locate the leak. She closed her eyes and let a long, slow breath brush across her lips.

How am I supposed to do this?

She waited for an answer. A small sign. A burning bush. Something to assure her that she would get through this. Because on this side of the pain, it sure didn't feel like that would ever happen. She wrapped her arms around her legs and laid her cheek against the Bible.

The nightmare that had shattered her sleep blasted through her. Micah on the surgery table, opening his eyes. Only it was too late. The surgeons had already removed his organs.

She squeezed her eyes shut in an attempt to press away the image. The doctors had assured her Micah was gone. That nothing would bring him back. But still…

What if they were wrong? What if she'd given it some more time? What if next month, or next year, they discovered a way to reverse extensive brain damage? Or what if she'd insisted he stay home from work that day to nurse his headache? She'd done nothing except get the bottle of aspirin and told him to take two. Maybe if he'd stayed home she would have insisted on taking him to the hospital before the bleeding did so much damage. Maybe then she'd be rejoicing with her husband over their pregnancy instead of crouched in the back of their closet, hiding from a pain that was much too quick to find her. She knocked the back of her skull against the wall, trying to tap away the direction of her thoughts.

She had gone into the closet to find a way back to Micah. She'd heard somewhere that smell was the only one of the five senses that bypassed the rational brain. Smell traveled straight to the limbic system. She wanted to drown herself in Micah's scent and forget he was gone. But her brain wouldn't cooperate.

I need Micah. He was my partner. My best friend. My everything. I can't do this on my own. I can't work my way through this grief and raise a child at the same time. You're asking too much. This burden is too heavy for one person.

She envisioned Jesus, scars on his hands, reaching out, inviting her to lay her troubles on His shoulders. He was strong enough to take them. She knew that. But her heart wouldn't listen. Her heart needed someone tangible. Someone she could touch and feel.

Jesus, how do I give You something when You aren't here to take it?

Her hand fluttered to the Bible. She clutched it to her chest, curled into a ball, and lay on the floor. The fuzzy carpet rubbed against her cheek. She closed her eyes and surrendered to the appealing call of slumber.

Somewhere in the distant recesses of her mind, a baby cried. A high pitched wail she couldn't soothe. And then a doorbell.

Her doorbell.

Robin bolted upright, brushing hair from her face. She wasn't expecting any visitors. Bryan, Amy, and the kids had flown back to Arizona yesterday. Bryan had to get back to his job. And with the funeral over, there was no reason for them to stay. Loraine and Jim were still in town, staying at Gavin's until after Christmas, but they always called before stopping by.

She crept out from underneath Micah's clothes and made her way down the steps, wiping her tears away with the crumpled sleeve of her sweatshirt. When she reached the door, she drew in a shaky breath and attempted to look composed. Attempted to look like she hadn't just been hiding in a closet, sniffing Micah's shirtsleeves. She blotted her face one last time and opened the door.

Bethany stood on the other side.

Robin brought her hand to her chest. She'd expected one of the women from her Bible study, another ready-made casserole in hand. The last person—aside from Micah himself—she expected to find on her doorstep, was Bethany. "I thought you left."

"May I come in?"

Robin stepped aside, thankful for the unexpected distraction. If someone would have told her two weeks ago that Bethany Quinn would be standing in her living room, she never would have believed it. But then, she wouldn't have believed she'd be a pregnant widow either. She pulled long sleeves over her hands and redirected her thoughts. Even though Bethany wore tailored clothes and had straightened her posture, her face and body looked just as they did ten years ago. Robin clung to the familiarity like a life preserver. "Is everything okay?"

"I should be asking you that question." Bethany didn't frown or cock her head or look at Robin like she'd swallowed a bomb. She had a way about handling grief. A way that soothed Robin in high school after her mother died. A way that soothed her now.

Robin had the sudden urge to take Bethany's hands, lead her into her living room, and sit knee-to-knee like they'd done so often as girls. She suddenly wanted to tell Bethany everything. Like how she had a hard time getting out of bed in the morning. How she spent the majority of her days with her nose buried in Micah's pillow. How she wasn't sure she wanted the baby. And how this last thought consumed her with a grief more powerful than losing her husband. She settled on something a bit more simplistic.

"Trying to take one day at a time, I guess." She walked to the kitchen and opened the refrigerator. "Can I get you something to drink? We have water." She disregarded Micah's iced coffees lining the top shelf. Those were his. She looked from the dinners her church family had cooked over the past two weeks to the side panel and found three cans of Pepsi. "Or pop."

"No thanks. I'm not thirsty."

Neither was Robin, but she grabbed a bottled water anyway. Before she left the hospital, the doctor made her promise to drink plenty of fluids throughout the day. When she twisted off the top, the dripping faucet caught her attention. Five drops splashed into the basin of the sink. Her stomach clenched tighter with each one that fell. Before his collapse, Micah promised to fix that leak. She pried her attention away and caught Bethany staring at her. "What did you say?"

"I asked if we could talk."

"Oh. Yeah. Sure."

The two of them settled on the sofa in the living room. Robin took a sip of her water.

Bethany clasped her hands in her lap. "I really hate to ask you this. And you can totally say no. I won't blame you at all for saying no. But I need a place to stay for a few weeks. Evan kicked me out. And you know I can't go stay with my mom in that trailer. So I thought I'd ask if—well—if maybe I could stay here. It's really not a big deal if I can't. I'll understand if you want your privacy."

Robin stared for an extended moment, mouth agape, waiting for the sluggish synapses in her brain to process the information that had tumbled from Bethany's mouth. "Evan kicked you out?"

Bethany nodded.

"I thought you were going back to Chicago."

"I was. But we met with Dan's lawyer after the funeral. Apparently, Dan left me his farm. And by the time the meeting was over, the weather was too bad to drive back."

"Dan left you his farm?" Robin didn't mean to sound like such a parrot, but she was having a hard time keeping up. "Then how could Evan kick you out if it belongs to you?"

"Dan left Evan the house."

"Oh."

"Yeah."

The bottle crackled inside her grip. "Why would he do that?"

Bethany looked toward the closed blinds. "I'm sure he had a reason."

"And you *want* to stay in Peaks?" Robin's eyebrows knotted together. Bethany had spent most of her life trying to escape this town. She didn't see why Dan's farm would induce her to stay. "What about your job? What about Dominic—that's your boyfriend's name, right? Whenever I talked to your mom, she made it sound like you two were pretty serious."

Bethany stared hard at something on the floor. "I lost my job. My lease is up. And Dominic's moving to Atlanta. I mean, it would almost be funny if it wasn't so sad. This train wreck of things going wrong." Her cheeks tinged with color, as if she realized, as soon as the words left her mouth, that maybe her train wreck wasn't as bad as Robin's. "Anyway, I need a place to stay while I figure out what to do."

Robin's brain was fuzzy from lack of sleep. And grief—piles and piles of grief. She rewound. Went back to the beginning. Forced herself to focus on one thing at a time. "Why did Evan kick you out? That doesn't sound like something he'd do."

"He said if I stayed there, I'd drive him insane. He also said I'm not a nice person."

Robin almost laughed. Almost. The sensation felt odd, as if she hadn't experienced such an urge in years instead of weeks. "So you'd like to stay here? With me?"

"Just for a few weeks. I'd understand if you didn't want me to."

Robin studied the woman sitting next to her. This was Bethany. And even though she'd shut Robin out of her life over the past ten years—for reasons Robin understood—Bethany had come back when it mattered. Robin blinked away the gathering tears. Just a few moments ago, she'd sat in a closet and told God she couldn't carry this burden alone—this awful, heavy, unbearable burden. That she needed somebody to help her.

Is Bethany your answer, Lord?

Despite her traumatized mind, the irony was not lost on Robin. Only a confident God would use Bethany—a woman who wanted nothing to do with Him—to comfort one of His broken children. The sheen of tears thickened, blurring Robin's vision. She wanted Bethany to stay. Regardless if this was God answering prayer, or just her gasping for a breath, she suddenly needed Bethany to stay. She'd told God she couldn't do this on her own. Maybe she wouldn't have to. Not completely.

"You can stay as long as you like."

Bethany did something then. Something surprising yet altogether welcoming. She took Robin's hand and squeezed. "Just until I figure out what I'm doing. I promise."

Robin found herself hoping the task would take longer than Bethany expected. "What do you think you'll do with the farm?"

"Sell it. What else can I do?"

Robin wondered what Evan thought of that idea. He loved farming. And over the past five years, she and Micah had watched him fall in love with Dan's land and make peace with his past. She wanted to ask Bethany to reconsider. She wanted to suggest that maybe she could rent the land to Evan. That farm held many fond memories. She would be sad to see it go. And sad to see Evan lose it. But now that she had Bethany back, she didn't want to lose her again so quickly. So instead, she closed her eyes, and said a silent prayer.

Lord, if it's not too much to ask, I'd really like Bethany to stay.

Eighteen

Perched on the sleigh bed in Robin's guest bedroom, Bethany leaned against the oak headboard, her laptop opened, legs extended, a small, blue ring spinning in the middle of her screen. Internet didn't usually take so long to load. She double clicked on the icon, letting out an impatient sigh. She wanted to post her resume and search for local Realtors who specialized in farmland. She couldn't do either of those things without the internet.

She crossed one leg over the other and jiggled her foot, her mind ambling from one bad thought to the next. Dominic. Dan. The farm. Her empty desk at Parker Crane. The humiliating way she'd broken down—not once, but twice—in front of Evan. She clicked on the spinning blue ring, attempting to block out their most troubling encounter. After seeing the vet pull out those two syringes, she'd lost it. Everything Evan and that lady had said touched too close to a past she'd rather forget.

The blue ring disappeared. Her display changed from Chicago's skyline to a white screen. *Internet Explorer cannot find webpage?* She checked her wireless connection. It was on. She shifted her laptop from her legs to the bed and crept down the hall, the carpeted floor creaking in several places. She flinched each time, especially when she walked past Robin's room, the half-opened door revealing a curled up lump in bed. After Robin had helped

Bethany get settled in earlier this morning, she disappeared inside her room and fell asleep. Bethany didn't want to wake her up.

When she entered the office, she sat down in front of Micah's desk and swiveled the chair to face the credenza. An Ethernet cable attached the modem to the router, but the power light wasn't on. She rolled the chair back and looked down at the surge protector. A plug was out of the socket. After plugging it back in, she pressed the power button and drummed her fingers against the desktop. While she waited, she noticed a large picture frame of Robin and Micah, the former swathed in white, the latter dressed in a fancy, black tuxedo.

With Robin's dark, silky hair pulled into an elegant twist, she looked more like the Robin from Bethany's past and less like the haunted, washed-out figure who'd answered the door this morning. Bethany reached for the frame and brought it closer, studying the pair. She'd only seen Micah in a hospital room, surrounded by machines, his eyes closed and face blank. The Micah in this picture was smiling, flashing a mouthful of straight white teeth, a thick head of wavy hair, and premature laugh lines. His eyes sparkled through the frame, the color a familiar hazel. She hadn't noticed in the hospital, but Evan and Micah looked very much alike.

She set the frame in its place and drew back, her elbow brushing over a yellow legal notepad opened on the desk. Penciled sketches—almost like blueprints—covered the front page. Curious, she picked up the notepad and photos spilled out. The glossy three-by-fives splattered across the floor in a scattered puzzle of black-and-white. Bethany bent down and examined them. The images were taken at artistic angles and featured a variety of cafés—or, rather, more like parts of cafés. Robin graced a few of the photos, eyes dancing as the camera captured her laughing against an unfocused backdrop.

Bethany gathered the pictures into a pile and examined the sketches.

She flipped the page and found more drawings—chairs, tables, light fixtures. Even one of a piano, bathed in the glow of pendant lighting. A variety of paint colors and wall art collections were listed beneath the sketches, written in Robin's bubbly handwriting.

The lights from the router blinked and held steady. She flipped to the first page and looked again at the drawing on the front. Even in feathery pencil lines, it looked good. Classy, cozy, intimate. She could imagine the inside. She could see herself sitting at a booth, working on one of her projects while she sipped a mocha and munched on a lemon scone.

A toilet flushed, tearing Bethany from the pleasant vision she'd created for herself. She swiveled to the doorway and walked out into the hall, sketches in hand, wanting to ask about them. Robin emerged from the bedroom. Her hair stuck up in a few different directions and a red crease ran from her ear to her jaw line—a far cry from the beauty she'd examined in the picture frame.

"Are you feeling okay?" What a stupid question. "Physically, I mean."

"Nauseous." Robin pulled her oversized sleeves over her hands. The sweatshirt hung from her body, much too big to be her own. "Were you looking for something?"

"I was just plugging in the router. The internet wasn't working."

Robin pinched her lips together, as if she had a vendetta against the World Wide Web.

"I hope that's okay."

"Oh yeah. Of course." Robin looked toward the office, back at Bethany, then motioned toward the notepad in her hand. "What's that?"

"I found some drawings on the desk. Did you make them?"

Robin eyed the sketches.

"They look like a café or a coffee shop." Bethany held them up. "They're really good."

Robin hugged her middle, her face turning an alarming shade of pale.

Was she about to be sick? Bethany came forward, prepared to catch her friend in case she fainted. "Robin?"

But Robin didn't faint. She grabbed the notepad from Bethany's hand, tore out the sheets, and ripped them to pieces. Bethany's mouth fell open, her body frozen in place as the last scrap of paper fell to the ground. Robin clapped her hand over her mouth, like she couldn't believe what she'd just done, then fled to her bedroom while Bethany stared at the jagged paper fragments littering the floor.

What in the world had just happened?

Bethany eyed Robin's closed door. She should have left the drawings alone. But they'd been sitting there so out in the open, almost begging for attention. Generally she had no idea what to talk to Robin about. This had felt like such neutral territory. Obviously not.

She crept to Robin's bedroom and lifted her fist to knock on the door. Hesitated. Brought it down. Lifted it again. What was she going to say? Sorry? For what? She didn't know what she did wrong, except for unintentionally dredging up something painful.

She lowered her hand and let out a long breath before kneeling to gather the shreds into a pile. As she crumpled them into her palm, the door behind her creaked. She swiveled around on her knees. Robin stood in the doorway—a shadow, a wisp. Hardly there at all. Bethany's heart twisted. She tried to untwist it, but it wouldn't budge. Why, after ten years of separation, did she feel so protective, so invested, so much like a mother hen? She hadn't felt like this a week ago. What had changed?

Robin bent over and helped collect the mess, curling trembling fingers around a few scraps. "I'm sorry. I didn't mean to react like that."

Bethany didn't say anything. Really, what was there to say? They collected the rest of the mess in silence. When the carpet was paper-free,

Bethany reached out to take the crumpled shreds from Robin's hand. "I'm going to throw these away," she said. She didn't know what else to do, what else to say. So she walked to the stairs.

"Micah wanted me to open a café."

The disembodied words floated into Bethany's ears. A hollow sound with no inflection. She stopped and turned. Robin was still on her knees.

"When we went to Europe for our honeymoon, we must have visited at least twenty cafés. He watched me fall in love twenty different times." Robin picked at a loose thread of carpet. "It took Micah seven years, but he finally convinced me to go for it. I made those sketches the day before he collapsed." Her soft voice caught on something in her throat. "He would've done anything for me."

Bethany took a tentative step toward Robin, an idea percolating in her mind. She couldn't sit around, pat Robin's back, and talk her through this. That just wasn't her. It never had been. She needed a purpose, a goal, something to keep her moving and sane. She stepped closer, toying with the idea in her head. She had no idea how Robin would take it, but it was the only way she knew to help.

"Do you still want to build it?"

Robin sat back on her heels, her eyes unfocused. "Without Micah?"

The idea continued to roil, taking shape, filling with appeal and promise. Robin needed something to distract her from her loss, something to give her a sense of purpose again. Right now, she was floundering, flailing in a sea of pain without a life jacket. Maybe Bethany could get her going again. Reel her to safety. And not only would the project be good for Robin, it would give Bethany something to do while she waited for job offers to roll in. A fun project to build her resume.

"The sketches were really good, Robin." She held up the crumpled ball in her hand. "I could help you. We could draw up blueprints."

Robin tugged on her sleeves.

"Even if we don't actually go through with it, it would give us something to do. I have a program on my computer." She nodded her head toward the guest bedroom. "We could enter in the dimensions. Play around with some ideas."

Robin's hands were completely hidden now. The ends of her sweatshirt sleeves were twisted and stretched.

"It would give us something fun to do while I'm here."

Her eyes dimmed. She probably couldn't imagine anything being fun at the moment.

Bethany's shoulders sagged. What could she say that might penetrate Robin's grief? She stepped closer. "The truth is, I don't know how else to help you."

Bethany looked into Robin's eyes, pleading, knowing this would be good for her. Money wasn't an issue. Robin's mother had been independently wealthy, and her father was a lawyer. The only thing holding her back was grief. "So, what do you think?"

One of Robin's fingers ventured out and fiddled with a hole in the knee of her jeans. "Maybe you could show me the program you're talking about."

Bethany smiled. Grief might have a hold of Robin's ankle, tugging her into dark, murky water, but Bethany had just grabbed on to her wrist. She wasn't going to let Robin drown if she could help it.

Nineteen

Two years ago, Dominic took me to Vail for Christmas. He was charming and sophisticated and terribly flirtatious. I'd catch women staring at him and then at me. No doubt wondering what he saw in such an ordinary-looking woman. I spent a considerable amount of time that week reminding myself I wasn't Bethany from Peaks anymore.

The fact that I was a Chicago architect, skiing in the Rockies with my handsome lawyer boyfriend, and drinking fine wine at fancy restaurants was proof of how far I'd come. How far removed I was from the girl who had been forced to endure Christmas in our hunk-of-junk-home.

I loathed those Christmases.

Mom, either in her attempt to hide the ugliness of our house or in a sincere effort to spread Christmas cheer, would string lights around every inch of our trailer and cover the entire inside with tacky cutouts of baby Jesus and the three wise men. On Christmas Eve we'd go to the service at First Light, and afterward, we'd come back to drink eggnog while Pastor Fenton came to visit.

I'd sit in that dingy recliner Mom bought from Goodwill and yearn for the farm. Yearn for Grandpa Dan and Dad. Yearn for the Christmases before the accident, when we'd buy one of those cookie dough logs—the kind with a picture stamped in the center of each cookie—and bake them for

Santa while Dan read from Luke chapter two and Mom played Christmas music on our old phonograph. She would hum along while David and I rattled the wrapped boxes beneath the tree.

Christmas Eve away from the farm was depressing. I hated watching my worn-out mother struggle to stay awake because of her third shifts at Alcoa. I hated that a real Christmas tree wouldn't fit inside the door. I hated that I ached so badly for someone whose name had become taboo. And I hated that Pastor Fenton would come over and ruin Luke chapter two.

I spent nine miserable Christmas Eves in such conditions and thanks to David, there's only one of those I can look back on with any hint of fondness. My brother decided to steal, on Christmas Eve of all days, a pack of bubble gum from the gas station near the trailer park. He snuck the pack into church and nudged me just as everybody stood and opened their hymnals to sing We Three Kings of Orient Are.

My eyes darted downward to the miniature purple block he offered me. Without saying anything, he slid it into my hand and I watched in awe as he stuck a piece into his mouth and started chewing, peering at me from the corner of his eyes.

Gum in church.

We had become young rebels, fighting against the institution.

My cheeks stung from suppressing a grin. As discreetly as possible, I copied my brother. The tangy flavor tasted so wonderfully...purple. For forty-five glorious minutes, David and I moved our gum from cheek to cheek until the flavor ran dry and the juicy gob turned into something hard and cardboard-like. We were never caught. Not even by Uncle Phil, who was a dentist and could smell sugar-coated, cavity-causing goodies from a mile away.

Right before Pastor Fenton gave his benediction, I watched David fake a sneeze. His hand flew up to his mouth and he spit the lavender wad into his palm. My eyes followed his fingers as they curled under the wooden pew and stuck the gum out of sight. I tried to think of a way to get rid of my own, before Mom or Aunt Sharon asked me a question and I would be forced to open my mouth and reveal the aroma of our rebellion.

I imagined the scented evidence floating up the holly-decorated aisle and wafting up Pastor Fenton's nose. I imagined him stopping mid-sentence in his sermon, surrounded by all those poinsettias, his nostrils flaring as he kicked me out of the sanctuary. I needed to think of something quick. But my mind came up blank. So instead, just as Fenton finished the benediction, I gulped. The hard lump squeezed down my throat. Years later, when Robin told me it was impossible to digest gum, I imagined that seven-year old grape gob sitting in my stomach, and smiled.

My fondest memory of church.

Twenty

Dad, I promise. You don't need to fly in." Robin took the phone in her other hand and sat on the edge of the bed. "You were just here."

"But tomorrow's Christmas. I could catch a flight in two or three hours and be there before bedtime."

She searched for something to say, something that might appease his worry, but she came back empty. Losing Micah had rendered her mute. She had words. Lots of them. They swelled inside of her—questions mainly, for God. But her tongue refused to give them a voice. "Dad, you and Uncle Jay might not have many more Christmases with Grandma. You should stay in Ohio."

"I could fly you out here."

"Dad…"

"It would help you, Robin."

She recoiled at his words. Spend Christmas with two widowers and her ninety-year-old grandmother? How could that possibly help? Just because her dad spoke from experience, didn't make him an expert on pain. She wedged the phone in the crook of her shoulder and picked at one of her cuticles.

"I think a change of scenery would be good for you."

Her cuticle burned, then oozed red. "I promised Loraine and Jim I'd go to the Christmas Eve service with them tonight. They're going back to Tucson after the holiday and they want to spend some time with me before they go." She stuck her finger in her mouth and sucked away the stinging.

He sighed into the receiver. "I hate to think of you alone in that house."

"I'm not alone. Bethany's here."

"Bethany?"

"She's been staying with me for the last week."

"I didn't realize the pair of you were still friends."

She brought her hand over her abdomen.

"Are you sure you don't want me to fly out?"

I'm pregnant.

She tested the words out in her mind, but they refused to transfer to her mouth. What was it about those two words? Why couldn't she say them out loud?

"I'm positive. Wish Grandma and Uncle Jay a Merry Christmas for me." She gazed at the clock. "I really have to go. Church is in an hour." And she had to shower, maybe shave—both tasks took so much longer now than they did a couple weeks ago.

Thirty minutes later, Robin's fingers shook as she brushed mascara on her lashes. By the time she was dressed and ready to go, the tremor in her fingers had spread to her hands and arms, landing somewhere in the pit of her stomach.

Bethany sat at the kitchen table, laptop in front of her as she clicked back and forth between her e-mail and AutoCad—the computer software program they were using to design their potential café. At times, Robin caught herself growing attached to the project. The brainstorming and designing had become a much needed distraction. Something to take her mind off her new reality. With each passing day, the realization that Micah was gone—really gone—dug its nails deeper into her soul.

Robin poured herself a glass of milk and forced down a few sips. Bethany stopped her typing and stared at the shaking cup. "You don't have to go, you know."

"Yes, I do." She and Micah had gone to the six o'clock Christmas Eve service at Grace Assembly for the past eight years. There was no reason to stop now. "You can come with me if you want."

Bethany looked at Robin as if she'd just invited her to go Christmas caroling with Pastor Fenton, then returned her attention to the computer screen.

"Any bites on your resume yet?"

Bethany gave her head a stiff shake, clicked back to AutoCAD, and changed the dimension of the windows while Robin watched over her shoulder, more than half-way tempted to stay home and do some more brainstorming. Instead, she pulled herself away and said goodbye.

Evan had offered to pick her up, but she'd declined. She and Micah drove her Jetta to the Christmas Eve service. That's how it had always been, and that's how it would stay.

When Robin stepped inside the crowded church, several familiar faces turned to look at her. Micah's parents smiled from across the lobby. One minute Loraine was talking to an older couple by the double doors near the south entrance, and the next she had taken Robin's coat and wrapped her in a hug. Jim approached at a slower pace, delayed by chronic arthritis. He gave Robin a side-hug before placing his palm beneath Loraine's elbow. Amanda stood beside them. Evan and Gavin were missing from the ranks.

As if reading her mind, Loraine's face seemed to lengthen, adding ten years to her appearance. "Gavin's not coming and Evan should be here any minute." Loraine took Robin's hand and squeezed. "How are you doing?"

A gust of cold wind saved her from answering. It blew into the lobby and swept strands of hair into her eyes. A shiver ran up her backbone and spread to her shoulders as Evan entered through the double doors. He hugged her and searched her face, a question in his eyes. She gave her head a subtle shake. No, she hadn't told anybody else about her pregnancy. She hadn't been able to get the words out.

Jim collected her coat and went to hang it up. Several paces away, the sanctuary awaited—full of life and the beauty of Advent, when she felt gray and dead. She took a deep breath and reminded herself that Christmas Eve services were short. Just forty-five minutes. She could handle forty-five minutes.

Amanda placed her hand on Robin's elbow. "We were thinking of sitting somewhere different this year."

"We always sit in the balcony," Robin said.

Jim rejoined them and took Loraine's unoccupied hand.

A lump filled the hollow space between Robin's clavicle.

Why did it have to be Micah? Of all the husbands in the world, why hers? Why did Loraine get to hold on to Jim's hand, when she was left with nothing but wispy memories? The sudden and fierce desire to rip their hands apart gripped her.

"We just thought it would be a good idea to sit somewhere else," Jim said.

Robin peeled her eyes away from their hands and nodded her head toward the staircase. "I'm going to sit up there." She and Micah sat in the balcony every single Sunday. They had their own special spot. His family could exchange glances all they wanted, she needed to be in the balcony now. She turned and walked up the stairs, and Micah's family followed.

As the sanctuary filled to capacity, Robin played with the small, white candle the usher had handed her upon entrance, rolling it back and forth in her fingers until the music started—the slow, haunting melody of *Silent Night*. Micah's family stood, but she stayed in her seat. She couldn't stand. She couldn't sing. She couldn't even breathe. Gravity had singled her out, gathering in all its force to rest solely on her shoulders.

A couple months ago, she'd talked to a woman in Bible study about God and how He had a plan for all things. She had believed that, felt amazed by it. But now? She wasn't so sure. Not with anger pulling her out to sea. With every crashing wave, it sucked her farther and farther away from shore, away from God, away from the Christian she'd become over the past ten years. While the Christmas music floated around her, she let herself drift away, unsure if she wanted to swim back. Unsure if she had the energy or the faith to fight against the forceful waves.

I can't do this. I can't, Lord. It's too much.

The pianist started another song. *Joy to the World.* But how could there ever be joy in a world without Micah? The gravity pressed harder. Her lungs could not expand. Her brain demanded she stand up. She needed to get her body out of the sanctuary. She no longer had control of herself. Nothing about her felt like her. It was as if her body had separated into disconnected parts. Her eyes and her lips and her arms and legs. All of them had become their own entity. She, as a whole, no longer existed.

Forcing her muscles to move, she rose to her feet, shuffled past an eternity of knees, and hurried down the stairs. She didn't let out her breath until the cold winter air splashed against her face. She sucked in gulps of it while she stumbled to her car. But even as she ran, there was no escaping the grief.

⚜

Evan slammed the car door, eying the silver Audi parked in Robin's driveway, his heart giving an unwelcome blip. He knew Bethany was staying here. He just hadn't prepared himself for a run-in with her tonight. He figured she was spending the holiday back in Chicago. With her boyfriend.

Over the past week, thoughts of the woman popped into his head more times than he cared to admit. He liked to think it was because she held his fragile future in her hands. But truth was, he couldn't figure Bethany out, and anytime he couldn't figure something out, it drove him nuts. It was the same reason he'd spent an entire week as a kid twisting and turning Bryan's old Rubik's Cube. And that was just a cube.

He gripped the coat Robin had left at the church and walked toward the house. Unlit Christmas lights wrapped around the gutters. Micah always put the lights up at the beginning of November. They were *that* couple. The couple that skipped right over Thanksgiving in their eagerness to spread yuletide cheer. As far as he knew, the lights hadn't been turned on since Micah's collapse. This year, come January, Evan would be the one to take them down. He shook away the depressing thought, stepped onto Robin's stoop, and pressed the doorbell.

Five seconds later, Bethany swung open the door, clutching the knob with one hand and the door jamb with the other, as though blocking his entrance. "Yes?"

"Merry Christmas to you, too," he said. "Have you decided what you're going to do with the farm yet?"

"Is that why you came? To interrogate me about my plans?"

"I came to check on Robin."

"Robin's at church. I assumed you'd be with her."

"She's not here?"

A crease formed between Bethany's eyebrows.

Great. Robin was missing in subzero temperature. Without her coat. He shouldn't have listened to his dad. He should have gone after her as soon as she hightailed it out of the sanctuary. "May I come in?"

She hesitated.

Before he could remind her that this was his brother's house, her hand slipped off the knob and she stepped back into the living room. Wearing faded jeans, a hooded sweatshirt, and her hair pulled back and messy, she looked much more like a carefree college student than an overly ambitious professional. His eyes moved down the length of her body and landed on her unpolished, neatly trimmed toenails. She must have caught him staring, because she curled her toes and tucked a strand of hair behind her ear. Something warm tiptoed up his spine. He wasn't used to seeing her like this, without her makeup, without her tailored clothes, without every strand of hair in its proper place.

It was refreshing.

Evan stepped inside, greeted by the smell of sugar cookies and the sound of Christmas music—a familiar melody without any lyrics. An opened laptop, a can of Coke, a crumpled napkin, and some papers littered the top of the coffee table. Bethany lunged at the mess and swiped up the can and napkin as if he'd caught her with a smoking gun. When she straightened, she ran a hand down her rumpled sweatshirt, then over the crown of her head.

The gesture was cute, but something about the sight of her listening to Christmas music all alone on Christmas Eve pulled strings in his chest that he didn't want pulled. Nobody should be alone on Christmas Eve. Not even Bethany. "Do you know where Robin is?"

"I told you. She went to church." She glanced at the wall clock and went into the kitchen.

He followed. "She left in the middle of a song. I wanted to check on her."

Bethany threw away the napkin and peeked into the oven. The smell of warm sugar and butter escaped into the room.

"I didn't peg you as the baking type," he said.

She put on an over mitt and pulled out a sheet of cookies—the cutaway kind with green Christmas trees stamped in the middle of each one. "I knew Robin shouldn't have gone." Bethany set the sheet on top of the stove. "She needs time to heal. Not go to church. Your family shouldn't have pressured her."

"What makes you think we pressured her?"

"Why else would she want to go to church right now?"

"I don't know. Because that's what she and Micah did on Christmas Eve. They went to church." He looped his thumbs into his pockets. "Maybe she was hoping to find some comfort."

Bethany shook her head, like he didn't have a clue. She used a spatula to scoop the cookies off the sheet and onto a cooling rack. "Do you want my opinion?"

"Since you're so eager to give it."

"I don't think God is going to help her through this."

He crossed his arms, intrigued. "Why not?"

"Not everybody needs a crutch. Sometimes, the crutch just gets in the way."

So that's what she thought? She saw God as a crutch, helping weak-minded people like himself get through life. "Do you want my opinion?" he asked.

She stopped her scooping, put one hand on the counter, held the spatula with the other, and raised her eyebrows at him. "Since you're so eager to give it."

"Everybody has a crutch."

She shook her head again. "I don't."

"You don't?"

"No."

He smirked and took a few steps toward her. "What about your career? Or your success? What about that fancy car out in the driveway? If all those things were taken away, you think you'd still be standing?"

"I've had a pretty rough go of it this month," she motioned to her legs, "and I'm still on my feet. I stopped thinking about God a long time ago and I'm doing just fine."

"Are you?"

Her eyes flickered, but she turned away from him and scooped three more cookies onto the rack. He came to her side, so close he could feel the warmth from the oven and smell the vanilla clinging to her skin. "You're a duck, standing in a puddle."

She furrowed her brow. "Did you just call me a duck?"

"Standing in a puddle." He placed his palm against the countertop and leaned in to it. "It's something my dad used to say when we were younger. Whenever any of us would step away from God, he'd warn us not to go flying into puddles. You know, not to be like those ducks you see in town, standing on the side of the road, ankle deep in a puddle of water. He'd tell us to fly back to the pond."

Bethany looked at him as if he'd tracked cow manure into the kitchen.

"You lean on things that will dry up. Like a puddle. I lean on God." And just to make sure she understood the analogy? "God's the pond."

"Doesn't your dad know that ponds can dry up too?"

"Not God's pond."

Bethany rolled her eyes.

"I know. It's an annoying metaphor, isn't it?" It used to drive him crazy when he was a kid. Even crazier when he turned into an angry teenager.

She opened her mouth, but the rumbling of the garage door stopped her from saying whatever she was going to say. A few moments later, Robin stepped inside the kitchen, her nose red, her hands trembling. He hurried to her side and took her elbow. "Where were you?"

Unlike Bethany, she didn't fight away his offered hand. She let him lead her to a nearby stool, her teeth clicking together like an old fashioned type-writer. "The cemetery," she said.

His heart twisted. The cold couldn't be good for her health. Or the baby's. And hanging out at Micah's grave didn't sound like a good idea. He turned to the cupboards and began searching for a mug, so he could make her something hot and steamy.

"I'm okay, Evan. I promise."

He turned from his quest, cupboard door ajar. Nothing about her looked okay.

"I'm sorry for leaving church." Her ears were red. Her cheeks even redder. "You don't have to be worried about me."

But he was. He was very worried. She looked like she'd shrunk three sizes over the past couple weeks when she should be expanding. With Micah gone, he felt an obligation to take care of her. "Do you want me to stay?"

Bethany held up the rack of cookies. "Do you want a cookie?"

"I'll be fine. I just have to lie down for a bit." She patted his hand, like he was the one who needed comforting, and shuffled out of the kitchen.

He and Bethany stared after her.

"I'm worried about her," Bethany finally said.

He plunked down at the table. "Me too."

"She barely eats." Bethany eased onto the seat across from him. "She says it's because of morning sickness, but I'm not sure I believe her."

An instrumental version of *Drummer Boy* floated in from the living room.

She rested her chin in her hands. "This was my dad's favorite song."

"It was Dan's, too."

They sat there, listening to the melody, the words playing through Evan's mind. *I have no gift to bring... That's fit to give the King...* What did Bethany think about those lyrics? Did she know them like he knew them?

"Why do you think he did it?" she asked.

Evan didn't have to ask what Bethany meant. He knew she was talking about Dan's farm and the way he'd split his inheritance. It was something he'd thought about frequently over the past week. "I don't know."

"I wish I could ask him."

"Would it change your decision?"

The song ended, replaced by *Blue Christmas*.

Bethany pulled her chin out of her hand and sat up straighter, as if noticing him—really noticing him—for the first time that evening. "Is your family expecting you to be somewhere?"

His family was probably on their way out to the farm right now. Waiting for him. Waiting for Robin. But something about that kitchen and the music and the smell of store-bought cookie dough kept him still in his seat. "I can stay a while longer."

"Do you want some cookies?"

He nodded.

And then he ate cookies with Bethany on Christmas Eve. They weren't homemade. They weren't even baked all the way through. But they were warm. And there was milk. And even though he hated what Bethany was planning to do with the farm, even though he couldn't stand the thought of her selling it, he couldn't help feeling grateful that she was here. That Robin wasn't alone. That Bethany was watching out for her.

Twenty-One

Sitting on the floor of Robin's guest bedroom, Bethany ripped open the last of her moving boxes and searched for her favorite cashmere sweater. When she didn't find it, she pushed the box away, set her elbows on her knees, and fisted her hands through her hair. After accepting a short but civil visit from her mother on Christmas Day, followed by an unexpected, but much welcomed phone call from her brother, Bethany had driven back to Chicago and spent two days packing her things. Moving most to storage and stuffing a few boxes in the back of her car to take with her.

Dominic had stopped by and helped for a while. Their goodbye was awkward and anti-climactic. He said she could visit whenever she wanted, and Bethany said maybe she would come down in January, but they were empty words. They'd reached a stalemate in their three-year relationship, only neither one of them wanted to say it out loud.

So now there she was, back in Peaks, on the floor of Robin's guest bedroom, unable to find what she was looking for. She pulled out a pair of shoes and placed them in the closet while Robin talked with whoever downstairs. Bethany heard snatches of their conversation. The flood of visitors who came the week before Christmas had slowed in to a steady trickle after. Mostly people from Robin's church.

Robin endured the company, answering questions and smiling when appropriate, but Bethany doubted anything penetrated the invisible barrier of grief Micah's death had erected. The sound of the front door opening and closing told her the visitor had left.

She plopped down on the bed and opened her laptop. Her empty inbox made her want to scream. She'd posted her resume on every site imaginable and called architect firms across the entire United States, only to be met by a barrage of rejection and silence. To keep her sanity, she fiddled around on AutoCAD, creating designs for art museums that would never exist and skyscrapers that didn't need building. She changed the layout to Robin's café so often that all the designs blended together like an indiscernible pile of mush.

Three days post-Christmas, sitting in that room folding and refolding her clothes, checking her e-mail every thirty seconds—finding nothing but spam—and her sanity finally snapped. She found a phonebook in the kitchen, pulled the number of a Realtor from the yellow pages, dialed, squeezed her eyes shut, and convinced herself Dan was not rolling in his grave.

Sixty minutes later, Bethany stood in front of the farmhouse and pulled at the door, but it stuck in place. She tried again, but with no luck. Her breath froze as soon as it escaped her lips and with each inhalation, her nose hairs tingled with frost. She rubbed her gloved hands together and considered peeking under the rock near the kitchen door. Maybe Evan kept a key underneath.

She looked over her shoulder—nervous, jittery. She hadn't seen or talked to Evan since his drop-in visit on Christmas Eve, when they established some unspoken truce. Once he found out what she was up to, the truce would end. Whatever peace they'd found would combust into flame.

"Excuse me, are you Bethany Quinn?"

Bethany spun around and came face-to-face with a stork-like woman bundled in a coat much thicker than her own, and behind her, a shiny van parked next to Bethany's car. The fresh layer of snow blanketing the drive must have muffled the woman's approaching vehicle.

"Yes, I am." Bethany stuck out her hand. "And you must be Susan. Thanks for coming at such short notice."

Susan pumped Bethany's hand. "That's my job." She motioned to her surroundings. "So, this is the farm. How many acres did you say it was?"

Bethany opened her shoulder bag and pulled out the file Drew had given her. "Five hundred. I have the property details right here."

"Shall we go inside?"

"The door's locked."

"Don't you have a key?"

Bethany folded one corner of the folder over and back until it lost its shape. "I don't own the house."

Susan's beaklike nose twitched. She turned slowly and surveyed the land stretching past the horizon.

"I don't own the surrounding ten acres either." Bethany winced along with the admission, hoping this tidbit of information wouldn't cause trouble. She tried to assess Susan's expression, but her poker face revealed nothing. "Will that be a problem?"

"That depends." Susan held out her hand and Bethany gave her the folder. The Realtor sifted through the papers, puckering incredibly thin lips as she surveyed the information. "Says here the acreage wraps around the house, sort of like a horseshoe. And it's boxed in by a creek."

"Is that bad?"

"It's not ideal." Susan straightened the papers, tapped them inside the folder, and gave them back. She surveyed the drive. "Access to the home cuts through the property." She muttered the words to herself, as if making a mental note. "So who owns the farmhouse? Would that person be willing to sell?"

Bethany looked over Susan's shoulder to the empty paddock. "There's a possibility."

As if sensing the lie, Evan pulled down the lane in his Bronco. He came to a stop, jumped out of his vehicle, and clomped toward them.

"What are you doing here?" he asked.

Bethany ignored the writhing in her stomach. She had no reason to feel guilty. She wasn't doing anything wrong. "Evan, this is Susan Sparks, my Realtor. Susan, this is Evan—"

"You're a piece of work, you know that."

Bethany stiffened. "I told you I was going to sell."

"You also told me you'd keep me informed."

She pulled back her shoulders and gripped the folder with both hands. "Well, consider this your information."

"If you think I'm going to let you stand on my front porch while you—"

"Evan?"

Bethany and Evan swiveled their heads at the sound of Susan's voice. The scowl on his face melted away and recognition lit his features. "Susan?"

Bethany groaned. Of all the Realtors in the county, Bethany had to pick one who knew Evan?

Susan touched Bethany's arm. "I used to babysit Evan's little sister when I was in college. What a small world." Susan frowned and cocked her head, her face morphing into the same expression people kept throwing at Robin. "How are you holding up?"

Bethany bit her tongue. Evan wasn't going to die if somebody looked at him wrong, and neither would Robin. She shifted her weight and addressed Susan. "What steps do we need to take to get the ball rolling?"

Susan blinked, her allegiance obviously torn. Bethany watched the war play out across her features. Finally, her eyes settled on Evan. "Bethany said you might consider selling. Is that—"

Evan balked. "She lied. I'm not selling."

Heat climbed up Bethany's torso. "So you'd keep the house, even if that meant living here with no farm?"

"That's right."

"Even if that meant you'd be surrounded by a new housing development?"

He stuck out his chin. "I said, that's right."

Now it was her turn to balk. "That's ridiculous. And really stubborn."

"Dan gave it to me for a reason, and I intend to take care of it." He turned to Susan. "I don't know what Bethany told you, but I'm not selling. You might want to write that down in your notes." He stepped around them and fished a key from his pocket. "I'm sorry you got sucked into the middle of this, Susan. I hope you understand why I can't invite you in, at least not as someone who wants to sell my farm."

"It's *my* farm." Bethany gritted her teeth.

"That's just semantics." He jammed the key in the lock and addressed the Realtor. "But you're more than welcome to come inside as a friend."

With her hands buried in her pockets and her shoulders hunched up by her ears, Susan looked tempted by the offer. "Thanks, unfortunately I'm on the clock."

Unfortunately?

Evan nodded goodbye and stepped inside, leaving the pair of them standing in the cold.

"You might want to discuss your plans with Evan, Ms. Quinn." Susan dug in her purse. "Honestly, you have time. Land development has slowed quite a bit in the recession. And winter isn't the optimum time to sell. In fact, it's almost impossible. I think you'll save some energy by waiting until spring." She pulled out a business card. "Give me a call when you've figured out what you want to do."

Bethany forced a smile but didn't touch the card. "Thank you, Ms. Sparks, but I think I'll be working with somebody else."

✺

Bethany barged inside Robin's house, fuming over Evan's stubborn refusal to sell. Job interviews weren't coming in. Most of the companies she had solicited were probably running on maintenance staff during the holidays. She couldn't look for another apartment until she knew where she'd be working. And getting rid of the farm might prove more difficult than she hoped. Bethany was stuck in her own personal hell, right alongside Robin.

Well, enough was enough.

Maybe she couldn't do anything at the moment about her own situation, but she could try to do something for Robin's. She marched up the stairs to Robin's room and poked her head through the half-opened door. Her friend lay in bed, staring at the ceiling.

"Hey," Bethany said, rapping her knuckles against the trim.

Robin pulled herself up, her hair in tangles.

"Want to go to Lowe's?" Bethany asked. "We could get out of the house. Look at paint colors for the café."

"No thanks." Robin lay back down, her disheveled hair fanning across the pillow.

"Please?" She held on to the doorframe and did her best impersonation of puppy-dog eyes. "I need a distraction. I'm going crazy cooped up in here."

Robin's eyes closed for a long moment. Bethany forced herself to wait.

"Okay, fine."

A sense of victory flitted through her. A simple trip to Lowe's and she was ready to pump her fist in the air. Not a good sign. Batting away the disquiet rustling around in her mind, she tapped the door frame with her palm. "Great. I'll meet you downstairs in fifteen."

❧

The ends of Robin's damp hair darkened the shoulders of her blue sweatshirt. Her face hung slack, eyes glassed over and far away. Bethany forced her attention back to the interstate and passed a pickup hauling a trailer loaded with farm equipment and scattered bits of hay. "When's your next doctor's appointment?" she asked.

"Two weeks."

"Are you excited?"

Robin shrugged.

"You'll get to hear the heartbeat this time, right? That'll be cool. Don't you think?"

Robin replied with nothing more than a whispered *hmmm*. An acknowledgment of her question—not to be mistaken for an actual answer. Out of conversation starters, Bethany stopped fighting the silence in the car and let it have its way. She flipped her blinker and steered into the right lane when a sonata—possibly Chopin—issued from Robin's lap.

Robin yanked the phone from her purse and pressed it against her ear. Bethany stared at her from the corner of her eye. Sometimes the sound of Robin's phone would ring and ring and ring through the walls of their bedrooms, until whoever called got shuffled to voice mail. Other times—like now—Robin acted as if her phone held some sort of magical solution. Like if she answered it quickly enough, Micah would come back from the dead.

Bethany exited Interstate 80 and turned through a green arrow while Robin propped her elbow on the console, her face no longer the expressionless mask she'd worn moments earlier.

"On Saturday?" The confused words swooshed into the air.

A muted chattering sounded from the other end of the phone line.

"Will I have to say something?"

More vague chattering.

"Thank you. I'll try to make it." Robin pressed the end button with the pad of her thumb and let the phone drop into her lap. She'd either forgotten to say goodbye, or hadn't bothered.

Bethany turned into Lowe's parking lot. "Who was that?"

"The mayor."

"Of Peaks?"

"They want to recognize Micah."

"Who's 'they'?"

"Mayor Ford said he's going to recognize Micah at the New Year's Eve Ball. For his service to Peaks." Robin's eyelids fluttered. She gave her head a slight shake and brought her fingertips over her lips. "He organized a county-wide coat drive for the homeless each winter and he was a volunteer firefighter. He served on the county fair board too."

The fair board? Chicago most definitely did not have a fair board.

"The mayor called to invite me."

"Are you going to go?"

"Will you come?"

Bethany recoiled. Go to Peaks' New Years Eve Ball? Socialize with the locals? Sit through a meal while her table mates discussed cash crops and pigs? The idea reeked of small-town. But Robin looked at her as if saying no to the invitation might push her off the edge of some invisible precipice. The whole purpose of going to Lowe's was to pull Robin away from the edge, not scoot her closer.

"Evan will go, won't he? I bet he would take you."

"I need you to be there."

She squirmed. Why her, exactly? Over the past few days, Bethany hadn't been much more than a houseguest. Beyond the mandatory *Hi, how are you*, the two of them coexisted in solitude. "Why do you need me, specifically?"

Robin didn't answer right away. She looked out the window while Bethany pulled in to a parking spot and shut off the ignition. "Remember senior year, when Mr. Burny asked us all to write an essay about the most important relationship in our life?"

Bethany nodded slowly. She'd forgotten all about that essay.

"He made us stand in front of the class and read them out loud. Genevieve Winters quoted second Corinthians and dedicate the whole thing to her future husband."

"Debbie Carter wrote about Chris Samson."

"His head swelled to the size of a watermelon."

"You wrote about me."

Bethany's smile fell away. She had.

"You said we knew how to be there for each other without filling up the space with words. You said we didn't try to pretend things were good when they were crappy." A ghost of a smile tugged at Robin's lips. "I remember you used that word too, and Mr. Burny scrunched his nose."

"Mr. Burny always scrunched his nose."

"You said when we first met, I made breathing a little easier." Robin picked at the black rubber lining of the window. "I remember sitting in class, thinking the same thing. I never would have made it through my mother's death without you."

A heavy something rolled onto Bethany's chest. Mrs. Delner had been the mother she had always wanted—warm and outgoing and beautiful. Her death had been incredibly hard. But being there for Robin had provided some distraction from her own grief.

"Micah was my whole world, Bethy. And now he's gone, and having you with me—I don't know—it just makes breathing a little easier."

Bethany chewed the inside of her cheek. She didn't want to encourage Robin's inexplicable dependence. When she left—and she would be leaving soon—she wanted to make it as painless as possible for her old friend, but despite her misgivings, she caught herself nodding. Agreeing to escort Robin.

It wasn't until they were inside Lowe's, browsing the display of paint samples, that Bethany remembered something. She'd just agreed to go to Peaks' annual New Year's Eve Ball. The one honoring Pastor Fenton.

Twenty-Two

Bethany fingered the black twill fabric of her dress as she walked toward Shorney's Terrace, the only banquet hall in Peaks. She attended the ball once before, way back in junior high, when she'd gone as Robin's guest. As a kid, she'd worn a corduroy skirt one size too big and a mustard colored cardigan her mother found at the local Goodwill. The stark contrast between her outfit and Robin's brand-new party dress dominated her memory so much that she couldn't recall what the adults had worn. So she settled on the sheath, knee-length number she'd purchased last year for one of Dominic's business dinners and crossed her fingers that she wouldn't repeat her childhood offense.

When she and Robin approached the queue of people lining behind the double doors, she let out a long breath, unaware she'd been holding it in. She would support Robin through the evening and ignore as many familiar faces as possible. Still, just in case she did get roped into awkward conversation with old classmates, she'd spent a long time in front of the mirror, hoping for the right look. As opposed to her previous experience, she found that her high-belted waist and black pumps gave her a sophistication others in the crowd lacked.

She raised her chin, pulled her winter wrap over her bare shoulders, and hugged her Marc Jacobs clutch purse to her chest. The winter chill nipping at her cheeks and fingertips subsided as soon as she stepped inside the banquet hall. At one time, the oak floor and wide-set staircase leading to the second story ballroom might have impressed her. Now all she could think was that the place could use some renovation. Palladian windows, marbled flooring, and well-placed pillars would add some visual weight to the ground floor. She moved to the staircase with Robin and grazed her fingertips over the metal balustrade. The urn-shaped, pewter balusters looked out of place in the otherwise unrefined Great Room.

As she ascended the staircase, she angled to study the throng of guests filing through the doors and spotted the tops of three familiar heads. Clean-cut Bryan held hands with Amy—her corn silk hair styled into a French twist. Robin said they flew into town for the evening, wanting to honor Micah, and left their kids in Arizona with Loraine and Jim. Evan entered behind them, his suit coat covering impossibly broad shoulders.

Bethany's stomach tightened. She covered the silly reaction with her hand when something sparkly caught her attention. Light reflecting off a shimmery red gown. The wearer looped her arm through Evan's. Bethany stopped at the top of the steps. Someone bumped into her from behind and mumbled an apology. She didn't know Evan had a girlfriend.

Robin leaned over and searched the crowd. "Who are you looking at?"

Bethany nodded toward the doorway. "Bryan and Amy are here. And Evan and his date."

A smile took shape on Robin's face—the first real one Bethany had seen since losing Micah. "I didn't know Diane was coming. She's great. You'll love her."

Bethany relinquished her grip on the balustrade. Judging by the woman's sparkly, full length gown and the pile of platinum curls on her head, Bethany doubted she would love her. The woman was obviously trying too hard. Bethany undid the clasp on her purse, retrieved a pack of wintergreen breath mints, and frowned at her shaking fingers. This was ridiculous. She'd come tonight out of obligation. She knew three people would be in attendance. Pastor Fenton. Her mother. And Evan. She had every intention of avoiding all of them. Especially after her and Evan's fight in front of Susan Sparks.

Popping the mint between her lips and rolling it to one side of her mouth, she turned and entered the ballroom. Floral arrangements adorned the center of every table. Strings of balloons hung from the ceiling, and gold, twinkly lights wound their way up plastic pillars. At the front of the hall, underneath a large banner, was a platform with a lectern positioned in the middle. The younger version of herself would have felt like a princess in this place. She took pleasure that her reaction today was nothing more than an indifferent acknowledgment that the committee who organized the event had tried very hard to dress up a country banquet hall.

A line of people mingled while waiting to order drinks from the bar. Bethany made eye contact with a pair of familiar faces—two girls who graduated in her class—and quickly turned away. Taking a deep breath, she reminded herself that she'd moved on to bigger and better things. She had nothing to be ashamed about. It had taken two solid years in college before she stopped ducking away from unwanted attention. Two solid years before she stopped slouching her shoulders as if her diminished posture might hide her from some figurative spotlight. She wasn't going to revert back to that nasty habit now.

She straightened her back, squared her shoulders, and raised her chin. She didn't need a sign on her forehead announcing her level of education, her major, her accomplishments. Let them see it in her posture. And if anybody asked, she'd be ready to share.

"Do you want to find a table?" she asked Robin.

"The mayor reserved one for us in the front—for all of Micah's family."

The thought of spending the evening sitting with Evan and his date made her queasy, especially if Evan planned to interrogate her about the farm. Before Bethany could suggest a different table, Evan was beside them, wrapping Robin in a hug. When he let go, Bryan was next. Then Amy. Then the woman in the sparkly red dress.

"I didn't know you were in town," Robin said.

"Oh, honey, you know me. I couldn't miss an opportunity to dress up." A thick southern drawl saturated every syllable.

Robin smiled, the second one that night. And Diane had been responsible for both. "This is my friend, Bethany," Robin said. Diane's green eyes sparkled with amusement as she gave Bethany a long and deliberate once over.

Warmth crept into Bethany's cheeks. Looking at Evan's date was like staring at the tonal inversion of her picture. Diane was Bethany's own personal negative. Her full-figured frame filled that ostentatious dress with curves, while Bethany stood like a fence post. Diane's white-blond curls bounced around her heart-shaped face, while Bethany's brown locks hung straight past her shoulders. Where Diane's smile came quick and easy, Bethany guarded hers carefully. Even their voices oozed opposition. Diane's dripped with sweetness, while Bethany had cultivated her own into something like red wine. If Diane symbolized Evan's type, Bethany landed herself on the opposite end of the spectrum.

But why should Bethany care about that? She stuck out her hand, but the woman bypassed all personal space for a hug. Not just a friendly pat either, but an actual squeeze.

When Diane pulled her arms away, she flashed a sugar-sweet smile. "It's so nice to meet you," she said, leaning back on her heels and bumping Evan's hip with her own. "Shame on you. You didn't tell me Bethany was such a pretty young thing."

Bethany's attention darted to Evan, but he avoided eye contact. He stared at Diane instead, who looped her arm through his. Heat stirred in Bethany's chest. She looked away from the pair, annoyed at her reaction. So Evan had a girlfriend. One who looked like Marilyn Monroe's identical twin. So what?

When they reached the table, Evan slid out Diane's chair, and before Bethany could object, he slid hers out as well. She draped her wrap over the back of her seat, picked up her glass of ice water, and motioned to the two empty chairs at the end of the table. "Are Gavin and Amanda coming?"

Bryan and Evan exchanged somber looks while Bethany took a sip.

"No," Bryan said. "Gavin can't make it. And Amanda left. Spring semester doesn't start for a couple weeks, but she wanted to get back."

Diane eyed the two brothers before slapping Evan on the wrist. "Speaking of that little brother of yours. Wouldn't Bethany look lovely on his arm?"

Bethany coughed several times and forced the water down her throat.

"Are you okay?" Robin asked.

Amy patted Bethany's back. "Isn't Gavin a bit young?"

"He's twenty-four," Diane said. "And shoot me dead if Bethany is a day over that."

Maybe any other woman would be flattered by Diane's words. Bethany was not. She took her hand away from her mouth. "I'm twenty-eight."

Diane's chin dropped. To her credit, she seemed genuinely shocked. "And she has a boyfriend."

Bethany's gaze snapped to Evan, who had spoken the words, but he fiddled with his rolled up silverware and stared at the tablecloth. So far, he hadn't looked at her once. Not even when he pulled out her chair. Obviously, he was still upset about the Realtor.

Diane placed her elbow on the table, rested her chin on the top of her fist, and wagged her eyebrows. "And where's the lucky man? He's handsome, I'm sure."

Bethany brought her napkin to her mouth and used one corner to pat her bottom lip dry. "He moved to Atlanta. We're...no longer together."

Diane leaned closer. "So you're available?"

Heat crept up her neck. Every single eye except Evan's looked in her direction. Available? She hadn't thought of herself in that way for the past three years. And even if she was interested, Diane setting her up with Evan's younger brother would not be a good idea. "I'm not looking right now. So no, I'm not available."

"Until you find the right guy, you mean?"

Right for what? "Sure, until then."

Diane tapped Evan's forearm and arched an eyebrow. A muscle in his jaw pulsed out and in, and he gave his head a very discreet shake—something Bethany wouldn't have noticed if she hadn't been watching him from the corner of her eye. Obviously, he didn't want her dating Gavin anymore than she did. She bristled at the implications. He probably thought she wasn't good enough for anyone in his family. She turned her attention to the front of the hall.

A thin man dressed in a tuxedo, most likely Mayor Ford, stepped on the platform and the humming chatter quieted around them. Bethany turned and scanned the banquet hall, which looked filled to capacity. The mayor's family sat in the seats behind the lectern while he tapped the microphone, greeted the guests, and informed them all that dinner would be served before the speeches and awards. After finishing his announcement, he helped his family off the stage and sat at the table directly in front, two away from their own.

Bethany rubbed her thumb over the hem of the linen napkin she'd draped across her lap just as a server came and took their drink orders. She requested the merlot, her mouth watering for the rich, intoxicating flavor. When the server finished pouring, her fingertips clasped the long stem of the glass, twirled the scarlet liquid in rhythmic circles, and inhaled the fragrance of the wine, just as Dominic had taught her over the years. When she brought her lips to the crystal, a voice jarred her from the hypnotic effects of her drink.

"Bethany? I didn't know you were coming."

Bethany pulled the glass away from her lips and looked into the face of her mother. She was so used to seeing the worn-out version, that seeing Mom now, in a dress, with makeup and curled hair, made her do a giant double take.

"Robin invited me."

Fenton stepped behind her mother. He removed her shawl, pulled out one of the chairs for Mom, and sat in his own with immaculate posture. Everything inside Bethany froze. Pastor Fenton was sitting at their table.

His gaze lingered on her wine glass, his brown eyes moving from the drink to her face, filled with the same accusation she saw too many times as a child. *Sinner.* She was always a sinner. She refused to endure an entire dinner sitting across from him and her mother. As individuals, she might be able to handle them, but not when they sat like a unified force, her mother playing a terrified, infatuated mouse, and Fenton the handsome, intimidating house cat. Without excusing herself, she rose from her chair and left the table, unable to stand one more second of Fenton's scrutiny.

Evan clamped his hands on the edges of his chair, his eyes darting between Ruth, who worried her lip, and Robin, whose body was poised much like his, ready to chase after Bethany as she navigated her way through the maze of tables. Pastor Fenton ignored Bethany's departure, introduced himself to Bryan and Amy, and struck up a conversation. Evan turned his attention to Diane, the line of her brow furrowed into a sharp V as she watched Bethany disappear into the hall.

She shifted toward Evan, close enough to whisper. "What was that about?"

"I'm not sure."

"You should go find out," she said, giving him an animated wink.

Evan rolled his eyes. "Easy there, Cupid. Retract the arrow."

She raised her eyebrows and shoulders in unison. "I'm just sayin'."

He knew exactly what she was just saying. As soon as Bethany revealed her age, he could see the cogs turning in Diane's head. Evan scooted his chair back the same time as Robin. He placed his hand on her shoulder, letting her know he would take care of it. The look of relief she gave him tore at his heart. Prior to Micah's death, Robin wouldn't have thought twice about maneuvering her way through a crowded room. She would have stopped to mingle with several friends and acquaintances on her way out. Now, however, the thought seemed to terrify her.

Evan moved toward the exit, trying not to let his thoughts go in directions they didn't need to. Like the way Bethany looked in that dress. Or the fact that she no longer had a boyfriend. He didn't care if he had an irrepressible urge to push back the brown lock that kept falling over her eye. The woman wanted to sell Dan's farm and hightail it out of Peaks. He had no business entertaining romantic thoughts for someone so totally wrong for him.

Emptiness filled the hallway. He looked one way, then the other. After a failed search, he trotted down the steps and made his way outside, stepping around a few late guests straggling through the door. His muscles tensed against the nighttime air. He peered at the parking lot, searching for the shadow of a figure hurrying toward a car. After her desertion the day the doctors took Micah off life support, he wouldn't put it past her to do the same tonight. But she wasn't out there.

Rubbing warmth into his hands, he turned back to the door and spotted a silhouette. The glow from the moon reflected off Bethany's bare shoulders, making her look almost translucent as she stood at the edge of the terrace overlooking the Mississippi River. She was nuts. Certifiably nuts. Nobody in their right mind stood outside in weather this cold wearing nothing but a thin dress.

If she heard him approaching, she didn't turn her head. She faced the water, watching waves circle over the dangerous currents pulling beneath the surface. When he stepped by her side, she looked up, like a doe hearing the cock of a rifle. Her eyes matched the tumultuous river, swirling with hidden depth.

"Are you okay?" he asked.

A slight breeze sent Bethany's hair floating around her shoulders. Goose bumps marched up her arms. She shivered, drawing her arms around herself as Evan shrugged off his coat.

She held out her hand to stop him. "I'm fine."

Evan draped his suit coat over her shoulders anyway. Despite her initial protest, she pulled the jacket close to her body and turned her nose to the fabric. His insides dipped as if he'd slipped a few rungs down a silo ladder. Was it his imagination, or was Bethany smelling his clothes? He rubbed his hands together and blew hot air into them. "Are you going to tell me why you hightailed it out of the banquet hall?"

No response.

That was okay. He was good at digging. "Does it have to do with your mom?"

Her head jerked. Whether she meant it as a yes or no, he couldn't tell.

"You two don't get along so well."

A small muscle twitched in her neck.

Evan prepared to push the shovel down further, hoping to divot her hard, winter exterior with the spade of his questions. "Does it have to do with her date?"

This time her head jerk was obvious. She aimed her stare at him, pinning him beneath the barrel of a loaded gun. "How is this any of your business?" A controlled sharpness laced each word.

"Robin looked ready to go after you. And since she has enough on her plate at the moment, I thought taking her place was the right thing to do." His insides balked at the lie. If he was being honest, he'd have to admit he came after her for more complicated reasons. In the milliseconds before she fled the table, she'd granted him access into something vulnerable. Something broken. And it had pinched his chest with the strong desire to fix whatever hurt.

"I'm an adult. I don't need to be taken care of."

Evan leaned over the railing, the cold metal stinging his palms. "Everybody needs to be taken care of, Bethany."

"Not me."

Evan glanced at his coat wrapped around her shoulders and smiled. *Sure she didn't.* She jutted her jaw forward and started to remove the offensive evidence. Evan placed his hand over the fabric. She twisted out from under his grasp. "Don't you have anything better to do? Like go entertain your date? I hardly think she appreciates you running after another woman."

"Diane won't care." Quite the opposite, in fact. Evan was sure Diane was plotting a number of schemes that all involved getting him and Bethany on the dance floor later that night.

Bethany arched a brow. "So it's that kind of a relationship?"

"Relationship?"

"Whatever you've got going on with Diane?"

He blinked, taking in Bethany's hardened features. Did she think Diane was his girlfriend? That he was in a relationship with the vivacious blonde on his arm—the one he used to wrestle with over his Big Wheel? He started laughing—a deep vibration that warmed his lungs.

Her face pinched. "What's so amusing?"

"You think Diane and I are in a relationship?"

"Aren't you?"

"Diane's my cousin. She flew in from Kentucky for the dinner. She wanted to be here when they honor Micah." He chuckled. "Plus, she loves a good party."

Something changed in Bethany's posture and expression. Was she relieved? The thought amused him, and on the heels of his amusement came something deeper, something that warmed his insides despite the frigid temperature. He didn't like it.

"Are you going to come back in?" He took a hopeful step toward the door. "It is winter you know. Not the best time to stand outside and appreciate the scenery." He took another step, hoping she'd follow.

"You assume I appreciate what I see."

Her enticing response hugged the ends of her breath and evaporated into the night. He cocked his head to one side. "You don't appreciate the Mississippi River?" Dismissing such a powerful piece of nature seemed reckless somehow, like she was dismissing the river's creator as well.

"All of it." She swept her hand over the horizon, her forearm poking through the front gap of his jacket. "Nothing ever changes here. I've been away for ten years and it's still the same Peaks."

Did she have blinders on? Things around Peaks were changing every day—and much too fast. Suburbia crept closer and closer, like a glutton's ever-expanding waist line. New housing developments swelled against previously set boundaries. Every year, the glutton purchased a new pair of pants to accommodate its increasing girth. And Bethany wanted to feed it.

"This place is like my own personal purgatory. Ever since I came back, my life just stopped moving, and I can't get it going again."

"I thought you didn't believe in heaven and purgatory and all that."

She didn't respond. She was lost out in the river, staring as if the cold didn't exist.

But it did to him. The freezing temperature seeped through his starched shirt and settled on his shoulders. He wanted to ask her about their last encounter, with Susan on the front porch. He wanted to ask if and when she planned on putting the farm up for sale, but he couldn't get the words out. He preferred to ignore them all together.

Bethany let out a long breath. "Robin asked me to stay."

His chin dropped. "Permanently?"

She shook her head. "Through her pregnancy."

"Are you going to?"

"It doesn't make sense to lease an apartment in Chicago without knowing if I'll find work there. I could end up anywhere."

Evan imagined her resume floating in cyberspace, searching for the biggest cities. He tried to picture her in New York, or London, or Tokyo. But he couldn't. When he closed his eyes, all he could see was her curled up in Dan's recliner, keeping her grandfather company while the pair of them watched black-and-white sitcoms. Dan wouldn't have sat through those for anyone other than Bethany.

She picked at the frozen banister. "And since you're holding on to the farmhouse…" She shot him an irritated look. "Selling might take longer than I thought, especially in the winter."

Evan fought to keep his expression neutral.

"I told Robin I would stay until I found a job. Right after my promise, I get Fenton shoved in my face. It's like the Universe is reminding me why I hate this place."

"What is it about that guy? Why do you hate him so much?" Sure, the guy came across a smidge self-righteousness, but whatever Bethany felt toward Fenton went much deeper than a simple distaste. It was something very personal.

She grimaced but didn't answer.

He gave an involuntary shudder, his body protesting against the cold, and stuck out his arm. "Are you ready to go back inside?"

She handed back his coat and ignored his offered elbow. Despite the ripple of bumps spreading up her arms, she straightened her shoulders, tilted her chin, and together, they rejoined the masses. For the rest of dinner, she hovered somewhere a little bit above everybody else. What he might have considered arrogance before, now became nothing but a defense mechanism. How could anybody hurt her when she couldn't be touched?

✤

While music played and people danced, Bethany stared at Pastor Fenton and her mother as they mingled with a group of First Light attendees at a far-off table. Annoyed by Fenton's deceptive good looks and her mother's rapt attention, she wrapped one leg over the other, hooked her foot around the back of her ankle, and crossed her arms. Suffering through an entire dinner next to him, then listening to his exorbitant speech afterward, had wound her nerves tight.

It was time to go.

She glanced over her shoulder, toward the front of the stage, where Mayor Ford's wife droned on and on to Robin, who nodded vacantly, gripping Micah's post-mortem plaque to her chest. They came. They honored Micah's memory. But enough was enough. Bethany unwound her legs, ready to go rescue Robin, so they could make their escape. Somebody beside her let out an exaggerated sigh. She looked over to find Evan standing there.

He plopped down in a chair and drummed his fingers against the table.

"What?" The word came out snappier than she'd intended.

He leaned toward her. "Do you want to dance?"

She laughed. "You're kidding."

He stared—his face completely deadpan. "Does it look like I'm kidding?"

Bethany swiveled her head around and stared once again at Fenton and her mother.

He leaned closer. "This past month hasn't been very fun. For you or for me."

She turned around. "No kidding."

He studied her for a bit, as if considering something, until Glenn Miller's *In the Mood* sounded through the banquet hall and a smile lighted across his face—one that made his cheeks dimple and her insides flop in a very silly way. He stood suddenly, took her hand, and pulled her up next to him.

"What are you doing?"

"Time for some fun," he said, dragging her toward the mass of moving bodies.

He pulled her to the edge of the dance floor before she managed to dig in her heels and twist her hand from his grip. Panic knocked through her body. "Are you nuts? I'm not going to dance."

"Why not?"

"Because I'm not about to make a fool out of myself."

"Who says you're going to look like a fool?"

She raised her hand. "Me. I don't dance."

"Do you always have to be in such control?"

She crossed her arms.

"It's frightening how two people can be so much alike yet so very different."

"I have no idea what you're talking about."

"I have a hard time letting go, too. Thankfully, it's an acquired skill." A stupid, devilish grin spread across his face, and before she could react, he took her hand again and spun her onto the dance floor—her heart tumbling and crashing with the spin. The way he moved forced her to move with him—stiffly, awkwardly. She was all too aware of her body. And all too aware of his. Heat pooled in her cheeks. She was not going to do this. Not here. At this banquet. With this man. With all these people she used to know watching.

"We can't both lead here, Bethany." His breath tickled her ear.

"I'm not leading."

"You're not following either."

"That's because I don't want to dance." She stepped on his foot and the heat in her cheeks exploded. "Evan, I have no idea what I'm doing."

"Bethany, it doesn't matter." He pulled her closer. "Because I do."

The heat from his body and the hardness of his chest made warmth pool inside her belly. She tried to yank away, but he refused to let go, and the uppity beat of the music played on. "Evan."

"Bethany." He raised his eyebrows in mock challenge, but a seriousness burned in his eyes and his feet continued to move. In perfect, annoying rhythm. "Just trust me."

"You say it like it's so easy."

Evan spun her around him. "Of course it's not."

"Then how am I supposed to *just trust you?*"

"Funny thing about trust." He let go of one of her hands and made her move in a way she didn't think possible. Her eyes widened. "Sometimes you have to give it before you can experience it."

"That doesn't make sense."

"Of course it does."

He twirled her around. Did some loopy-thing with their arms. Twirled her again. Faster this time. And all of a sudden, Bethany wasn't thinking about her feet anymore. Evan whirled her around the dance floor and Bethany caught herself smiling. Wanting to laugh, even. Because he was right—this was fun. And his steps were so sure that she didn't have to think. She lost herself in the music and found that the more she let go, the more fun the dance became. They moved to the fast-paced melody, and Bethany felt flushed. Exhilarated. Freer than she could remember feeling in long, long time.

Evan spun her around. Pulled her close. Flung her back out. And then he dipped her, and the song was over, and they were both out of breath, and his face was inches from hers, and he was smiling too—a giant grin that made his eyes crinkle in the corners.

"Bethany?"

"What?"

He pulled her out of the dip and they stood in the middle of the dance floor, Bethany becoming more and more aware of the crowd. Of her body. Of herself. She tucked her hair behind her ears, embarrassed by the heat in her neck and cheeks.

Evan's face grew serious. Intense again.

"Not all Christians are like him," he whispered.

She didn't have to ask who he meant. She knew exactly who he was talking about. And she had no idea what to do with the words.

Twenty-Three

P urgatory trickled into something much longer than she anticipated. Bethany's life became a series of gray, five o'clock sunsets, all infused with the dismal admission that another day had passed, and she was no closer to a job than when she first moved in with Robin three months ago. Nobody had even called her for an interview.

She munched on the last bit of apple and cheese she prepared for lunch, and stared at the slip of paper in her hand. Yesterday, one of Robin's friends stopped by, and when Robin mentioned Bethany's predicament with the farm, the woman wrote down the contact information of a local Realtor.

Today Bethany was determined to get her life moving forward again. She dumped the last slice of Colby Jack cheese into the garbage. Her attention snagged on the dripping sink, and above that, the calendar. March twenty-second was circled in red ink—the date of Robin's twenty-week ultrasound. Just like the other three appointments, she'd asked Bethany to go. And just like the other three, Bethany couldn't bring herself to say no, especially after hearing the heartbeat for the first time two months ago. Proof that life not only grew but thrived inside Robin's womb.

For a woman who didn't have much of a maternal instinct, the quick patter had obliterated the growing frustration in Bethany's chest. When the tiny heartbeat filled the examination room, she'd looked to Robin in awe but quickly checked her expression. She could tell by the look on her friend's face that the sound of that heart was breaking Robin's own.

Many times, Bethany had attempted and failed to coerce Robin from her long-standing stupor, usually by trying to elicit some excitement over the café. But their plans had stalled out. The café turned in to nothing more than a saved project on AutoCAD, while Bethany grew more and more attached to Robin and her baby.

And it had to stop.

She snatched the phone, picked up the slip of paper, and dialed the number. When the lady on the other line started asking questions, Bethany dug out the paperwork from one of the dresser drawers in the guest bedroom. The woman sounded very pleased and asked if Bethany could meet her at her office in an hour. Bethany readily agreed, relieved at such quick timing.

Throughout the interim, she refused to dwell on the what-ifs. She forced herself to focus on the possibilities. And after three months of hibernation, her heart stepped out into the sunlight, and the warm blood of purpose pulsed through her veins. Her heart rate increased, her temperature rose, until a healthy, warm sensation tingled through her. It didn't falter. Not when she sat in her car. And not when she drove out of town. She hummed the entire way, tapping the steering wheel, pleased with her decision.

Until she drove past the farm.

Bethany's foot eased off the gas pedal when she passed the gravel road leading to Dan's farmhouse. She caught herself staring in her rearview mirror, searching for Evan out in the fields. After New Year's Eve and that dance she couldn't get out of her head, he'd been very intentional about visiting Robin at least once a week. Once he showed up with his younger brother, Gavin, who looked to be faring just as well, if not worse, than Robin. But in late February, his visits started tapering off. And now, by mid-March, she hadn't seen him for at least two weeks. She refused to ask about his absence and ignored the correlation between his waning presence and her darkening mood.

Bethany blinked several times and forced her eyes away from the mirror, exhaling as the farm fell out of sight.

Her stomach dipped, and it had nothing to do with the rolling hills. Here she was, plunging ahead with her decision to sell, while Evan labored in the fields. She tightened her grip on the steering wheel and swallowed, imagining a lump of self-assurance sliding down her throat—a much needed nutrient.

Yes, Evan would be upset. Yes, she was taking away his job, but she had her own life to consider. Her own goals. Over the past few months, she'd let other people's feelings and opinions influence her decisions. Robin's grief threw her off course. Evan's opinions churned her emotions into chaos. Dominic's doubt scared her away from taking a chance. And Susan Sparks delayed her plans. She sat straighter. No more of that. She needed to take control. She needed to do what was best for her.

Just when she convinced herself, the steering wheel jerked under her hands. The car lurched, and a loud rumbling filled the cab of her vehicle. Was it the muffler? How in the world could a muffler go bad on a new car? Her foot shifted from the gas to the brake. She attempted to pull over to the side of the road, only the steering wheel wouldn't cooperate. Did faulty mufflers impact the steering? She cranked the wheel, forcing it to submit.

After turning off the engine, she stepped out to survey the damage. It didn't take long to find the problem—a flat tire. And it wasn't just kind of flat either. It was flat-flat. She brought her hands to her hips. Great, this was just great. Of course something like this would happen. Just when she pushed her life back in motion, Peaks reached out its dirty claws and popped her tire.

She let out a frustrated sigh, the gravel crunching beneath her feet as she pivoted in a circle, scolding herself for not knowing how to change a tire. It was a skill she should have taken the time to learn. Precisely so she wouldn't end up in a situation like this.

She looked down at her new shoes. She wouldn't make it more than a mile without getting horrendous blisters and where would that get her? Next to some cows? Her phone was inside her purse on the console, but who was she going to call? She didn't want to upset Robin with her plans, there was no way she was calling Evan, and her mother was probably sleeping. She strode to her trunk, popped it open, and pulled out the spare tire. She rolled it next to the flat and went back for the jack. She turned the tool over in her hand, examining the shiny metal before getting on her hands and knees. The sharp gravel dug into her palms, and even through the cotton fabric of her Calvin Klein's, her knees protested against the sting.

Thinking one place was as good as any, she set the jack beneath the car and rejoiced when she elevated the vehicle enough that the offensive tire hung a few centimeters above the ground.

Her joy, however, was short lived. She tried to remove the screw things from the hubcap, but no matter how hard she yanked on the L-shaped iron device, those four metal pieces wouldn't budge. Surrendering to defeat, she chucked the worthless tool against the ground and plopped onto her butt. Melted snow seeped through her jeans. She checked her wristwatch and put her face in her hands. She was already ten minutes late.

With nothing else to do, she retrieved her purse from inside the car, fished out her cell, and dialed information for the number to a local towing service. Maybe they could change her tire. When the operator connected her to Study's Towing and nobody answered, Bethany stifled a scream. What kind of business didn't answer their phone in the middle of a weekday?

She decided to try Robin, who didn't answer. Then the Realtor, who didn't answer. Then her mother, who didn't answer. The scream in her chest wanted out. The Universe was against her. Bethany sunk down in the driver's seat, the door open, her dirty knees facing a random field, and considered her options. Walking was out, unless she wanted to grow a dozen blisters on each toe. Nobody was answering their stupid phone. And Evan was a couple miles away—his number typed out in Times New Roman on the paperwork Drew McCarty had given her.

What other option did she have?

Letting out a shaky breath, she dialed his number, half hoping he wouldn't answer. The phone rang three times. After the fourth, her shoulders relaxed as she prepared to get a voice recording, but the gruff sound of his hello propelled her heart into a series of irregular beats. Her thumb flew to the end button. For a brief second, she considered hanging up. But then what? She couldn't hang out on the side of the road and wait until somebody drove past. That might be hours.

"Hello?" he said again.

"Evan? It's Bethany Quinn." She squeezed her eyes shut. Why did she say her last name? He knew who she was. "I'm sorry to call. But I have a flat tire and I'm stuck on the side of the road about two miles away from the farm." Her cheeks grew hotter with every word that poured from her mouth. Why had she never learned to change a tire?

"Out of town or toward town?"

"Out."

"I'll be there in just a bit."

And that was that. No other questions. He was more than willing to pause from his day to help her out. She doubted he'd be so willing if he knew where she was headed.

Ten minutes later, she spotted his Bronco cresting the hill and scolded her heart for its erratic behavior. He pulled up behind her, stepped out of his car, and clomped over in a pair of muddied work boots laced beneath dirt-stained Wranglers. His once-white shirt revealed two strong forearms, slightly tanned from the indecisive sun. She eyed his windblown hair and caught the smile spreading across his face. He obviously found this amusing. She pretended to study her flat tire.

"So what seems to be the problem, little miss?"

Bethany put her hands into the pockets of her down vest. Maybe he could prance around in fifty degree weather wearing short-sleeves. She, however, was cold. And messy. And annoyed. She kicked the tire as he approached.

His eyes hesitated on her dirty knees. She shifted, careful to hide her wet backside. During her ten minute wait, she'd put the spare tire and the tool thingy back in the trunk, but she left the jack, hiding her incompetence and highlighting her accomplishment.

He crouched over his knees and surveyed the damage. His hand found the lever of the jack and he started bringing the car down. She stepped forward. "What are you doing?" Why was he undoing her only successful foray into tire-changing?

"You have your car jacked wrong." He moved to his belly, unconcerned about the wet gravel, and tapped the underside of her vehicle. "You want to put it here, beneath the jack flan, so you don't damage your car."

Bethany faked indifference but watched from the corner of her eye. Next time her tire went flat, she would be prepared to fix it herself.

Once the car was back to its original position, he propped himself onto his toes and messed with the bolt things, like he had the strength to undo them with his bare hands. Wanting to provide at least the appearance of self-sufficiency, she retrieved the metal tool from her trunk.

"Don't you need this?" she asked, bringing it into view.

"Do you have the key for these lug nuts?"

Lug nuts. So that's what they were called. "I didn't realize lug nuts needed a key."

"These ones do. They're locking lug nuts. They protect your wheels from getting stolen. I'm sure it comes in handy in Chicago. Don't need 'em in Peaks."

It took a bit for Evan's words to sink in. Her tire needed to be changed if she was going to get anywhere. The lug nuts needed to be removed before any tire-changing happened. The lug nuts wouldn't budge without a key. "What happens if I don't have a key?"

Evan nodded at the metal tool dangling at her side. "Then that tire iron won't do us any good." He stood up and swiped at his pants. "We can drive into Peaks. They'll have what we need at the hardware store."

She blanched. She was supposed to be heading in the opposite direction. She glanced at her watch. Thirty minutes late. While waiting for Evan to arrive, she'd tried calling the Realtor again to inform her of the delay, but she got the lady's voice mail.

"Do you have somewhere you need to be?"

Her lips pressed together. If only he knew.

He crossed his arms in front of his chest and cocked an eyebrow. "It's about the farm, isn't it?"

She watched the muscles clench in his jaw, his carefree mood vanishing as he waited for her to answer. She refused to wither beneath his stare. "I was going to meet with another Realtor."

He turned his face away and surveyed the tire. "I guess that plan didn't work so well, did it?"

She looked at her watch again. Thirty-five minutes late.

"How are you planning on getting there now? I'll help you fix your tire, but I am not driving you *there*."

Bethany fisted her hand and placed it on her hip. "Would you stop taking this so personally?"

He took a step closer.

She held her ground.

"You don't think Dan meant this to be personal?" He took another step toward her and brought his hand to his chest. "You're planning on selling *my* farm."

"Do you need to see the paperwork again?"

"Did you take it personal when your boss fired you from your job?"

"How is that the same thing?"

"It's the exact same thing. You're tossing the farm around like it means nothing." He was very close now. Too close. Her feet begged to step back, to put some distance between them so the building tension could have some room to breathe. But she wasn't going to back down. She lifted her chin.

"Farming is what I do. And you're so eager to pull that from underneath me."

Bethany swung her hand around, motioning to their surroundings. "You can get another farm." That's all this place was. An eternity of corn and cattle. "I can't imagine one is very much different from the next."

"How in the world am I supposed to *get* another farm?" He didn't wait for her to answer. "And anyway, I love *that* farm."

She gritted her teeth. "And I love architecture. I'm just trying to get that back. It's the same thing you would do."

"Not at the expense of somebody else's dreams."

"Keeping the farm is expending *my* dreams."

"It doesn't have to." Evan's face softened. "Let me rent the land. You can make some money without even lifting a finger."

She let a frustrated breath push past her lips. He was impossible. Unreasonable. Stubborn. He was pitting her dreams against his, and nothing she could say or do would convince him that hers had equal value. They could stand there all day, and neither one of them would give in. What a waste of time. She picked up her phone lying on the driver's seat and dialed the Realtor's number. No answer. The scream in her chest came back, but instead of letting it loose, she threw her phone on the seat and gave him a stony look.

"Can we please go get whatever key we need to get?"

"Fine." He walked to the car, his big boots clomping against the graveled shoulder. Before she could stop him, he had the passenger door open. Why did he have to do that? Even she could tell he didn't want to. He gave her an are-you-coming-or-what look. She followed. The sooner they finished this, the sooner she could get away from him.

They started the fifteen minute drive to town in unyielding silence, until about halfway, when Evan decided to turn on his radio. She cringed at the twang emitting from the speakers. He turned up the music, as if goading her, and tapped his thumb against the steering wheel to the beat of each redneck song. She gritted her teeth and refused to the take the bait.

It wasn't until Evan slowed his Bronco and they passed the pharmacy on the outskirts of town that she let out her breath. She could get the stupid key, get back to her stupid car, and catalog this stupid day away with every other disaster she'd encountered since returning to Peaks. She brought her fingertips to her temples. It seemed to be the hub of her growing headache, and if she could get the throbbing under control there, the pain shooting to the base of her skull would lose its power. She rubbed soothing circles into the spot and looked out the window.

Evan turned down his music, which abated some of the pounding, and she spotted a For Sale sign perched in the window of Sunshine Daisies—a former flower shop. It was next to the antique store she and Robin used to poke around in when they were younger.

The slightly rundown shop exhibited the usual wear and tear of an old building with few updates over the years. But the yard outside enchanted her, with a quaint gravel walk through what could soon be a lovely garden in a month or two. The shop sat back from the road, nestled on top of a small hill.

"Can you stop?"

"The hardware store is up this way."

"I'm not interested in the hardware store right now. I want to check something out."

He hesitated, then pulled the car over to the curb. She unbuckled her seatbelt and stepped out of the vehicle before it had completely stopped. She walked up the steps leading to the shop and smiled. It truly was a perfect spot. Especially with the park across the street, which would bring in customers. She ran her hand over the rusticated brick façade and studied the fenestration of the windows. There was even a second story. She tried the door, but it was locked. So she brought her face to the darkened window pane and peered through the dingy glass.

"What exactly, are you doing?" Evan asked.

She brought her face away, disappointed that she couldn't see anything but curtains. She looked at the For Sale sign, noted the phone number posted below it, and plugged it in to her phone before addressing Evan's question. "Amusing myself."

He didn't need to know the particulars. She wasn't going to divulge Robin's secret, if that's what the café was. The excitement that had coursed through her veins earlier in the morning returned.

This was her favorite part. The vision. The potential. Knowing her ideas could become a wonderful, appealing reality. She breathed in the sense of purpose, feeling useful for the first time in months. This project could keep her occupied until she could find a Realtor who answered her phone and was enthusiastic about selling the farm, or until the job offers started rolling in. And she was suddenly very confident they would. Now all she needed to do was convince Robin that Sunshine Daisies was the perfect spot for her and Micah's café.

Twenty-Four

A twelve-year-old should not be in love with a dollhouse. But I couldn't help myself. Robin had the most immaculate dollhouse I'd ever seen in my life. It had five rooms, a gigantic kitchen, arched windows, and a second-story balcony. It sat in the corner of her bedroom, on top of white carpet, in what seemed to be a perpetual stream of sunlight that slanted in from her lace-curtained windows.

We'd sit on her canopy bed, beading necklaces, braiding our hair, talking and laughing, while I snuck glances at that house, no doubt worth more than the entirety of our trailer. Ever since our chance meeting at the Laundromat, I spent every moment possible in Robin's home. Unlike my own, everything was beautiful there. Especially Mrs. Delner, who was slim, without being waif-like, and had shiny dark hair and the most vibrant blue eyes. Her laugh sounded like wind chimes, and she showered me with hugs at a time when everybody else treated me like I had leprosy.

I became so infatuated with Robin's life and Robin's family—and in awe that I could be a part of it—that my obsession with the farm started to ebb. I would lay awake at night in my creaky old bed listening to David mutter in his sleep and instead of dreaming about the farmhouse and Grandpa Dan, I imagined living in a life-sized version of Robin's dollhouse. Of course, I never shared this obsession with Robin. I didn't want my best friend to know I was an almost thirteen-year-old coveting a toy she'd probably grown out of years ago.

So at the end of July, on my thirteenth birthday, when Robin blindfolded me and pulled me out to her garage with Mrs. Delner, I had no idea what to expect. I was even more confused when they took the blindfold off, and I stood facing sheets of wood and cardboard, a box of tools, paints and paintbrushes, different rolls of wallpaper, and a stack of shingles. I turned around and looked at them, their faces split with identical grins.

"Happy birthday!" Mrs. Delner said.

"What do you think?" Robin's voice was a bit breathless.

"What is it?" I asked.

"Your future dollhouse."

My cheeks grew hot. Robin knew? This whole time she knew?

"We tried to find the same one I have in one of our old catalogs, but they don't make it anymore. So Mom thought we could do the next best thing. We could build one together."

I attempted to hide my mortification. Or at least undo the uncertainty creeping into Robin's eyes. But I couldn't find the right words.

"Don't you like it?" she asked.

"I love it. It's just... I don't know how to build a dollhouse." At least not one as beautiful as Robin's.

"Mom said we can learn together." Robin stepped forward and picked up a hammer. "I think it'll be fun."

And she was right. It was.

For two whole months, we drank Snapple in the garage and listened to Hootie and the Blowfish on Mrs. Delner's CD player. With our hair tied up in handkerchiefs, we trimmed and painted the wood, assembled the walls, glued on the shingles, and chose just the right wallpaper and flooring and finishing touches. In the end, it was nothing like Robin's dollhouse. But I loved it anyway.

When we finished, we draped a sheet over the roof, eager for our big reveal once Mr. Delner returned from work. As soon as he walked in the door, Robin grabbed his hand and tugged him into the garage. I tore off the sheet like a regular magician, and Mr. Delner didn't disappoint. His eyes widened. "Wow, girls. This is impressive."

"Didn't they do a great job?" Mrs. Delner asked.

"I'd say so." Mr. Delner came closer to give our handiwork his full attention. "What an intriguing design."

Robin beamed. "That was Bethy's idea."

Mr. Delner looked at me then, and smiled so handsomely it reminded me of my dad. Before his accident. Warmth filled my entire body.

He turned to Mrs. Delner, his smile still firmly in place, my warmth growing all the warmer. "Looks like we have a budding architect on our hands."

Two things stuck in my mind. Mr. Delner said *we*, like I belonged to them. And Mr. Delner called me an architect.

Twenty-Five

Robin pulled two shirts off the hanger and clutched them to her chest. Something inside her refused to toss them onto the sparse pile on the floor. So far, she'd taken four of Micah's sweatshirts from the back of their closet—the ones he hadn't worn in a good two years—and dumped them onto the carpet, proud of her accomplishment.

She'd just talked with her father on the phone. He'd asked how she was doing. Fine, she'd said. Then he inquired about Micah's clothes. He told her cleaning out her mother's closet had been one of the hardest things he'd done after she died, but also necessary. He told her to buck up and clean it out. Tough love.

So that's what she was doing. Or attempting to do. Three months and Micah wasn't coming back to wear his clothes. If she thought those first couple days before the funeral had been difficult, it was nothing compared to the emptiness that made up her current existence. At least then shock had cushioned the blow. Now a pressing darkness weighed upon her soul, and there was nothing she could do to get out from beneath its suffocating presence.

She took another of his shirts from the hanger and pressed it against her nose. It didn't smell like Micah. She inhaled deeper, trying to pry the buried scent from the fabric, but nothing came. She pulled another shirt from its place and breathed it in.

Nothing.

"No." The sharp word sliced through the closet.

She snatched another. Then another. And another. Until she'd ripped every single shirt from its spot, and the barren hangers rocked on the bar. None of the clothes smelled like Micah. Not a single one. They lay like an odious pile, mocking her from the floor.

"I'll get it back. You can't have his smell too."

She didn't stop to examine the logic of her one-way conversation with God, or the fact that He hadn't stolen Micah's scent to heaven like she accused Him of doing. Nothing about her actions was logical anymore anyway.

She clutched the discarded clothing against her chest, hurried to the basement, and stuffed the washer full. She dumped in a large dose of fabric softener, the kind Micah loved, and stared at the wall for the entire twenty-five minute cycle. As soon as it buzzed, she threw the load into the dryer and waited for his clothes to dry. Before the cycle finished, she wrenched out the heavy bundle, raced up to their bedroom, uncapped his cologne, and doused his clothes in the fragrance.

Come back to me, Micah. Come back.

She repeated her plea with every spritz from the bottle. When there was nothing left to spray, she got down on her knees and buried her face in the cloying scent, her tears staining the fabric, her sobs muffled by the warm, semi-damp laundry until a throat cleared behind her.

Robin sat up, hair plastered to the wetness on her cheek. She pushed the strands away and found Bethany standing in the doorway, surveying the pile of dress shirts and pants on the floor. The concern on Bethany's face brought Robin back to her senses. She was a mess. An absolute mess. Her attempt to clean out Micah's closet could not have gone any worse. The look on Bethany's face was nothing compared to the look that would be on Micah's if he could see her now.

"Robin? What are you doing?"

She tried to give Bethany a self-deprecating smile, but the gesture fell short. So she held up a shirt with one hand and wiped at her eyes with the other. "I thought I would clean out Micah's closet. It's not going so well."

Bethany walked into the room and sat on the edge of the bed.

"Why does this have to be so hard?" Robin asked.

Bethany didn't answer right away. Probably because there was no answer to give. Difficulty came with death. Robin knew that. She'd experienced it when she lost her mother.

Yesterday, she'd Googled the stages of grief, searching for an end to her own, and had no problem diagnosing herself. She was stuck somewhere between anger and depression, her mind waffling between the two. When she read the last stage—acceptance—she'd burst into an irrational bout of tears. Not because the stage felt so far away but because she was afraid of reaching it. As taxing as this was right now, with every breath a battle, at least her pain linked her to her husband. If she let go of the pain, wouldn't that mean letting go of Micah? How could that ever be a good thing?

"Why don't you let me do it?"

Robin brought the shirt into her lap. "Because it's my job."

"Says who? Why should it be your job to clean out Micah's closet?" Bethany slid down the bed and joined her on the floor. "Since when did you become so masochistic? If cleaning out Micah's closet causes you pain, don't do it." Bethany looked at her belly. Robin's over-sized T-shirt rested over the small protruding bump. "You have enough to deal with."

She envisioned Micah up in heaven, cheering. He'd tell her to stop holding on so tight. He'd tell her to let go. She stared at the pile of clothes.

They were just clothes. No amount of cologne would turn them into any-thing else.

"I have something that might distract you." Bethany reached out and touched Robin's hand, a smile on her face. "I found you a café."

"A café?"

Bethany nodded. "Sunshine Daisies is going out of business. It would be the perfect place to build it."

Robin couldn't match Bethany's enthusiasm.

"It's a two-story building. We could rip out some of the second-story flooring. Open it up into a vaulted ceiling with a cozy loft. Customers could look down at you playing the piano and enjoy a view of the Mississippi out the windows. Honestly, it's perfect."

Something inside Robin recoiled. "I don't want to build it." She said the words without thinking.

"You haven't even seen the space yet."

"I don't need to see it. I don't want one without the other."

Bethany furrowed her brow. "What do you mean?"

"The café. I don't want it without Micah."

"Why not?"

"Because it's not how it was supposed to be."

Bethany motioned to the pair of them sitting on her bedroom floor amidst a pile of cologne-soaked laundry. "And you think this is?"

Robin wasn't trying to be difficult. She really wasn't. But she couldn't just jump into the plans Bethany had laid out while Micah's clothes spun through the wash. She couldn't shift gears that quickly. "I think I need to be alone right now." She hoped her request didn't come out rude. She wasn't trying to be mean, or selfish. Especially not with Bethany, who had sup-ported her over these last three months.

Frowning, Bethany stood. Before she exited the room, she stopped and rested her hand on the door knob. "Please just think about it, Robin. It would be good for both of us. And maybe even fun." She left, letting Robin contemplate that last thought.

Fun.

It was a foreign word. One that had long since fallen out of her vocabulary. Something she used to know the meaning to—a long, long time ago. All that remained now was a niggling familiarity.

Bethany rapped on the door. Although the farm belonged to her, the farmhouse didn't, and her presence felt presumptuous. She took a deep breath and knocked again. No answer. She glanced at her watch, and just to make sure, looked at the sky. The sun sank toward the horizon, leaving the east an inky blue and the west a mixture of pinks and oranges. She turned away from the front door and peered at the fields. A misty fog hovered over the ground. Pretty soon, all remnants of daylight would disappear. Evan's Bronco parked in the driveway told her he had to be there somewhere.

Her flat tire this morning felt like ages ago.

She stepped off the front porch and walked to the side of the house to peek in one of the windows. The hallway light illuminated an empty living room. She tried to see into the kitchen, but the angle wasn't right. Just as she considered peeking in the window by the back door or walking to the machine shed, something snapped behind her. She turned around to find Evan staring at her, his eyebrows raised, his two faithful border collies panting at his side.

"This is quite an odd habit you've developed, spying in windows."

She took a quick step out of the mulch like a naughty child who'd been caught peeking at Christmas presents. Evan wore the same clothes as earlier, only he had thrown a stained sweatshirt on over his white tee, probably to combat the falling temperatures.

"Sorry," she said, more mortified by her flaming cheeks than being caught nosing around the bushes.

"What are you doing here?" His words came out curious instead of harsh, although she was sure she deserved the latter. After some distance, she could understand his anger. Evan loved the farm as much as she loved her career. She'd be just as angry if somebody tried to take that away from her.

"I have a favor to ask," she said.

One of the border collies wagged its tail and barked. Evan ignored the dog and crossed his arms in front of him. "Two in one day? That must be a record for you."

Her shoulders stiffened and she turned to go, but Evan reached out and took her elbow. "Bethany..."

Her breath caught in her throat. It was the first time he'd touched her since their New Year's Eve dance, and something warm spread through her arm, as if she'd dipped her elbow into a pool of sunshine.

"I'm sorry." He let go of her elbow and took a step back. "I didn't mean to be rude. What can I do for you?"

She blinked away the fuzz from her brain. She had to make it clear that his help would benefit Robin, not her. She couldn't imagine he'd agree to help her with anything after their morning together. "I'm worried about Robin. And the baby."

"Is everything okay?"

She held up her hands. Rushing to his car and driving to Robin's to check for himself would be just like him. "The baby's fine. But I'm not so sure about the mother. You haven't been over in a while."

"I've been sort of busy. It's calving season."

"I'm not accusing you of anything. I'm only updating you on your sister-in-law."

He looped his thumbs inside his front pockets and sighed. "She's not doing any better?"

"Did you really expect her to be?"

He stared past the barn, out into the darkening fields. "I don't know what to do. It's like she's shut herself off."

"I have an idea. But I need your help."

His eyes flicked toward hers. He waited a beat, then nodded for her to continue.

Bethany took a deep breath. "Did Robin or Micah ever talk about a café?"

"What kind of café?"

"One they could open together."

Evan smiled—not at Bethany, but at her words. "That sounds like them."

"I guess it was something they were planning before…" She let the thought fall away, unspoken but certainly understood. "Anyway, Robin has some great ideas for it. And the two of us have been playing around with the design. Drawing up dimensions, looking at paint colors."

"That sounds like more than just playing."

"It was something to do. But these past few weeks, we haven't talked about it. Robin's been kind of…distracted." More like comatose. But she didn't need to tell him that. "Today, when I saw that flower shop for sale…"

One corner of his mouth quirked. "You want to make the flower shop into their café?"

"It would be a healthy distraction. Cathartic, maybe."

"Have you talked to her about it?"

"Just a little bit ago."

"And?"

"She wasn't very interested."

Doubt crept into his eyes. She could see the response on his face—he was two seconds away from telling her to respect Robin's wishes. But she couldn't let him shut the door on this. Not yet.

"One of the very first renovation projects I did was an art gallery outside Chicago. An older couple wanted to turn a rundown bank in to an art gallery. Their son was an artist. He died in a boating accident. They had all sorts of paintings stored away in their basement. They built the place to honor him."

Bethany hadn't thought about that couple in years. At the time, she'd resented such a low-budget assignment, but looking back, it had been one of her most satisfying accomplishments. In all the rest of her years at Parker Crane, she'd never received a thank you as heartfelt as that couple's.

"I remember the lady telling me how good it felt to be doing something. She said the project helped them heal."

"And you think building this café will do the same for Robin?"

Bethany nodded.

Evan shifted on his heels. The two border collies no longer sat alert at his side. One had wandered to the house to sniff around. The other lay in the grass, licking Evan's boot. She watched them while she waited for his answer.

"It sounds like a good idea. But I have a concern."

Bethany frowned. "What?"

"Aren't you going to leave? So you start building the café. Then what? You get halfway through, someone puts down a tempting bid on the farm, and you hightail it out of town. You think *that* would be good for Robin?"

"When I start a project, I finish it."

Evan studied her face, as if looking for an expression, or a muscle, or a feature that might contradict her statement. He wouldn't find one.

"So what's my role in all this?"

Bethany smiled. She couldn't help herself. Evan was on board. "I'd like to do most of the renovations without contracting out."

"Why? Robin has plenty of money."

"Her pockets are deep, but they aren't bottomless. I don't think it's smart to spend a bunch of money if we don't need to." Bethany had learned, over the past few months, that the future was a murky, uncertain thing. Who knows? Maybe someday, Robin might need all that money, especially with a kid on the way. "Robin says you helped Micah finish their basement."

Evan chuckled. "Or more like Micah helped me."

She turned up her palm, as if he'd proven her own point. "So you're the perfect man for the job. Together we convince Robin that this is a great idea. And when the time comes, you help us with the building." The thought of working side-by-side with Evan did all kinds of funky things to her nerves, but if it meant getting out of her current rut, and pulling Robin out with her, then she'd just have to suffer through.

Evan's chest expanded, paused, deflated. "I have this problem, Bethany."

Her heartbeat fluttered at the way he spoke her name. "What?"

"I'd sure love to get the fields ready for planting. But I sort of have my hands tied at the moment."

Bethany shoved her hands inside her pockets.

"Planting is a lot of work. Eighteen-hour days, usually for a month straight. Not to mention the cost. It's not something I can commit to without knowing I'll be here in October to harvest."

It sounded like blackmail. Agree to keep the farm or else he wouldn't help with the café. She considered his words and ticked the months off in her head. Seven more until October. She refused to imagine herself in Peaks seven months from now. But who said keeping the farm meant she had to stay? She could let Dan's farm produce another year's worth of crop, collect some profit from Evan, and say goodbye in the fall. It would be an act of kindness on her part. Give him one last year. Perhaps it would even make her feel less self-serving when the time came to sell.

"When I meet with a Realtor, I can make sure they know not to put the farm on the market until after your harvest."

Evan scratched his jaw and studied her beneath a darkening sky. "You'd really do that?"

"Yes."

"And you honestly think this café will help Robin and the baby?"

"I'm sure of it."

He stuck out his hand. "Then count me in."

Bethany stared at his offering. She usually didn't shake on a deal. She was more of a pen-and-paper type gal. But she swallowed and stuck her hand in his. The heat returned. Instead of pulling away, Evan held her hand captive and gave her a calculating look, as if measuring her word with his stare. She pulled herself up straighter, determined to show him something he could count on.

Twenty-Six

Robin peered across the waiting room. A woman rested her hand on top of her swollen belly and leaned back in her seat, lengthening her body to accommodate the large cargo in front. Her husband—or at least Robin assumed he was her husband—sat in a more natural position beside her, a parent magazine held in one hand while he pointed at something on the page. The woman pinched her eyebrows together and pushed the magazine away. Robin closed her eyes and shook her head, but the image of the couple's interaction refused to dissipate.

According to the doctor, Robin was moments away from seeing her child. The baby Micah and she had made together. While she had an initial ultrasound to ensure the health of the embryo, all she saw then was a miniscule, flashing blip on the computer screen. Supposedly now she would be able to see the entire baby—head, body, hands, and feet. Robin stared at her abdomen. How would she react to seeing the fingers and toes of a baby that was half Micah?

A nurse appeared from the hallway. Robin sat straighter. Bethany shifted beside her, as if sensing Robin's distress. The nurse opened the manila folder in her hand and called out an unfamiliar name. The woman with the large belly rocked back and forth in her seat while grabbing on to her husband's hand. With both of their efforts, she managed to uncork herself from the chair and waddle toward the nurse.

Robin's heart stopped its gymnastics routine, leaving behind a familiar exhaustion. She closed her eyes and clasped her hands between her knees. Praying was the only way she knew to combat the oppressive lethargy, and she needed God's help if she was going to get through this.

With a bowed head, she asked God to take the black brew of resentment and apathy percolating in her soul. She envisioned that couple again, and the fissure in her chest widened. Did that woman appreciate her blessings? Did she understand how easy she had it, with her husband by her side? As much as Robin appreciated Bethany's support, it was Micah she wanted. Micah she yearned for.

"Robin Price?"

She brought her head up. A woman holding a file stood inside the waiting room. Robin retrieved her purse from the floor, stood, and tried to smile at the blond-haired woman who introduced herself as Mandy, the ultrasound technician. She led them in the opposite direction of the doctor's offices, toward a small room with an ultrasound machine.

"If you lie down here, we can get started," Mandy said, motioning toward the inclined bed.

Robin eased onto the side of the bed and swung her legs around while Bethany sat in a nearby chair—the one usually designated for husbands.

"If you'll just lift your shirt." Mandy bent over to retrieve something from below the monitor and put on a pair of plastic gloves.

After Robin exposed her rounded belly, Mandy lowered the waistline of Robin's pants, her face splitting into a giant grin. "Is this your first ultrasound?"

Robin shook her head. "I had one in the very beginning."

It didn't seem possible, but somehow the lady's smile widened. "Well, this will be quite different. We'll be able to see all kinds of things. Before we get started, would you like to know the sex of your child?"

Her muscles tightened. Micah would want to know. He couldn't wait for anything to save his life. He would have jumped out of his seat with an enthusiastic yes. She swallowed the image and looked to Bethany, as if her friend might be able to answer the question for her. But this wasn't Bethany's decision. It was Robin's.

"No, thank you."

Lord, does Micah know? Does he know he has a child?

She pressed her lips together. One of the hardest things about all this, one of the things she wrestled with every evening before bed, was that her husband died never knowing. They'd tried for a baby for a year and a half, and Micah never got to reap the joy of all the waiting and uncertainty. She never showed him the positive pregnancy test. She never felt him pick her up in his arms and twirl her in an excited circle. She never saw him jump up on the bed and do one of those victory dances football players do in the end zone. She never watched him get down on his knees, bring her alongside, and thank his Lord and Savior for blessing them with such a gift. Robin blinked away the burning in her eyes.

"Okay, then." Mandy sat down on a stool and wheeled over to the bedside. "This is going to be cold." She squirted a dollop of clear jelly onto Robin's abdomen.

Robin stared straight ahead, stomach clenched against the coolness, avoiding the screen as Mandy brought the Doppler to her belly and began gliding it over her skin.

Bethany scooted closer, her chair scraping against the linoleum. "Oh, wow."

"Do you want to see your baby, Mrs. Price?"

Robin turned toward Mandy, who held the Doppler in place. Did people ever tell her no?

No, sorry, I would not like to see my baby. Not without my husband. And since he's never coming back, I guess I'll never want to see my baby.

Mandy's smile faltered and a trace of confusion flickered in her eyes. Robin forced the corners of her mouth up. She took a deep breath. She let it out. She turned her head. And she gasped at the image on the screen.

Clear as could be. Not the blob of black-and-white fuzz she'd been expecting but the image of a baby's profile. An upturned nose, a small body, and a tiny arm raised above its head, as if waving hello. Robin's throat closed. Something light and warm crept up her legs, filled her stomach, and spread throughout her chest. Her hand fluttered to her mouth. Moments earlier, she couldn't look. Now, she couldn't look away.

This baby was real. And this baby was hers.

She wanted to reach out and trace the tiny features over the glass screen.

Mandy moved the Doppler, explaining the different images of Robin's child—the top of the head, the baby's bottom, arms, legs, the heart. Ten fingers. Ten toes.

The burning returned, pricking her eyes. And this time no amount of blinking would help. A tear dripped on to her cheek and plummeted off her chin, followed by another, and another. In four-and-a-half months this baby would be out of her womb and into the world. A tiny, helpless infant. One that depended on her for survival. In that small ultrasound room, as Robin watched images of her child roll across the screen, she came face-to-face with the choice God laid before her.

Life or death.

No amount of bargaining. No amount of crying. No amount of anger would bring this baby's father back. Micah was dead. And for the past several months, she'd joined him. Her heart might beat, the synapses in her brain might fire, but she'd gone to the grave the same day Micah did. She declared herself dead right alongside her husband. Only she had life growing inside her. Life that needed her. Life that depended on her. Life that belonged to her.

In the confines of that small ultrasound room, Robin became the rope in a nasty game of tug-of-war. Death pulling from one end and life from the other. Which would it be? What side would win? The gentle whisper of God's spirit brushed up against her soul.

Choose life, beloved, so that you may live. Choose life, for the sake of your child.

Robin squeezed her eyes against the tears, her breathing dense and painful.

I want to choose life, Lord. But how do I let go of this grief?

She imagined God prying her arms open, loosening her hold on the pain she cradled so tightly to her chest. She could think of this tiny baby—half her and half Micah, the epitome of two becoming one—as a heavy burden. A cruel joke. An unwanted offering. Or she could think of this tiny baby as a wonderful blessing. An awesome challenge. A merciful gift. A piece of Micah. Robin drew in a ragged breath. And in the deepest recesses of her soul, she let go. She released her sorrow to God.

She chose life.

Bethany tossed her keys on the counter, where they slid a few inches before resting by the sink. Robin stepped inside behind her, quiet and pale. She hadn't said a word the entire drive home from the doctor's office.

Rubbing her fingers beneath her eyes, Bethany stared at the steady drip issuing from the faucet. For whatever reason, Robin didn't want it fixed. Shaking her head, she dropped her hands to her side, strode to her room, and flipped open her laptop, unsettled by her growing infatuation with the life inside Robin's womb.

Bethany had never been the type to dream about motherhood, yet as soon as that baby appeared on the monitor, finger-like tentacles wound their way around her heart, forming an attachment she didn't want. Building a café was one thing. It had limits. It had closure. A clear beginning and end. But a baby? Babies didn't come with any boundaries. She couldn't let her strange infatuation with Robin's unborn child alter the course of her future.

She flopped on the bed, slipped off her shoes, and let them fall to the floor. Maybe today would be the day. Maybe when she opened her inbox, a flood of job offers would greet her and erase her preoccupation with Robin's child. Bolstered by the thought, Bethany stretched her legs on the bed just as Robin appeared like a phantom in the doorway, a trace of a smile shadowing her lips.

"Can I come in?" she asked.

This was new.

Bethany brought her legs to her chest and scooted to the wall. Robin joined her on the bed, catapulting Bethany back in time, when they'd sat in similar fashion, sharing secrets, hopes, fears. She couldn't think of another person she'd laughed or cried with more than Robin. Not even Dominic, who after three years of coupledom, should have at least been competition.

While Bethany waited for Robin to begin, her mind teetered between polar desires. Disengagement and yearning. With Robin sitting in front of her and the images from the ultrasound still fresh in her memory, Bethany grasped at disengagement. She looked at the computer screen where she'd typed the address to her e-mail account in the browser. She pressed enter just as Robin found her voice.

"I've been thinking about what you said the other day." Robin picked the fuzz off her slippers. "About Sunshine Daisies and our café."

Bethany's mind honed in on her choice of words. *Our* café. After the pseudo-agreement she'd made with Evan a few days ago, she tried to bring the café up with Robin several times. Talking with her proved as fruitful as communicating with a brick wall. So Bethany had tucked the idea away, floundering as she reposted her resume to several websites and scheduled a meeting with yet another Realtor.

"I know I said I didn't want to do it. And I'm still not completely convinced it's a good idea. But I was thinking…" Robin glanced up from her feet. "I'm tired of feeling like this."

The tentacle-like fingers drew tighter around Bethany's heart. She looked at her computer screen and saw three new messages in her inbox. Her finger twitched over the touchpad.

"I know this isn't logical. But part of me is afraid letting go of the pain will mean losing Micah all over again."

Bethany took a deep breath and pried her eyes away from the e-mails screaming her name.

"Now, after that ultrasound…" The trace of a smile returned. "That was something else, wasn't it?"

Bethany closed the lid to her laptop and set it aside.

"Seeing that baby…" Robin's smile solidified. "*My* baby. It was like God's wake-up call."

More like the advancement of technology.

"I started thinking about Micah and what he would want." Robin tucked her legs beneath her. "He'd want me to open the café. He'd want me to do it."

A slow smile crept across Bethany's lips. "The place is great."

"You already checked it out?"

Bethany nodded. After her conversation with Evan, she had called the owner and walked through the shop. It was old. It needed work. But it was perfect. She could close her eyes and imagine all of it. Which walls needed to be removed. Where new ones could be erected. The work they could do to the ceiling, the roof, the flooring.

"Did you like it?" Robin asked.

"The space has great potential. And the owner is selling it dirt cheap. She's not using a Realtor." Only in Peaks would a business owner not use a Realtor. "She's ready to retire and none of her kids are interested in carrying on the business."

Robin took a deep breath, studied the wall behind Bethany, and screwed her up her face in determination. "Let's do it, then. Let's build us a café."

Bethany couldn't help herself. Robin's smile was too contagious. Her e-mail would have to wait until later. Because right then, they had some planning to do.

Twenty-Seven

T he next morning, Bethany took Robin to Sunshine Daisies. Sharing her vision didn't take long. A few well-chosen words, and the potential which had been so glaringly obvious to Bethany became just as obvious to Robin.

They were twelve-year-olds all over again. Standing side-by-side, the building before them bursting with possibilities. Only this wasn't a dollhouse. This was Robin's future.

That evening Robin spoke with her dad to get legal advice, and conferred with her financial advisor. Both offered a few words of caution before giving their blessing. So the following day, Robin hired an accountant and made an offer. The owner accepted without a counter-offer, asked that Robin's dad draw up the papers, and made one simple request. To love and appreciate the space as much as she had throughout the years. Since the lady didn't mention anything about tearing the inside apart, they gave their word free of guilt.

The impetus from such a bold purchase hurled Bethany into a whirlwind of activity. Before they could start tearing out walls, improving the electrical, or adding a commercial kitchen, she had an architectural plan to solidify, a building permit to fill out, zoning laws to research, supplies to acquire, and a never-ending slew of decisions to make. Her pulse came back to life. She had a project again. Maybe not the next Sistine Chapel, but it was a project nonetheless.

By the time Bethany had muddled through the details, received the permit, and prepared for some actual renovation, Robin had written an entire business plan for the café and her belly had grown twice its former size. Bethany had also acquired fourteen unreturned voice messages from her mother—none of them about David—and the farm had swallowed Evan whole. Even with Gavin's help, who took over tagging the calves, his availability varied between barely there and nonexistent.

Bethany stayed in sporadic contact with him, trying to figure out what they could renovate on their own and what they'd be better off contracting. After here-and-there conversation, she decided to contract the kitchen. Even in a small town, all the codes and regulations weren't worth the headache of doing it herself.

Evan's time started to free up around the same time she received three bids from three different construction companies specializing in commercial kitchens. On the second Sunday in May, instead of just dropping Robin off after church, he stopped in to discuss building plans. As soon as Robin left the room, he leaned in close.

"How's she doing?" he asked.

"She's fine."

"Care to elaborate on that?"

Bethany resisted the urge to roll her eyes. Why didn't he just ask Robin himself? Did he think she would break under such a simple question? Sarcasm crept to the edge of her tongue, but his hazel eyes, much brighter from his tanned skin, stared at her with imploring seriousness.

"She's trying," she said.

"She doesn't sing in church anymore."

"Maybe she realizes there's nothing to sing about."

Evan cocked his head, his stare reminding her of Storm's. He didn't just look at her, he looked through her—inside of her—and whatever he found seemed to make him sad.

She stiffened. "What?"

He stepped closer and stared so intently that for a second, she thought he might reach out and touch her cheek. "Someday, Bethany, I hope you find out that you're wrong. There's so much to sing about."

The understanding look in his eyes and the tenderness in his voice thumped her in the chest. She could not find a comeback. He could have slapped her and it would have shocked her less.

"Let me know when you need me to start working on the café."

Before she could respond, he exited the kitchen and closed the door behind him, leaving Bethany alone with his words.

Evan didn't know it, but he worried for nothing. Robin not singing in church had no bearing on the time she spent reading her Bible at home. She read that book with matchless ferocity, and each time Bethany caught her in the act, something hot would bubble inside Bethany's chest. Once, during one of her more impulsive moments, the burning question building in her lungs whooshed past her self-control before she could squelch the words.

"Why do you bother with that?" she'd asked.

Robin looked up from the pages.

Bethany ducked behind the pantry door and pretended to search for something to eat, hoping her busyness might negate Robin's desire to answer the question.

So what if she read the Bible? As long as she didn't become the next Pastor Fenton, why should it matter to Bethany if Robin chose to spend her time worshipping *that* type of God? Bethany straightened the clip on a bag of chips, re-stacked cans of peas, and picked a cinnamon raison granola bar from its box before resurfacing from her hidey-hole.

Robin stared at a red spot on the table—last night's marinara. Bethany thought she'd wiped off the counters yesterday.

"It's the only thing that gets me through the day," she said.

Bethany turned her attention away from the crusted spaghetti sauce and studied her pregnant roommate. "Robin, you get *yourself* through the day."

Robin shook her head.

Bethany wrapped her fingers around the granola bar. The wrapper crinkled. "Why do you insist on giving God credit for something you're doing on your own?"

Robin was a pregnant widow, for crying out loud, reading her Bible like she owed God her thanks and devotion. But for what? For taking Micah? Despite Bethany's attempt at calm, the heat bubbling in her chest gave way to a roiling boil. She had the sudden urge to rip Robin's damaging faith away, to strip it bare, expose it for the louse it was, so Robin would step over to her side again. Bethany reined in the harshness of her tone and laced her expression with a composure she didn't feel. "What has believing in God done for you?"

Robin's simple answer, and the peaceful way she delivered it, invaded the hidden places in Bethany's soul.

"Everything."

�֍

Between Robin's open exhibitions of faith and Pastor Fenton's successful ministry with Project MAC saturating the local news, Bethany was more than eager to meet with the contractor they'd chosen, call in a building inspector, and make sure plans were up to code.

But there had been a delay. A temporary standstill while the contractor met a deadline for another project. They postponed their meeting—twice. She was two seconds away from contracting somebody else when the project manager called, apologized, and suggested they meet the following day. The meeting was productive. They didn't need a large kitchen, not for a simple café. The floral shop already had a walk-in refrigerator. The guy sounded confident they'd be finished in two weeks. Mid June. Impressive timing.

Despite the misty drizzle, Bethany strolled from her car toward the house, arms swinging by her side, glad to finally have some news to share with Robin. She stepped inside the living room, the smell of fresh baked goods wafting up her nose.

Inhaling the chocolaty aroma, she slipped off her shoes, muddied from the afternoon rainfall, and entered the kitchen. Robin stood in front of the sink with a crescent wrench in her hand and stared at the dripping faucet. A dirtied mixing bowl and a cake pan sat on the counter.

"Who's the cake for?" Bethany asked, pulling her arm out of her jacket.

"Evan. It's his birthday tomorrow."

Bethany stopped. "Really?"

Robin tapped her finger on the marbled countertop, her eyes following each drip that escaped the faucet. "I was thinking about fixing the sink."

Fix the sink? The one she hadn't let anybody touch over the past several months? Talk about progress. Bethany hung her coat on the back of a chair and pushed up her shirtsleeves. So what if she'd never fixed a sink before. It couldn't be that hard. "Want some help?"

"You bet."

Bethany spent the next two hours tinkering around with a wrench and the pipes, updating Robin on the café renovations. They took a break so Robin could whip up some frosting and slather it on the cake, then went back to work.

"I still can't believe we're really doing this," Robin said, coming out from the opened cabinet and setting down the heavy tool. She stood up, brushed her hands against her pants, and turned on the faucet.

Bethany scrambled from the floor just as Robin turned the faucet off. Bethany held her breath and counted to ten. Not a single drip. Her chest swelled. She turned to Robin and caught her wearing a matching grin. They slapped each other a high five, and Bethany motioned toward the treat on the counter.

"Do you always bake a cake for Evan on his birthday?"

Robin covered the top with a plastic lid and licked her thumb. "I promised him and Gavin I would until they found a wife to do it for them."

Warmth fizzled up Bethany's torso. An uncensored image of whisking cake batter while Evan baled hay in the field whispered through her mind. Where had that come from? She cleared her throat and grabbed her jacket from the back of a chair. "I need to run to the grocery store. I can pick up some dinner if you want."

Robin held up the pan. "Could you run this over to Evan while you're out?"

Bethany blinked. "But his birthday's tomorrow."

Robin lowered the cake and peered out the window above the sink. Rain ran down the glass pane in winding trails. "He won't be working tonight. Besides, you said you needed to talk to him about tearing out some walls."

Bethany's stomach tightened. She grappled for an excuse. The idea of being alone with Evan on a dark and rainy night did not sit well. "Why don't you come?"

"I can't. A friend from church is coming over to drop off a stroller, and I promised I'd be here when she came." She held the pan higher. "And since you're already going out..."

Bethany chided her squirming insides for acting silly. She did have a few questions for Evan about the café. And she hadn't spoken with him face-to-face in a while. She eyed the container, brought her arm through her other sleeve, and took the gift. Bringing him a cake on a dark, rainy evening was nothing to worry about.

⁂

Evan threw a log into the fire, the dry heat from the flames going to war with the damp air in his living room. A cold front had insisted on moving through the area, unconcerned that late May did not usually welcome weather so reminiscent of early spring.

The rain had persisted over the past week, turning the sun into a rare commodity. Evan didn't mind. He'd just finished planting his corn, and the more it rained, the thicker his hay would grow. After last year's drought, he'd love to get at least two good cuttings in over the summer with enough to feed his cattle and have some left over for profit. He could use all the money he could get, seeing as this might be his last year farming the land.

He jabbed the wrought iron poker into the flames, watching red flakes materialize from the logs. Nothing was set in stone. Bethany was willing to wait to sell after harvest. Many things could happen between now and then. Maybe she wouldn't sell at all. Maybe she'd agree to let him rent the land from her indefinitely.

He watched the burning embers hover, then float back down into the fire. He imagined his dreams going with them. Who was he kidding? Bethany keeping the farm was about as likely as Tootsie Rolls becoming Iowa's next biggest cash crop.

Evan sat on the carpet, brought his elbows to his knees, and thought about the simplicity life offered last year when Dan was alive. When his livelihood hadn't depended on the decision of a woman who moved full-steam ahead in whatever direction best suited her needs.

Lord, what am I supposed to do without this farm?

He'd been preparing his heart for the inevitable, even checking a few websites to research the cost of renting local farmland. Prices were higher than he expected, and even if they weren't, it was this land he wanted, this land he'd fallen in love with. He could always fall back on repairing cars and farm equipment. Money wasn't the issue. The life that he loved was. Bethany put his dreams on the end of a stake and threatened to light them on fire.

The flames in the fireplace grew and popped and an ember landed by his big toe. He jerked his feet back and closed the screen. Maybe it was the weather that had his mood so jumbled. Or maybe it was the fact that tomorrow he'd be thirty-two. He thought by now he'd have a farm of his own and a wife by his side. Kids, even. He never thought he'd be a thirty-two-year-old bachelor who owned nothing but a farmhouse and a bunch of potentially homeless cattle.

To stop his mind from falling into a black hole, he stood from the floor and retrieved his Bible from the end table. He went to the kitchen to make some coffee. As he waited for the brew to percolate, he leaned over the counter and feathered through the thin pages. He scanned the small words until he reached a familiar verse in Jeremiah.

"For I know the plans I have for you," declares the LORD, "plans to prosper you, and not to harm you, plans to give you hope and a future."

Evan rolled the verse through his head several times and poured himself a cup of coffee. After his car accident when his buddy died, well-intending church-folk would quote that verse at him. His parents even had it hanging somewhere in their living room. But surely, when Jeremiah penned those words, he never intended them to be plastered across coffee mugs. Evan wasn't an Israelite and he wasn't stuck in Babylon.

But the God who prospered a fickle, thoughtless people was the same God who recaptured Evan's heart and refused to let go. He shut the book, rested his palm over the leather cover, and bowed his head. Before he could start his prayer, however, a knock on the front door echoed in the kitchen.

His head snapped up. He reached for his cup and knocked it over. The spilled liquid raced over the counter, spread around his Bible, and colored the edges a soggy brown. He scooped up the book and shook it off over the sink. Who would come calling on a Monday evening? Gavin? His younger brother was finally starting to come around. Rejoin the living. Perhaps he was stopping by to wish Evan an early happy birthday.

He snatched a bundle of paper towels, soaked up the spilled coffee, and returned his damp Bible to the counter. A few seconds later he swung the door wide expecting to see Gavin on the other side.

Instead, Bethany stood, one foot on the porch, the other on the step, as if she couldn't decide if she should stay or go, the slanted rain soaking through her clothes.

"What are you doing here?"

She turned on her heel, wide-eyed and pink-cheeked, holding a cake pan in her hands. Her eyes moved up his body before resting on his face. "I'm sorry to interrupt." She stepped under the awning, out from the rain, and handed him the container, raindrops darkening her long eyelashes. "Robin made cake for your birthday."

He tried to get out a thank you, but his tongue wouldn't cooperate. She took a quick step away, back into the rain. Without thinking, he grabbed her elbow with his unoccupied hand. A simple gesture to keep her in place. The muscles in his chest did a funny twist. He let go, brought his hand to his side, to the cake container, then pushed it inside his pocket. "You're leaving?"

He didn't know why he wanted her to stay. Only that on such a rainy day, after so many hours keeping company with cows and seed, some human conversation would be nice. Even if it was with the woman who held his precarious future in her manicured hand.

She blinked away the spitting rain, her body as still as a statue.

"You're just going to bring me a cake and not wish me happy birthday?"

"Your birthday is tomorrow."

He fought back a smile. "So why'd you bring me a cake tonight?"

The pink staining her cheeks darkened to red.

He cocked his head. "And while we're at it, why did *you* bring it, if Robin made it?"

"Robin asked me to. And I had some information to relay about the café."

Of course. All business. "Why do you look so ready to leave, then?"

"You looked"—she motioned to his flannel pajama bottoms and Fruit of the Loom undershirt—"ready for bed."

Evan couldn't help it. The smile he'd attempted to suppress broke through. Bethany was embarrassed about catching him in his pajamas. It was cute. He stepped back and held the door wide. "Come on in. My bedtime isn't for another couple hours."

She hesitated.

"Come on, Bethany. I promise I won't bite." He held up the treat in his hands. "We can have some cake." This seemed to be the wrong thing to say. Too personal, he guessed, because she shifted away. He scrambled to erase his mistake. "It'll give us a chance to talk shop."

He left the door wide open and walked toward the kitchen. She stepped inside the foyer and shut the door, blocking out the patter of rain against the walkway. He set the cake on the counter, took off the lid, and breathed in through his nostrils. "Nobody can bake a cake like Robin."

Bethany followed him into the kitchen and placed her purse on the table. "I think she's the only person who still makes them from scratch."

Evan took out a cutting knife, sliced two pieces, plunked them onto paper plates, and handed one to her. She didn't take it. Instead, she stared at the mess on the counter. A glob of half -brown, half-white paper towels sat near his Bible.

He snatched the clump of coffee-soaked towels and threw them in the trash. He grabbed another mug from the cupboard, poured two cups of coffee, and jerked his head to the drawer by the sink. "Forks are in there."

She smirked. "I know. I used to live here, remember?"

"Oh. Right."

He took the plates in one hand and worked on getting the coffee mugs in the other. Bethany sighed. "Here, let me." She set a fork on each plate and picked up the mugs.

"Why thank you, Bethany."

She rolled her eyes.

Evan smiled and walked into the living room. He set the plates on the coffee table while Bethany cleared her throat, standing half in and half out of the kitchen, like she wasn't sure having cake and coffee on the couch in front of a crackling fire was the best idea.

"I discussed the plans for the kitchen with the owner of Roland and Sons."

Evan met her in the doorway and took the mugs.

Bethany swallowed. "They're going to start building tomorrow and should be finished in two weeks. They said we can work around them if we'd like."

He brought the coffee to the cake and sat on the couch.

"So I was thinking about ripping out the east wall. The sooner we get that done, the sooner we can start—"

"Bethany." He interrupted her monologue and patted the cushion next to his own.

She stood in the doorway, the embodiment of a professional, eying his invitation as if it might rear back and kick her. His mind wandered to New Year's Eve, out on the balcony of Shorney's Terrace, then later on the dance floor, when she'd let go and given him two minutes of her trust. Her unguarded smile when he dipped her had taken his breath away. He felt like interacting with *that* Bethany tonight—the vulnerable, slightly-mysterious Bethany. Not the businesswoman standing in his house, relaying information about the café with all the emotion of a fencepost.

"I can't stay," she said.

"Not even for birthday cake?"

"I don't like cake."

His lips twitched. Of course she didn't. He lifted his mug into the air. "Then stay for the coffee. And the company."

She eyed the rising steam. "Coffee at night?"

"It's decaf."

After standing in the opened door frame for a moment longer, she let out a sigh and joined him on the sofa, sitting as close to the opposite arm rest as possible.

"Now," he said, handing her a mug and taking a sip from his own. "When do you want to tear out that wall?"

She fingered the handle. "I'd like to get it done as soon as possible."

He'd just jumped the daunting hurdle of spring planting and thanks to the wet weather, his hay would be ready for its first cutting as soon as the rain dried. He had a busy week ahead, with the promise of a short break afterward. "I think I'll have some time in a week or so."

She examined the liquid in her mug, took a delicate sip, and made a face before setting it on the end table and scooting to the edge of the sofa. "Then I will call you tomorrow and we can arrange the details."

Evan reached out to stop her from standing. When his fingers found the bare skin of her arm, they prickled with warmth. Her line of vision darted toward his hand as if she'd felt it too, but she sprang from the couch and hurried to the door.

He jumped up after her. "Where are you going?"

"I have stuff to get done."

He stepped in front of the door. "What stuff?"

She dug inside the pocket of her jacket and pulled out her car keys. "Business stuff."

He crossed his arms in front of his chest, leaned against the door frame, and smirked. He didn't want to goad her, but negative attention was better than no attention at all. "You're a little on the obsessive side, aren't you?"

It worked. She brought her head up and gave him one of her looks. "All you ever think about is business."

"And all you ever think about is farming."

"Not true. In fact, tonight I was thinking about a lot of things."

She narrowed her eyes. "Like what?"

"A wife and children, actually."

The color drained from her cheeks, then flooded back into place. Crimson spread down her neck and disappeared beneath her jacket. Her hand fluttered to her throat as if to cover the incriminating blush.

Evan's pulse quickened, then purred as an image of Bethany in this house, not as a guest but as something more, tiptoed around the edges of his imagination. He didn't know what was more alarming. The idea of Bethany as his wife. Or the warmth spreading through his belly when he pictured it.

Silence stretched between them.

Evan didn't know how to break it, so he twisted the door knob and invited the patter of the rain back inside his living room. She moved to the door, closer to him. Her hair smelled of vanilla and he wondered what it might be like to run his hands through it. He reached out and grazed her arm.

Her breath caught.

And like hot cast iron searing into flesh, passion branded his soul. "Bethany."

He moved his free hand toward her neck and brushed her hair from her shoulder and for one glorious moment, the steel in her eyes melted into warm chocolate. His thumb traced over the frenzied tapping of the pulse in her throat. He curled his fingers behind her neck and brought her body closer.

Before he could bring his lips to hers, she ducked beneath him and stepped outside, her eyes no longer melted chocolate but the swirling waters of the Mississippi River. "I'm sorry," she said. "I have to go."

She hurried to her car, leaving him on the porch. He didn't move as she whipped down the drive. He didn't move when she turned on to the gravel road. He stood, framed in the doorway, left alone with his longing.

When he pictured his future wife, he imagined a woman who loved her family and wanted one of her own. A woman who understood the backbreaking work that came with living on a farm but loved it anyway. A woman who wouldn't be afraid to get her hands dirty alongside him. Someone easygoing and content. Someone who shared his faith.

How could his heart long for someone who didn't fit one part of that description?

Twenty-Eight

Bethany rushed toward Robin's house. As soon as she escaped the onslaught of raindrops plummeting from the sky, she closed the door, gulped in a big breath, and pressed her back against the cool mahogany, as if she could melt into it and disappear.

The place where Evan touched her neck hummed with unexplored energy, tingling up her jaw line. She pressed her palm against the spot and released an unsteady breath. Had Evan wanted to kiss her? Had she wanted to kiss him back?

Her mind conjured his chiseled jaw, deep-set eyes, dark waves curling over the tops of his ears. Men who looked like him did not kiss women who looked like her. Men who looked like him kissed women who looked like Robin. Still...the look in his eyes when they stood in the doorway. The timbre of his voice when he spoke her name.

A long-buried desire unfurled from its hiding spot and stretched inside her chest—an inexplicable need to be cherished, to be admired, to be loved. She tried to convince it to close its eyes and go back to sleep. But the memory of Evan's breath on her cheek—standing so close she could feel the heat of his body—provoked the awakening desire to sit up and face the day.

Bethany pressed cool fingers against her warm cheeks. She was being ridiculous. Even if Evan was, for whatever reason, attracted to her, she had no business being attracted to him. First of all, he made her feel completely off-balanced. And second of all, he lived in Peaks. On a farm she wanted to sell.

If she allowed herself to love him—to need him—she'd lose everything. The successful Bethany. The self-sufficient Bethany. The Bethany with ambitions as high as the sky. That Bethany could not afford to lose her heart to a man as intense, as tender, as unpredictable and maddening as Evan Price.

She pushed away from the door and climbed the stairs. No light filtered through the crack below Robin's door. She stepped inside the guest bedroom where the soft patter of rain against gutters and a distant train whistle floated in through the opened windows. She flipped on the light switch, removed her soggy jacket, and opened her laptop. As reflex, she double clicked on the internet icon and went to her e-mail.

A single unread message sat in her inbox. The two simple words of the subject line, bolded in black typeface, stared back from the screen. Interview Request. Her hands jerked away from her computer. She leaned forward and stared at those two words, her heartbeat quickening. Sending a hopeful plea out into the Universe, she clicked on the message.

When she saw who it was from, the air in her chest turned shallow. Gurtson and Bleeker Architectural Enterprises in Minneapolis—one of the biggest firms in the Midwest— wanted an interview. In three days. G&B was twice the size of Parker Crane. Every smaller firm trying to make it big modeled their business after Gurtson and Bleeker. And they were interested in her. A smile started in her thoughts, moved to her lips, then spread to her shoulders and beyond until her entire body morphed into one giant grin.

She opened Travelocity's website and began her search for plane tickets. She didn't have to be in Minneapolis until three o'clock on Thursday. But if she was going to clear her mind and focus all her attention and energy on this interview, then the sooner she left, the better.

In her temporary insomnia, she purchased an overpriced plane ticket and booked an overpriced hotel room. Apparently, traveling so close to Memorial Day weekend wasn't very economical. But she had no other choice, so she packed a small bag and lay in bed running potential interview questions through her mind. Slumber finally took her around two-thirty in the morning and held her captive until nine.

When she awoke, she told Robin the news and reminded her to meet the contractors at the café at noon since Bethany needed to be at the airport before then. Her stomach rolled in a thousand different directions at the thought of leaving, the thought of Evan, the thought of her upcoming interview. She needed a Tums. Only her bottle was tucked away inside her purse and she couldn't find her purse anywhere. It took her five minutes of tossing through her things before she realized where it was—in Dan's kitchen. And while she could buy another bottle of Tums, she needed her license to claim her boarding pass and get through security. Dread seeped into her pores and joined the jumble of nerves already protesting in her stomach. She searched the house for Robin, hoping her friend could pick up her purse for her. But she'd already left for her Tuesday morning Bible study. She wouldn't be back until eleven.

There was no getting around it. She had to go to the farmhouse.

As she slipped inside her car, she took note of the nice weather. Maybe Evan would be out in the fields. Maybe he didn't lock the door. Maybe she could sneak in, get her purse, and leave without ever having to see him. She tightened her grip around the steering wheel. A girl could hope.

Luck, however, was not on her side.

As soon as she pulled up the drive, she spotted him out front, carrying something in his arms as he walked from the shed to the house, the two border collies shadowing him. She stopped beside Evan's car and turned off the ignition. Her hands remained wrapped around the steering wheel, patches of white spreading across her knuckles. Why had she left her purse there? Of all the times to leave it behind, this was definitely the worst. She stayed in the cab and stared down into her lap.

Evan rapped on her window.

She startled and sucked in a quick breath. Then rolled her eyes at her own jumpiness.

Get a grip. Roll down your window. State your business and get your purse.

Before she could heed the logical side of her brain, he opened her door. He rested one hand on the roof of her car and leaned forward, the epitome of calm and collected. Her deluded mind must have somehow made up the entire almost-kiss scenario.

Evan tipped his head, his cheek dimpling with a suppressed grin "Bethany."

And then they spoke at the same time.

"To what do I owe this—"

"I need my purse."

He blinked.

Bethany swallowed. "I left it on your kitchen table."

He straightened and backed away. "And here I thought you were coming over to wish me a happy birthday."

The light-hearted tone of his voice baffled her. Seriously. Had last night not happened? Her eyebrows drew together. He stood there in his sleeveless T-shirt, showing off tanned, rippling biceps she didn't want to notice and looked nothing but amused.

Her impending interview couldn't have come at a more opportune time. She needed to get out of Peaks and gain some perspective. She stepped out of the car and forced herself to look into his face. She would not be attracted to Evan. Their relationship wouldn't be any more complicated than casual acquaintance and temporary business partner. The more distance between them, the easier it would be when Bethany sold the farm in the fall.

She cast a glance over the land, surveying her inheritance. The opened machine shed, where her grandpa spent many evenings repairing equipment. The barn, where she and David played when they were kids. Against their mother's wishes, they used to jump from the loft down into the round bales while Dan pitched hay, encouraging their rebellion by the amused smile on his face. Her attention wandered to the empty paddock. As a kid, several quarter horses grazed in that field. Before her father's accident, Dan taught her to ride them. He'd even convinced her mom to let Bethany join 4-H.

"Are you going to get another horse?" Her question came out without warning. Who cared if he bought another horse?

Evan tilted his head. "Do you want me to?"

Her stomach dipped. What if she said yes? Would he actually buy one? She shook her head. No, she did not want a horse. She wanted to sell the farm. Cut the strings. Say good-bye. So what if this place elicited fond memories? So what if it had once meant the world to her? Her longing then had been filtered through the eyes of a hurting child. While she thought she needed the farm as a girl, she knew better as an adult. She needed a job. Not a horse. Or a bushel of corn. Or any other thing associated with a farm.

Bethany cleared her throat and remembered her training. Spine straight, shoulders back, chin lifted. Give the illusion of confidence so the feeling would follow. "Can I get my purse?"

He threw his palm toward the house and gave a slight bow. "Be my guest."

Bethany marched to the side door, thankful he didn't follow. Her purse was where she'd left it. She grabbed it and turned right back around. This wasn't so bad. She could do this. Walk back to her car, thank Evan, and head to the airport. Look forward. That's what she had to do. The farm was her past. Evan and Robin were her present. She needed to look to her future. A job with a top-notch architectural firm. A new start in a new city. A place where she could forget about her six-month setback.

She rolled her shoulders, trying to regain some of the excitement she'd lost. The gravel crunched beneath her feet as she walked back to the car. She should be ecstatic, thrilled, relieved. Here was her chance to get out and move on, but her mind lingered on Robin and the baby. And the man leaning against her vehicle.

"Where are you going?" he asked.

She stopped. "What?"

He jerked his head to her backseat, the place she'd tossed her travel bag. She took two steps closer. "Minneapolis."

"Why?"

She reached for the car door handle, but Evan shifted his weight, blocking her from opening the door. "What's in Minneapolis?"

Her tongue pressed against the roof of her mouth.

"Bethany?"

"A job interview."

"A job interview?" A bolt of intensity flashed in his eyes.

Her insides thundered in response. He knew she was looking for a job. He had no right to look at her like that.

"I thought you said you finish your projects."

"I do." Bethany squished the two words between her teeth.

"Then what's all this crap about the café? What about the promise you made to Robin? What about—?" He stopped suddenly and a faint blush tinged his cheeks. She'd never seen Evan blush before. "You say you finish what you start. But what about what you started with the café? Why don't you finish that?"

"I am finishing it." She promised Evan she'd finish the café and she would. A job interview wasn't going to change that.

"What about Robin? You act like you care about her. How's she going to take it when you leave?"

"I promised Robin I'd stay until I found a job. She knows that." Bethany went so far as posting on her resume that she couldn't start until after Robin's due date. She was going above and beyond.

"And so what? You're just going to pack up your stuff and take off again?" He shook his head like he couldn't believe it. "I guess we'll see you in ten years then."

Something tore loose inside her. He was being impossible. Nothing would satisfy him. Nothing she gave would ever be enough. "What else do you want from me, Evan? I've forfeited six-and-a-half months of my life for Robin. How much more of it do I have to give to make you happy?"

"I'm not asking you to give up your life. I'm just asking you not to be in such a hurry to leave."

There was something behind his statement. An unspoken plea she couldn't decipher. It punctured the swelling heat inside her lungs. "If you're worried about Robin, don't. She has you and Gavin." And God. Despite Bethany's misgivings, she couldn't ignore the peaceful, almost appealing look on Robin's face whenever Bethany caught her in prayer. Bethany didn't understand it. It didn't make sense. But she couldn't refute the evidence. While faith had weakened her mother, it somehow strengthened her friend.

"Look, Evan. *You* can take care of her. *You* can help with the baby. *You* can support her." And maybe someday, he could take Micah's place. Even though her heart pinched together at the thought, she couldn't deny the fact that Robin fit beside Evan more than she ever would.

Evan's head dropped. He shifted his weight, then looked back up again. He stared at her with a mixture of desperation and doubt. Like she didn't get what he was trying to communicate and he wasn't sure he wanted to explain it. "Why are you so desperate to get out of Peaks?"

His words weren't what she expected. "What do you mean?"

"This place." He motioned to the farm and the world beyond. "You would never consider staying here, would you?"

A wave of heat rolled through her body. Did he mean here, as in *right* here? Or here, as in the general area? Her thoughts gathered, crowding her brain, tripping over one another. Did Evan want her to stay for Robin? Or did Evan want her to stay for him? She opened her mouth and closed it again. She didn't know what to say. And Evan wasn't helping her. She looked at the ground.

"I really have to go."

He stepped out of her way and for the first time since she met him last winter, he didn't open her door.

Twenty-Nine

B ethany stood in the airplane aisle and struggled to shove her luggage inside the overhead bin, then clicked the compartment door shut. A young couple blocked the path between her and her seat, holding hands, their foreheads touching. Bethany tapped the man's shoulder and gave them an apologetic smile as they pivoted their knees to one side. After jostling her way past, she sat in the narrow airplane seat and pressed her body as close to the window as possible, trying to ignore the passionate duo as they resumed their positions.

She leaned against the stiff headrest and closed her eyes, replaying the interview in her mind. It went well. Very well. Mr. Gurtson had beamed at her as she rattled off her experience. His face lit up when he browsed through her portfolio. He even asked his secretary to show Bethany around their office—their very large, two-story office. The place hummed with activity. She could smell the ideas and creativity coalescing in the air as architects and design engineers bustled through the hallways with elaborate models and stacks of blueprints.

She'd craved working for a company like G&B since she first declared her major in college. It was exactly what she wanted, exactly what she'd spent the last ten years of her life working toward. She'd be working with the best of the best—people and technology—earning the money and prestige she never had growing up. She'd no longer be stuck working in renovations, her creativity and vision no longer stifled by whatever run-down walls were already in place. So why wasn't she able to muster any enthusiasm? Why this vague sense of dissatisfaction? This unfamiliar ache for something she couldn't define?

The jet engine roared to life as one of the flight attendants stood up front and parroted a spiel about emergency procedures. Tapping her foot against the floor, Bethany peered out the circular window.

"Would you like a piece of gum?"

It took her a second before she realized the voice was speaking to her. She turned and found one half of the couple holding out a pack of Doublemint, sunlight glinting off the ends of each foiled wrapper. "My ears go crazy if I don't chew something. I found out last week."

"I'm fine, thanks."

Bubbling over with excitement, the young woman pointed at the man sitting beside her. "This is our second time flying."

Bethany liked the couple better with their foreheads glued together.

Miss Bubbly kept going. "I bet you've flown lots of times. You have that look about you."

Bethany gave a polite smile and a brief, affirmative nod. She leaned her head against the seat and faked a yawn.

"We're coming back from our honeymoon. It was our first time flying and our first time seeing the ocean."

It was probably their first time without adult supervision, too.

"We're excited to get home though. Now's when real life starts, you know?"

Real life? What did that even mean? Life was real by default.

"Don't get me wrong. The wedding and the honeymoon were great. More than great, actually. We're just excited to start our new life together."

Bethany's ears hummed. Of all the people on the plane, why did she get stuck next to motor-mouth? She gave another brief noncommittal nod and pulled out the airline's magazine tucked inside the back pocket of the seat in front of her.

"So where are you headed?"

Bethany crossed her leg and flipped one of the pages. "Home."

The word stuck in her throat like a wad of chewed-up bubble gum. Home? Now where had that come from? Peaks was not home. She paged through the magazine with unfocused eyes, bouncing her crossed leg as pictures of Robin and her belly invaded the unoccupied spaces of her mind. More pictures shimmied their way to the surface—pictures of the ultrasound photos hanging on the stainless steel refrigerator, pictures of the farm, the café, Evan. They gathered together, forming an unnamable collage that tugged at hidden places in her heart. She tried to sweep them up and shuffle them away, but they played through her mind like a reel of lucid vignettes.

Mr. Gurtson said she could expect to hear from them very soon. She'd been the last of their interviews. Bethany stopped fighting the collage. She surrendered to its beauty and allowed herself to pour over the images, knowing full well that in a few days, the collage wouldn't matter anymore. Her new home would be in Minnesota.

❦

Evan mopped the sweat beading off his forehead with a black bandana and returned it to his back pocket. He steered the hay mower inside the machine shed, bits of grass and dirt sticking to his skin. Peeling off his work gloves, he stepped down from the large machine and inhaled hay and humidity. The smell of home. He closed his eyes and pictured Dan's farmland covered with houses instead of corn—an image that had nagged him ever since Bethany left for that interview.

Lord, what am I supposed to do? I can't stick around and watch that happen.

Bethany was in Minnesota, chasing her dream, and in the process, squashing his. Come October she'd sell the farm without looking back, and although he told her he would keep Dan's house, he'd said it more as a threat, hoping his decision to hold on would make her decision to let go more difficult. He'd underestimated Bethany. After spending time with her over the past several months, he'd learned she wasn't the type of person to let a small obstacle like a farmhouse get in the way of her plans. Evan wiped his palms against his dirtied Wranglers. His last harvest crept closer with each passing day.

His back pocket vibrated. He pulled out his cell phone and pressed it against his ear. "Hello?"

"Evan. Hey, it's your favorite uncle."

Evan smiled despite his somber mood. Manny was his only uncle. He was also the man who introduced him to farming. And kindly kicked him off his farm when Evan grew destructive. "Hey Manny, it's been a while."

"Sure has. So listen, I talked with your mom last night."

Evan dug the heel of his boot in to a clump of grass.

"She told me you're in a bit of a pickle."

More like a giant cucumber.

"You're not going to believe this, but just this morning I was talking to Bill. You remember Bill. His farm runs on the other side of the creek, right next to mine. Well, anyway, Bill's looking to rent out the back four hundred acres of his property."

Evan's mind buzzed.

"He's renting it out for dirt cheap. I'm talking bottom line. Not sure why because the land's great. I can promise you that. He's gotten some local interest, so if you're interested, you should move fast."

The buzzing grew louder. He was a farmer. He needed a farm. And here was his uncle Manny, paving a path so he could keep living his dream. "How long before I have to make a decision?"

"A couple days at the most."

"It's a hard offer to resist."

"Sure is. And I have to say, I'd be delighted to have you as a neighbor."

Bethany wedged her cell phone between her shoulder and ear. She stood in the tool-lined aisle at Lowe's, blinking dumbly at the crowbars. "I don't understand. Mr. Gurtsen said my resume was the strongest he'd seen in six months." Her mind groped for a handhold, something to stop her from falling off the edge this woman had just pushed her toward.

"I'm sorry, Ms. Quinn. We really appreciate your time. But Mr. Gurtson decided to go with an architect who has more retail experience. He didn't want to leave the other applicants hanging over the long weekend."

A snarl built in Bethany's throat. Why had Mr. Gurtson chosen to hire someone who designed retail when he'd raved over her portfolio? She never hid the fact that her experience was entrenched in renovation. Bethany swallowed the snarl. "I see."

"He was very impressed by your interview and wanted you to know that if another position opens up, he will keep your resume on file."

"Thank you. I appreciate that."

"Have a happy Memorial Day, Ms. Quinn. Best of luck to you in your job search."

Bethany ground her teeth and hurled her phone inside her purse, wishing she could redo the past week. She'd wasted five hundred dollars on her flight to Minneapolis. Another five hundred on a hotel. And for what? She snatched up a crow bar and barreled through several aisles toward the front of the hardware store.

She wanted to get to the café, check on the kitchen, bring life to their carefully laid plans. In the wake of Mr. Gurtson's rejection, ripping out drywall sounded like a wonderful idea. But before she could immerse herself in any wall demolishing, Bethany had promised she'd help Robin put the baby's crib and dresser together. And tomorrow, Bethany would accompany Robin to the farm for a cookout. The Price family hosted one every year on Memorial Day Weekend. Evan's parents and Bryan and Amy had flown into town this morning.

The cool metal of the black-steeled tool rubbed against the pads of her thumbs. Although she hadn't seen Evan since Tuesday, he'd disrupted her thoughts, even her dreams, every day since. The back of her neck tingled as she stepped in line, as if Evan's hand materialized in the middle of the store and touched her in the same spot where he'd touched her several nights ago.

She replayed that evening through her mind a million different times from a million different angles. Each time, the footage revealed the same thing. Before she had fled the farmhouse, Evan wanted to kiss her. Of that, she was sure. She just wasn't sure what that meant. Or if she wanted to kiss him back.

Choosing not to examine the answer to that particular question, she paid the cashier and strode to her car. Why had he asked her if she'd ever consider staying in Peaks? Why, when she thought about staying, did the idea not tie her stomach into a knot of dread like it used to? And why, on the heels of losing the job of her dreams, was she more anxious about seeing Evan than she was about her architectural future?

Thirty

Evan prodded the hot charcoal with the end of his metal tongs and stepped away from the heat and smoke rising from the pile. A familiar ache swelled in his throat. He pictured Dan, sitting in a lawn chair, lip bulging with snuff, admiring the beginnings of corn stalks sprouting from the fields. He pictured Micah, tossing a Frisbee to his border collies. Three-hundred-and-sixty-five days later so much had changed.

The screen door let out a rusted groan and slammed shut, rattling away the bittersweet images. Bryan stepped beside him with a plate full of beef patties and hotdogs and started placing them on the grill. A slight breeze rustled over the countryside, and the smell of hay and mud swirled together with burning charcoal. Evan inhaled, hoping the summertime scent might loosen the tension in his jaw.

"We couldn't ask for a better day," Bryan said, plunking down the last of the meat.

Evan peered at the sky and grunted. The sun blazed naked and exposed against a cobalt blanket, not even the trace of a cloud offering it cover.

Bryan squeezed Evan's shoulder and headed toward the picnic tables to join the rest of the family. Evan poked the meat sizzling on the grill, turning over hotdogs and flipping burgers until the sound of spitting gravel broke through his trance. Bethany's car rumbled down the drive, followed by Gavin's rusted-out Durango. Evan's stomach dipped as the two mismatched cars pulled to a stop. The last time he saw Bethany, he'd almost blurted that she should stay in Peaks. Not for Robin. Not for her baby. But for him. Maybe *with* him. He'd exposed his heart to a woman who didn't want it, leaving it just as naked as the sun overhead.

Bethany's car door opened, bringing into view her sandaled foot and shapely calf. His heart faltered, then sputtered to life in a series of jolts and stammers. He tightened his grip on the tongs and studied the meat with unmerited intensity.

Three car doors slammed, followed by the sound of Gavin greeting both Robin and Bethany. Evan peeked at the approaching threesome over the top of his sunglasses. His younger brother walked so close to Bethany, that if he wanted, he could have grazed his knuckles across her thigh. Evan grabbed the hotdogs with the tongs and plunked them onto a serving plate.

When the threesome reached him, Gavin threw his arm around Evan's shoulder and noogied the top of his head. "What's up number two?"

Evan jerked out from Gavin's grasp and shoved him a bit harder than necessary. He appreciated that his younger brother finally had his spark back, but he was in no mood to roughhouse now. Or listen to Gavin call him number two in front of Bethany. He gave Robin a quick hug, her burgeoning belly pressing against his own, and avoided Bethany altogether, whose blue-green top revealed freckled shoulders and slim arms.

Gavin picked up a hotdog and juggled it like a hot potato. "How're the cows? They all dropped their calves yet?"

"I'm still waiting on one of the heifers."

"It's pretty late in the season, isn't it?"

"Really late." He flipped one of the burgers and frowned. Luna was younger than he liked. He didn't normally breed his cattle until they were two. "I didn't know she was pregnant until recently. Must've happened when one of the bulls got in the pasture last fall."

"Got to keep a better watch on your boys, Ev." Gavin took a bite out of his hotdog.

"I've been calving for five years. I don't need advice from my little brother."

Gavin bit another hunk out of his food and shrugged.

Robin patted Evan's shoulder. "We'll leave you two to talk cattle."

As soon as the two ladies exited hearing range, Gavin jiggled his eyebrows and let out a low whistle. "I never really noticed Bethany before. Diane said I'd appreciate her."

"She's kind of old for you, isn't she?"

Gavin's eyebrows disappeared behind his shaggy hair. "Did I hit a nerve?"

Evan scraped at the grit sticking to the grill while Gavin clucked his tongue. "Romance 101. If you love a woman, you should tell her."

"Give me a break, Gav."

"Come on. Just admit it. You're hot for Bethany."

Evan's glanced over his shoulder. "Will you shut up? What are you— twelve? I'm not hot for anyone."

Gavin slugged him in the arm. "Yeah, okay. So you're telling me, that if I asked her out, it wouldn't bother you?"

The muscles across Evan's jaw pulled tight. He ground his teeth and scowled at the charcoal. There was no reason for him to be territorial of Bethany. She didn't belong to him. He didn't even want her to. He scooped up the burgers and slid them next to the hotdogs. "I'm ninety-nine percent sure she would say no, but be my guest."

"I don't believe you."

"Believe whatever you want."

"I'm going to call your bluff."

"Go for it." He scraped away more grit. "Are we done with this topic?"

"Why? You have something better to discuss?"

"We're doing some demolition next week at the café. We have to tear out a wall. Can you help?"

"Count me in." Gavin slapped Evan's shoulder, then walked away with his usual carefree swagger, flip-flops smacking against his heels. Bryan and Amy's youngest son raced forward and catapulted his wiry body into Gavin's arms. Gavin tossed Brody high into the air amidst a delighted round of shrieks and giggles, then set the small boy down, sat on the edge of the picnic table, and whispered something in Bethany's ear.

Heat skittered through Evan's veins. Over the past couple months, Gavin had slowly started to come back to his old self. Evan should be happy to see him interested in life again. So what if that involved flirting with Bethany? He could call Evan's bluff all he wanted. There was no way Bethany would go on a date with him.

Evan hung the tongs on the side of the grill, brought the plate toppling with meat to the rest of the group, and set it on the table. Ignoring the enthusiastic banter issuing from his family members, he filled his plate with chips, coleslaw, potato salad, and a burger, took a seat, and forced himself not to glower.

Brody parked himself on Gavin's left, and Marshall—Bryan and Amy's oldest—sidled up on Gavin's right, squeezing himself into the small space between Gavin and Bethany. Evan couldn't help smiling at the kid. Dad picked up baby Lilly from the blanket on the grass and offered to bless the meal. Bethany speared a piece of cantaloupe and jammed it into her mouth as his family bowed their heads and prayed.

"So." Gavin reached across the table for the ketchup. "What do you do for fun, Bethany?"

Evan snorted.

Gavin looked at him. "What? Was that a weird question?"

"Bethany doesn't like fun." Evan didn't realize he'd spoken the words out loud until all seven adult heads turned in his direction.

His mother branded him with a look of disapproval. He could see the admonishment in her eyes. *If you don't have anything nice to say, don't say anything at all.*

Why was it he always had the hardest time with that rule?

"Wow. That's pretty harsh, Ev." Gavin gave Evan a peculiar look while spreading a large dollop of mayonnaise onto his bun. "So, Bethany, Robin tells us you went to Minneapolis for an interview. How'd it go?"

Bethany dabbed the corners of her mouth with a napkin. "They hired somebody else."

Evan coughed. She didn't get the job?

"That's a bummer. But who knows. Maybe something around here will open up."

"Bethany doesn't want to stay around here." Everybody looked at Evan again, but he was looking at Bethany. Maybe more like glaring. "When are you leaving, anyway?"

"Jeez, Evan. Did you wake up on the wrong side of the bed this morning?"

Evan ignored his brother and waited for Bethany's eyes to freeze over, like usual. Instead, they melted in to a puddle of confusion and uncertainty. The look punched him in the gut. What was the matter with him? Bethany had never hidden the fact that she didn't want to stay in Peaks. He had no right to take his frustrations out on her.

"Are you having a grumpy day, Uncle Evan?" Marshall asked.

Evan grimaced. "Yeah, I am, buddy." He tried to form an apology, but none came, so instead, he pushed away from the table. "Excuse me."

As he marched to the house, he unclenched his fists and stretched out his fingers. He'd turned Bethany into his scapegoat, when it was God he was frustrated with.

What am I supposed to do, God? Go to Missouri? Is that where you want me?

Did he really want to pack up his bags, his inheritance from Dan, and move six hours from Gavin and Robin and his future niece or nephew? Sure, he wanted to farm—needed to farm—but was this the only way he could do it? He flung open the screen door, its hinges protesting, and let it slam shut behind him. And what about Bethany? How had such a stubborn, impossible-to-read woman worked her way past the mortar of his heart? Why had he let her?

I need to know what to do, Lord. A burning bush would be nice.

Evan leaned over the counter and quieted his soul, waiting for something—anything. A whisper. A nudge. A hint at the right direction. He wasn't going to move until he had his answer. But the screen door opened and in walked the woman he couldn't get out of his head. She clutched a trash bag, her face a shade of crimson he'd never seen before.

"I was just coming to get a cutting knife for Robin's pie."

Avoiding her eyes, he slid a knife from the block near the toaster.

"Evan, I…" She let out a long sigh and pushed away a few wisps of hair lying across her forehead. "When I left, the other day. I didn't mean—"

"Look, Bethany, you don't need to explain anything to me. You were right. I was asking too much." He took the bag from her hand. "You never hid your intentions about the future." He was just delusional enough to hope they'd changed.

She opened her mouth.

But he cut her off before she could get anything out. "Why don't you bring this out to the others?" He handed her the knife. "Robin makes a killer peach pie."

Thirty-One

When are you leaving, anyway?

The sharp lines on Evan's face when he'd asked that question stuck in her mind. How could he go from asking her to stay, to asking her to leave? Yesterday, she'd gone to the cookout hoping to figure out how Evan felt about her, and in turn, how she felt about him. He couldn't have made his feelings any clearer if he'd doused them in a bottle of Windex. What could have caused such a dramatic shift in his attitude in the span of four days?

Did he think she didn't care about Robin or the baby? Did he think she would get the job and leave, abandon the café, abandon his sister-in-law? Her insides squirmed. She supposed he had cause to think that way, seeing as she'd done it ten years ago. And again after Robin took her husband off life support.

I think you're horrible because of the way you left.

He'd spoken those words before. Did he feel the same way now?

When Bethany awoke in the morning from a sleepless night, Evan's words still fresh in her mind, she decided to drive over and explain herself. She needed to set him straight. She needed for him to know she cared about Robin. Maybe she could even explain why living in Peaks was so hard for her. But as she stood outside his front door, late-morning heat pressing against her neck, fingertips tingling with nerves, she didn't know why any of it mattered. Why did she care what Evan thought? Especially after his blow-off yesterday?

She stood on his front porch, her insides writhing with conflicting desires. Explain herself to Evan and win back his favor. Or escape Peaks with her pride intact. She took a step back. She didn't need to do this. Evan could think what he wanted. His opinion of her shouldn't—*didn't*—matter. She'd learned a long time ago that people will think what they want to think. People will judge who they want to judge. None of it mattered.

She ran her hand through her hair. Who was she kidding? As much as she didn't want to admit it, as much as she didn't want it to be true, Evan's opinion mattered. She rested her forehead against the door. How in the world had she let this happen? Evan was the last person she needed to care about. Especially considering her plans for the farm. She moved her fingers to her lips and she blinked at the spot she'd stood several nights ago—on the eve of Evan's birthday.

A flush crept up her neck. She stepped off the front porch and walked to her car. But she didn't get in. Instead, she brought her elbows up on top of the warm roof and rested her chin on her hands. Late morning sunlight shone through the thin space between the barn and silo, and the rise and fall chorus of cicadas filled the humid air. She'd forgotten how loud they could get. As a kid, her mother would have to put a box fan in her bedroom window every summer to drown out their sound so Bethany could fall asleep at night.

A breeze rustled tall grass, bringing with it a familiar scent. Bethany inhaled—fresh cut alfalfa and a twinge of sweet. Another breeze fluttered her hair and like a bee attracted to nectar, she walked around the side of the farmhouse, where the backyard disappeared into cow pasture and cornfields. And farther off, around the side of the barn—wildflowers.

Before Bethany could take them in, Evan flew up to the barn on his four-wheeler, so focused on whatever it was he was doing, he didn't notice her at all. He hopped off before it stopped all the way and ran into the barn. Curious, Bethany picked up her pace. She half-walked, half-trotted down the rest of the hill and ran into him as he came barreling out the door.

He reached out to steady her with his free hand. A chain slipped down his shoulder and sudsy water slopped over the sides of the bucket in his other hand. "Bethany?"

She took him in—his panting chest, his knotted forehead, dried blood on his hands and arms. Confusion and alarm swarmed inside her chest. "Is everything okay?"

"Thank God you're here." He hitched the chains over his shoulder. "I tried to pull the calf out, but it's not working."

Pull the calf out? What was Evan talking about?

"I found Luna, one of my heifers, an hour ago, out in the pasture. I don't know how long she's been in labor." He grabbed her forearm and pulled her toward the four-wheeler. "The calf is stuck."

Bethany's heart lurched. She'd watched a cow and its calf die in labor once. When she was a kid. Dan called the vet, only the doctor arrived too late. She hadn't been able to do anything then. She didn't see how she could do anything now.

But Evan hopped on the four-wheeler and set the bucket by his feet, the knot in his forehead tightening, looking at her like she might be able to help. Without thinking, she climbed on behind him and grabbed on tight, hoping he couldn't feel the crashing of her heart against his back.

Evan sped off, past the paddock, out into the pasture. "The vet guessed wrong on her gestation. We thought she had more time. At least another few weeks. But now she's in labor and I let my neighbor borrow the calf puller."

Bethany's heart crashed harder as the air whipped through her hair. She didn't know what to say, so she said nothing at all. She just swallowed the dryness in her throat and tried not to think about the fact that she was wrapped around Evan, driving out to save a birthing cow.

He stopped as soon as they came upon the beast.

Bethany didn't have to be a farmer to know something was wrong. The large animal lay on her side in the middle of the field, her giant body straining like she'd never seen an animal strain. She released a groan and stilled, as if the pain had retracted its claws.

Evan jumped off the four wheeler and bent down on his knees beside her. "She's been in labor way too long. If we don't get that calf out, they're both going to die."

What did Evan expect her to do? She was an architect, not an Angus midwife. She gulped a mouthful of heavy air. Sweat beaded between her shoulder blades and trickled down her spine.

Evan moved to the back end of the heifer and waved for her to join him. "I'm going to wrap these chains around the calf's legs and every time she has a contraction, we're going to pull."

The loud whooshing in her ears blocked another groan from the animal. And perhaps Evan's words, too. Did he just say what she thought he said? Pull on the calf's feet? Was he nuts? "Evan, I can't deliver a calf. I'm not—"

"Bethany, you can do this. I'll be right here beside you." Evan came to her side—his sleeveless shirt covered in sweat and dirt and pieces of grass—wrapped his strong hand around her elbow and pulled her toward the distressed cow. She dug her heels in the ground, but Evan either didn't notice or didn't care.

No, I can't do this.

Evan yanked her forward, ignoring the frantic shake of her head. He brought her down, level with the cow's backside, and that's when Bethany saw them. Two tiny hooves sticking out from the cow's back end. Something caught in her chest. Something large and heavy and important. Everything else faded away. Everything except those two pathetic hooves. She could design skyscrapers and bridges. Why couldn't she help deliver a calf?

Evan wrapped the chains around the viscous-slicked ankles, twice around each leg, and handed her one of the chains. "When I say so, you pull with me as hard as you can. Down and slightly toward her belly."

Bethany blinked at the hooves. She didn't think about where her hands were. She didn't think about the intense heat emanating from the animal. She held on to that chain as if her life depended on it and prepared to pull like she'd never pulled before.

Evan looked into her eyes. "Are you ready?"

Bethany nodded.

And as if on cue, the cow strained.

"Okay, Bethany…pull!"

Bethany screwed up her face. And she pulled. As hard as she could. She clenched the muscles in her neck, her back, her shoulders. She clenched her toes inside her shoes. She clenched her fingers around that chain. She focused every fiber of her being on those two bony legs and getting that animal out alive. As if everything hinged upon the life of that calf. She tugged and tugged, and didn't stop until she felt something shift.

The hairs on her arms stood on end.

"The calf's coming," Evan yelled. "Get ready to pull again."

Bethany took a deep breath and braced herself.

The cow strained again.

"Pull!"

Bethany heard someone grunt. She didn't know if it was her or Evan. Her fingers whitened around the chain. She threw her body away from the animal, denying her lungs oxygen until she pulled that calf out alive.

"Come on Luna, push, girl. Keep pushing!"

Something shifted again.

"Great, Bethany! We're doing it! She's still contracting... Keep pulling!"

Her face contorted. Her mind focused on nothing but her muscles and the metal gripped tight between her fingers. Without Evan's command, she pulled again. And again. The calf's legs appeared, then its nose.

"One more time, Bethany!" Evan's voice echoed through the field, overtaking the cow's horrific groans.

With one last mighty tug, they fell back, bringing the rest of the calf's body with them. The calf was out.

She'd pulled the calf out.

Bethany gulped in the humid air, breathing in heaping mouthfuls, scented heavily with sweat and blood, the burning in her lungs spreading throughout her.

That weighty, important thing building in her chest rent loose and whirled away, leaving behind a lightness that might lift her off the ground and carry her to the sky.

The new mother came to her feet. She turned her giant head, nudged the calf on the ground, and began licking, cleaning her baby as if she'd done this a dozen times before. As if Bethany hadn't just been tugging the beast's insides out for all her life was worth.

Evan moved to the calf, did something to make it sneeze, then fell in to the grass. His eyes found Bethany's, and she stared in amazement at what they'd just done. At what she'd just done. She delivered a calf—she stood behind a twelve-hundred-pound animal and pulled a baby from its womb. Her breath came in airy waves. She could feel Evan watching her as she watched the two animals. Both alive. Both healthy.

Evan came to his feet, moved toward the mother-calf duo, and leaned close to the mother's ear. "This was your first one, Luna. I promise the rest won't be this hard."

He moved away, toward the four-wheeler. When he returned, he carried the bucket filled with soapy water and bent low to clean the cow's udders. Satisfied that her lungs were functioning and her legs would not collapse, Bethany stood and joined him. She'd watched Grandpa Dan do this same thing. Clean the cow's udders, so the calf could nurse.

"When I didn't see her with the rest of the herd, I thought I'd drive out and check. I've been worried about her. She's pretty small yet to calf." Evan dunked the rag into the sudsy water. "I didn't think she would make it."

Bethany could feel Evan looking at her, no doubt taking in the hair sticking to her neck, the dirt and blood covering her hands and arms. She had to look like a nightmare.

"Thank you, Beth. I don't know what I would've done if you hadn't shown up when you did."

The airiness in her chest hummed. *Beth.* Evan had called her Beth. Before she had time to dissect what that might mean, the calf did something amazing. Less than fifteen minutes ago, that animal had been fighting for its life. And now, there it was, getting to its feet. Bethany gasped and brought her hand to the base of her neck.

Evan dried the cow's udders and moved away. The calf took an unsteady step forward, bent its head, and latched on to its mother.

How did it know? Who taught that helpless animal to bend down and take that udder into its mouth?

Bethany looked at the sky, then scanned her surroundings. Something still, something peaceful, welled up inside her as she took in the view—a few distant round bales sitting in the fields, rows of corn stretching toward the horizon, the white-fenced paddock, and the spot she'd noticed earlier— where the stream gurgled through the pasture and wound behind the barn.

Her breath caught.

Wildflowers burst from the ground in vivid blues and whites and violets, creating a picture more pleasing than anything her hands could design. She didn't understand how it was possible, but Evan had been right. The abundance of snow had produced an abundance of wildflowers. More than she'd ever seen before. Somehow, those cold, lifeless winter months had prepared the land for something breathtaking. Something beautiful. Something brimming with life. And her newfound lightness grew lighter, warmer, as if the sight before her was reviving the dormant pieces of her soul.

Her father and grandfather had poured their sweat and heart into every inch of this land. Yet she'd been determined to get rid of it. As if keeping it would somehow mean forfeiting the woman she'd become. But sitting there, having witnessed such a miracle, with that heavy thing within her gone, she suddenly realized that it might be possible to have both. To be both. The little-girl Bethany who loved the farm and the adult Bethany who loved architecture. Maybe she didn't have to choose.

She breathed in the wide open space and embraced the deep-seeded longing germinating in her heart. A long-buried love took root and blossomed, and for the first time in a decade, it no longer felt like a weed.

Blood and dirt had soaked through the fabric of Bethany's shirt and would never come out. Thankfully, Evan lent her an oversized T-shirt, so she could discard her top. She rinsed her face with cold water and used a washrag to wipe her arms and legs, then pulled the T-shirt over her head. The scent of Old Spice clinging to the cotton didn't help her wobbling knees. Evan had given her a ride to the house on the back of his four-wheeler. Her body still felt like warm silly putty from pressing against his.

She slipped out of the bathroom and crept down the steps. The familiar creaking brought a gentle ache to her chest. On the cusp of such an exhilarating morning, she longed to talk to her grandfather. To share her experience with the man who could listen better than anyone. Instead, she tiptoed past his empty recliner—as if not to disturb his memory—stepped out onto the front porch, and found Evan sitting on the porch swing. She took a seat in the rocking chair beside him.

The shade of the porch didn't deter the heat. The mugginess crept underneath the awning and settled around her shoulders like a heavy blanket. Evan cracked open a Pepsi, grabbed an unopened one by his feet, and handed it over. The sweaty can felt like ice on her fingertips. She brought it to her neck and pressed the shock of cold against her skin.

They sat in comfortable silence while Bethany sipped her drink, rocking back and forth, the floorboards creaking a hypnotic lullaby. When she had nothing left but an empty can, Evan dropped his own to the ground and crushed it beneath his boot. The loud crackle may have interrupted the soothing cadence of the moment, but it was his words that obliterated her peace.

"You can sell the farm."

Bethany stopped rocking.

"You can tell your Realtor that I'll sell the house."

"I don't understand. I thought—"

"It's your farm. Not mine. My uncle has a friend in Missouri. He's going to rent me some land after harvest this fall."

Bethany's mind tripped over his words. Evan was leaving Peaks?

"I won't stand in your way anymore."

The word *hypocrite* flashed in her mind. He'd given her so much grief for wanting to leave, to find a job elsewhere. Now he was the one leaving. He was the one abandoning Robin. He was the one abandoning the farm.

Her hand pulsed with the angry desire to slap him. She wanted to scream at him for giving up, for relinquishing his dream. But she buried the words inside and gripped on to the sides of her rocking chair.

"Thanks for your permission."

The icy tone of her voice clashed against the simmering heat of the late morning and melted into a puddle of resentment at her feet. Bethany had nothing keeping her there. She had no excuses to hold on to the farm now. Not when her anchor had just let go.

Thirty-Two

A month after my eighteenth birthday, I packed up my car to leave Peaks, and the last place I planned to stop on my way out of town was the farm. I boxed up the few belongings worth taking and crammed them into the back of my Geo Metro—a horrid combination of teal and rust. Yet somehow better than Mom's Pinto, which thank the heavens, breathed its last dying breath two winters ago.

Mom stood to the side and watched, arms wrapped around her waist like she might spill into a puddle on the ground if she didn't hold on tight. She sniffed and dabbed her eyes with a crumpled pink tissue. David had left two years before and now she'd be all alone. In that tiny trailer.

I couldn't get away fast enough.

When I finished packing, we stood there. Awkwardly. My mother wasn't a hugger. And I supposed I didn't make it easy for her to hug me. So we said our goodbyes, Mom's eyes watering while mine stayed completely dry. She asked if I'd packed a lunch. I said yes.

And I drove away.

Without looking back.

I stopped at the Delner's next, my car, as always, completely out of place in their neighborhood. Robin had decided to stay in Peaks and go to St. Ambrose University—only fifteen minutes away—something I could never understand. Our goodbye wasn't awkward. We hugged. We promised to stay in touch. She said something that made me laugh, but I can't remember what. Mr. Delner came out and gave me one of his bear hugs. And I left before Mrs. Delner's absence could dampen our happy goodbye.

Then I went to the farm. To say goodbye to Grandpa Dan.

As I pulled up the long, graveled drive toward the farmhouse, I remember feeling surprised at how long it had been since I'd last visited. Once I started high school, with Mr. Delner's words about architecture firmly planted in my mind, I visited Dan less and less. When I wasn't busy hanging out with Robin, my studies consumed me. My grades were one of the few things I could control. Something that would ensure I could escape Peaks and make a life much different than the one I knew. It's what earned me a full-ride scholarship to one of the most prestigious schools of architecture in the country.

A smile spread across my face at the sight of Dan, riding atop a tractor, mowing a large circle around the machine shed. When he saw me get out of the car, he waved and cut the engine, and I had the strangest urge to join him. To kick off my shoes and run out to see the horses. To be, for just a moment, the carefree girl I was before everything went so sour.

The urge welled up so strong and sudden that it frightened me. I'd convinced myself that I was over the farm. My young-girl dreams of marrying a handsome farmer like my father were long gone. The farm was part of my past and I didn't want to feel nostalgic toward anything that would tie me to Peaks. I was eager to start fresh, where nobody knew me. Where nobody knew my past mistakes. Far, far away from my mother and her choices and the memory of my father and his death. I couldn't wait to recreate myself—to become Bethany the architect. Not Bethany the poor, fatherless trailer girl who tried to drown herself when she was twelve.

Dan shaded his eyes and we met at the end of the driveway. He held out his arms and I walked into them. I remember thinking how strong he was. Not at all like a typical sixty-five- year-old.

"My granddaughter, the college student," he said, his chest rumbling with a chuckle. He pulled back, took hold of my arms, and looked me up and down, like he wanted to capture a picture in his mind. "I have something for you. Wait right here."

He left before I could protest and trotted toward the house. I shoved my hands in my back pockets, kicked at some loose gravel, and scanned my surroundings—the paddock, the barn, that tall silo where everything changed. I fought hard against the lump building in my throat, perplexed by its arrival, until Dan returned with a box wrapped in newspaper.

"Grandpa, you didn't have to."

"I know," he said, handing the gift over, "but I wanted to."

I smiled, tore off the newspaper, opened the lid, and pulled out a maroon and gray Texas A&M T-shirt. Underneath, a biography about Frank Lloyd Wright. I draped the shirt over my arm and picked up the book, the lump in my throat growing bigger. "I don't know what to say."

"You're going to make a fine architect someday, Bethany. I have no doubt about that." His eyes crinkled when he smiled. "Just don't forget, you'll always have a home here too."

He didn't mean Peaks. He meant there, as in right there. The farm. And as I drove in to the sunset, toward my future—my new life—I couldn't help feeling comforted that the farm would always be there. My first home. My first love.

Thirty-Three

To avoid facing any decision about the farm, Bethany enmeshed herself in the café. The kitchen was complete. Evan and Gavin helped tear out the wall, replace the front windows, build the railing on the second floor, and make improvements in the two bathrooms. Robin planted flowers in the garden out front and browsed craigslist for used kitchen appliances and espresso machines. Bethany kept in touch with the building inspector.

Together, she and Robin found a great deal on fifteen marble-topped round tables with black iron chairs that looked exactly like the kind she imagined gracing the inside of an Italian bistro. Bethany convinced Robin to enlarge the photos of Italy that she and Micah had taken on their honeymoon. They turned them into square canvases and stored them away until they could hang them on the walls.

While the construction forced Bethany to keep in regular contact with Evan, she recaptured the cool indifference she'd lost over the course of her stay in Peaks and did not allow their conversations to slip anywhere beyond business. She buried whatever attraction she felt toward him and focused her efforts on bringing her vision to life.

The café would be finished well before Robin delivered her baby. While Bethany rejoiced over their accomplishment, part of her mourned its completion. Robin's due date crept closer. And soon she wouldn't have any more excuses for sticking around. With the café finished and Robin no longer pregnant, it would be time for Bethany to say goodbye to her odd, unexpected time in Peaks. She tapped the handle of the paint roller against her palm.

Gavin, Amanda, and Bethany just finished slathering on the first coat of paint, and Robin surveyed their handiwork from the door. She smiled her approval. "I can't believe how much you got done!"

Gavin sat back on his heels, wiping the beads of sweat trickling down his temples. "We did a pretty fine job, if I do say so myself. I think we ought to celebrate. What's everybody doing tonight?"

Bethany pressed the back of her hand against her forehead and shrugged. It was a Saturday night in Peaks. What was there to do?

Amanda groaned. "Gavin, we're not going to the fair."

Gavin turned to his sister. "What's your beef with the fair?"

"Every year, you somehow rope me into going. And every year, I somehow manage to step in a pile of horse—"

Gavin held up his palm. "Let's keep this G-rated, little sis."

Amanda smirked. "I was going to say manure."

How could Bethany forget about the fair? The town hosted the event every year, the week of the Fourth of July. As a kid, it was one of the few things she looked forward to. Grandpa Dan would let her and David go on some rides that made their insides wobble, buy them both a stick of cotton candy, then take them through the petting zoo. When she was seven, they had a white baby llama, and Bethany couldn't stop laughing while she petted the animal's long neck.

"What do you say, Bethany?" Gavin said. "Are you in for some fun?"

Corn dogs and funnel cakes didn't exactly fit her current definition of fun. Still, taking a night away from her disappointing job search to celebrate their accomplishments—even if it was at a small-town, Podunk event—did carry a certain appeal. She looked at Robin. "Do you want to go?"

Robin placed her hands on top of her belly. "I can't exactly go on any rides."

"We can sit out together. You know I can't stand being dizzy."

Gavin grabbed his phone from his back pocket. "I'll call Evan. The man works too hard. He needs to get his butt away from the farm for one night and have some country fun."

❧

The evening sun refused to look away. It glared at them over the horizon. Bethany moved her hand to her neck, twisted the loose tendrils together, and brought them up to her ponytail. She, Robin, and Gavin stood inside the fairgrounds, waiting for Evan, who had agreed to come out and celebrate.

Bethany forced her shoulders to relax. Tonight was about fun. Celebration. Enjoyment. Although those things would be harder to accomplish with Evan tagging along, she wasn't going to let his presence ruin her good intentions. She took a deep breath and attempted to see the fair through a fresh pair of eyes because hers had grown far too critical. She wasn't going to be that Bethany tonight. Although it was too hot to let her hair down in the literal sense, she intended to do so in the figurative.

Gavin leaned against the fair gate. "Hey, Number Two!" he said, calling through the wrought iron bars. "It's about time you showed up."

Bethany spotted Evan walking toward them with an easy gait—his shoulders back, his large hands swinging by his sides. He wore sandals, cargo shorts, and a navy blue St. Louis Cardinal T-shirt that hugged his broad chest and slim waist, the converse of Dominic's tailored suits which boasted of his impressive career. These two men couldn't be more opposite. While she'd claimed to love one for three years of her life, she couldn't remember her chest pulling as tight as it did now.

He handed the lady his ticket and joined them as they meandered through the crowded thoroughfare. Booths and beer tents lined both sides of the blacktopped road. But the sights and sounds didn't distract her from Evan, so close by her side that their arms bumped together when they wound their way through the crowd. Each time it happened, heat would burst against Bethany's skin and she'd lurch away.

Gavin led them down a lane filled with kids and adults, who forked over money hoping to shoot bottles off pedestals, or toss rings over rubber ducks, or shoot oversized balls through undersized hoops all for the sake of winning a stuffed bear.

"What do you say, Ev? Want to win these two pretty ladies here a little something?"

Evan turned to Robin, who hadn't said much since they arrived. "Is that what you'd like to do?"

It shouldn't have bothered Bethany that he addressed only her, but it did.

"Micah and I always looked at the animals first. He had a soft spot for the 4-H kids and their shows." Her far away expression flickered, then cleared. "But some games could be fun."

As they turned down the carnival lane, Bethany second-guessed their plans. The fair was something Robin and Micah used to go to together. The man had been on the fair board for crying out loud. Why hadn't Bethany thought about that? Or why hadn't Evan or Gavin? She was about to share her concern with Gavin when she saw two familiar faces several paces ahead.

Pastor Fenton stood behind a booth. And next to him, her mother collected bills from a girl's outstretched hand. Bethany stopped mid-stride. Evan bumped in to her from behind, but she ignored his mumbled apology. She'd kept in sporadic contact with her mother while staying in Peaks. She found she could handle her in small doses as long as they stuck to safe topics, like David. But handling her with Fenton was an entirely different story.

She pried her eyes away from her mother and noticed three other women, all from First Light, crowded inside the booth. A red banner that read *Project MAC* rippled in the muggy breeze. Before Bethany could duck undetected into the mass of bodies, her mother looked up from the overflowing canister of money. Bethany jerked back, but too late. She'd already been discovered. Her mother came out from the booth, her hands reaching out to her. "Bethany, I'm so happy you're here. I've been thinking about you. It seems you are making great progress on the café."

Bethany nodded toward the banner. "What are you doing?"

Her mother glanced over her shoulder at the booth. "Pastor Fenton came up with the idea. We're raising money for the church."

Bethany scrutinized the man doling out plastic balls and noticed a pallor in his face that she'd never seen before.

"Do you want to play? The money is going to a great cause."

"I'm sure."

"Bethany, please don't be so—"

But before Mom could ask Bethany to stop being whatever it was she was being, one of the women in the booth screamed. The sound of it pierced the air. Bethany spun around and saw Fenton slumped over the booth at an odd angle. The three ladies scrambled, calling out for help, grabbing on to Fenton's arms, while Evan and her mother raced to the booth.

The palpitation of Bethany's heart did not increase. Her breathing did not come in shallow, sporadic bursts. No part of her panicked. With the indifference of a curious spectator, she observed the scene unfolding in muted slow motion. She watched her mother bend over the crumpled man, her twisted mouth shouting for help. She watched Evan crawl over the counter and grab Fenton's shoulders. She watched Fenton shoo away the hands that tried to help him in an awkward one-armed bat, his contorted face drooping on one side.

Bethany retrieved her phone from her purse. With steady fingers, she dialed 911 and relayed the emergency with a coolness that might have confused the dispatcher.

"I'm at Peaks county fair and a man is having a stroke."

Thirty-Four

By the time the ambulance came, the sun had dipped toward the horizon. A crowd of onlookers parted and grew silent as a crew of paramedics scrambled out of the vehicle and got to work. They checked his vitals and asked questions, all while loading him onto a stretcher. Mom and the other women stood to one side, hugging and wringing their hands.

Bethany stood close enough to see Fenton's slack jaw and the fear nestled in his eyes as one of the first responders asked him questions. The right side of his mouth pulled downward in confusion, while the other remained slack and unmoving. He blinked, groaned, and turned his frightened eyes toward the EMT, a single tear leaking from the corner. It raced down his cheek and disappeared over the crest of his jaw line.

A furious heat pitched and rolled in Bethany's belly. What right did he have to cry? What right did he have to turn weak now, when he was finally receiving the same judgment he heaped upon her father? Bethany closed her eyes, unable to see any more tears. She imagined Fenton behind the pulpit, preaching about God's condemnation with a passion that made Bethany shrink back in her seat. Her mother had watched in rapt awe, clutching the tops of her thighs, while Bethany stared over the rows of wooden pews, thinking about her dad. At home. In a wheelchair. No longer welcome at First Light.

After the accident, her father stopped attending church. Not right away. But gradually. Pastor Fenton, it seemed, had a strong distaste for suffering and weakness. He didn't want it inside his church.

Her young mind couldn't wrap itself around the deterioration of her family unit. She only knew that Pastor Fenton rested at the core of their brokenness. Because ever since her father fell from that silo, the pastor hooked his claws into her mother and convinced her that the accident was proof of her husband's sin. His paralysis was God's punishment. According to Fenton, only sinners suffered.

But what now? What would the almighty Pastor Fenton say about this?

Flashing lights pulled Bethany from her thoughts. The paramedics loaded Fenton into the ambulance and left. As the siren wailed through the Fairgrounds, Bethany made eye contact with her mother, then turned around and walked away.

She wound through the rides, past ticket booths, past barns lined with pig and goat pens, cow stalls and enormous Clydesdales, kids and moms and dads and laughing teenagers. Her breath did not come until she escaped the crowd and found the shade of a large tree. She gulped in great heaping gobs of air and plopped down in the grass, her legs shaking.

The evening swaddled her in a blanket of chirping crickets and distant fair noises, but her mind was far from quiet. Her murky past stirred, and as hard as she tried, she couldn't force it to sleep any longer. She grabbed a tuft of tall weeds and braced herself for the onslaught of suppressed memories.

At the age of nine, Bethany found her father submerged in their bathtub. His opened eyes stared like lifeless orbs from the bottom of the tub, unblinking. But as frightening as his eyes were, it was his lips that flooded her soul with hysteria. The color of ripe plums. Parted and frozen. A scream had bubbled in her throat and split the air, echoing off the chambered walls of the bathroom.

According to the autopsy report, her father drowned. With puffy eyes, her mother explained to her and David that his death was an accident. A terrible, horrible, unfortunate accident. Her father must have lost his arm hold on the bathtub bars and had slipped down in the tub. Since he couldn't sit up on his own, or grab with his hands, he couldn't pull himself out of the water.

People talked. Speculated. Bethany heard the murmurs and defended her father with matchless ferocity, convinced his death was exactly as her mother had said.

All the while, her life turned inside out. Not only did she lose her father, her mom moved them into a dumpy trailer home—away from Dan and away from the farm. And every night, instead of tucking her and David into bed, Mom went away too. For the first time in Bethany's life, her mother had to take a job. Third shift. Every evening at seven o'clock Mom would leave for the local Alcoa plant.

Bethany mourned two deaths. Her father's and the life she loved. She spent many nights under David's watch, wondering why everything had to change. It was something that always confused her.

Until three years later.

The summer she turned twelve.

Bethany pedaled her bike through the rundown trailer park and stopped in front of the heap of metal they called home. Fenton's black sedan was in the driveway. He came over on Saturdays and drank coffee with her mom. Bethany knew she was to make herself scarce.

She stepped off her bike and crept to the front door, thinking if she snuck in real quiet, she could slip to her and David's room unnoticed. But when she reached the door, Fenton's voice carried through the opened window.

"The more you dwell on the past, the stronger foothold you give Satan."

Bethany's hand glued to the door knob.

"I just feel so guilty."

"Do you have reason to feel guilty? It was Tom who decided to take his life, wasn't it? It was Tom who decided to play God. He was an unrepentant sinner, Ruth. Please don't follow in his footsteps."

Bethany's hand fell to her side, her mind whirling around the pastor's words.

"I know, but I didn't make it easy for him. I kept pestering him. I was so worried about our future with him in that wheelchair. He was depressed, and all I did was urge him to seek God's forgiveness. Every time I did, things just became worse."

Bethany's heart thumped against her breastbone, her mouth as dry as cotton.

"You were right to urge him. He should have listened. But he didn't. He made his choice. And people who make that choice go to hell. Do you want to follow him?"

Bethany reared back, as if she'd been slapped. She hurled herself off the front step and sprinted away. Her two legs pumped, fueled by the urgent desire to escape Fenton's words. She ran from their implications. She ran until her lungs burned with the intensity of a raging bonfire. Only when the blood pounding in her ears reached its peak, did she collapse in a heap of exhaustion on the outskirts of town, right beneath that green population sign. Right in front of Jorner's General Store.

Even there, amidst haunting rows of corn and the gravel road, Fenton's words slithered around her throat and choked her with their inescapable, sickening truth.

Her dad killed himself.

And her mother was a liar.

He hadn't accidentally drowned in the bathtub. He had deliberately removed himself from the world. He left her behind, and according to the man with the black stare, sentenced himself to an eternity of fire. Too weak to face Pastor Fenton, too weak to win back his wife from the leader of First Light, too weak to overcome his injury, he'd taken the coward's way out. As Bethany sat on the shoulder of the road, the truth bore down on her thin, twelve-year-old shoulders. It bruised her soul and tore open tender scars that hadn't yet healed.

Shuddering, Bethany pulled herself from the horrible memory and sat perfectly still, until the peach horizon turned inky blue and the moon shone between the rustling leaves.

When she was a child, Pastor Fenton stood behind the pulpit every Sunday, his presence magnetic and larger than life. Her father had eaten his words like maggot-infested communion, shrinking beneath his judgment like it was the ultimate truth. Her mother revered Fenton. Loved him. Treated him like God. And Bethany had no reason to think he wasn't. In her little-girl mind, God and Fenton were one and the same. She had no idea how to tell the two apart.

Until now.

Seeing him so weak and fragile on that stretcher cracked the foundation of her beliefs. Beneath a star-strewn velvet sky, something simple, yet profound, shifted into place. Pastor Fenton was not God. He was a man. A broken, fallible man. Somehow, like her parents, she'd made him in to something more, when all he'd ever been was flesh and sinew.

A horse whinnied in the distance. Her phone buzzed. It was a text from her mom. Fenton was stable and in room 236.

Bethany wondered if Mom had turned delusional. Did she really think Bethany cared what condition Fenton was in or where he was staying? Did she really not understand how much Bethany loathed him?

Laughter approached in the form of three boys, most likely twelve or thirteen. They didn't notice her at all as they walked past with their cowboy boots and bags of taffy and rolls of tickets and sunburned cheeks. When Bethany turned to watch them go, she startled. Evan stood off to the side, watching her.

A humid breeze made strands of hair dance around Bethany's cheeks. She tucked them behind her ear and wrapped her arms around her legs. Evan had watched her since the paramedics arrived, transfixed by the emotions scrolling across her face. When she turned and walked away, he had every intention of going after her. Except Robin wasn't feeling well, and he and Gavin had to work out how she'd get home. As soon as Gavin escorted her away, he took off in the direction Bethany had gone. Hoping to find her. Needing to find her.

And now here she was, sitting beneath a tree on the outskirts of Peaks county fair.

"I'm glad I found you," he said.

She looked away, off into the distance. He had no idea what Pastor Fenton meant to Bethany or her mother. He didn't know what ties bound them together. He only knew what he saw—the pain on Bethany's face as they loaded him into the ambulance. Although he made a deliberate effort to detach himself over the last few weeks, to overcome whatever pull she had on him, he could not ignore the urge to go after her tonight.

He joined her beneath the tree and sat by her in the tall grass. "Are you okay?"

She looked at her fingers curled around her shins.

"I'd love to know what you're thinking about," he said.

A trace of a smile whisked over her lips and fell away. "God, actually."

Her answer slipped through his awareness. "What about Him?" He'd never met anyone more hardened to the concept of a loving Father than the woman sitting next to him. Except maybe himself four years ago. It was one more reason in a list of plenty why he shouldn't pursue her.

"I'm just trying to figure out who He is."

"Have you reached a conclusion?"

She sighed and rested her chin on the top of her knee. "I guess I know who He isn't."

He had never talked with Bethany like this. So intentionally unguarded. In the past, the only time she granted him access into her psyche was during times of distress—a fierce emotional outburst—usually one provoked by him. It had never been like this. With her sitting beside him—calm, reflective, open.

She picked a clover from the ground and twirled it between her fingers. "He's not Pastor Fenton."

"You thought he was?"

"When I was kid I did. I guess the belief sort of stuck with me." She shrugged. "But he can't be God. Not now. Not when he's lying in a hospital bed."

Evan sifted through her words, piecing them together. When the puzzle was complete in his mind, it spelled out a simple question. One that rarely came with a simple answer. One he asked her a long time ago, on a rock by the creek. Only she hadn't given him an honest answer then. "Bethany, why are you so angry with God?"

She furrowed her brow. "Because I hate what God does to people." She stared down into her lap. "At least I used to."

Evan didn't speak. He sat by her side and waited.

"I didn't like what believing in God did to the people I cared about. It destroyed my father and turned my mother into a cowering shadow." She picked the leaves off the clover, dropping them one at a time to the ground. "Christianity ruined them."

Evan stretched his legs out in front of him and leaned back on his hands. "I don't know your mom very well. And I never knew your dad. But what you just described… Bethany, that's not faith. Believing in Christ—knowing Him—it's not about fear. It's about freedom."

Bethany looked at him, and the desire to scoot closer ballooned inside his chest. He wanted to heal whatever wounds Fenton had branded into her soul. To erase her hurts and make her new. But just like his family couldn't save him during his angry years, he knew he couldn't save Bethany now. This was between her and God.

"Robin said she *gave her life to Christ*. Those were the words she used." Bethany turned to him, her eyes narrowed. Not with contempt or disapproval or mockery. But with concentration. Like whatever knot she strained to untangle was of utmost importance. "How does giving your life to someone lead to freedom?"

He contemplated her question, chewing it over in his mind while crickets chirped and the night settled between them. "Sometimes letting go is pretty liberating."

"Letting go, huh?" She hung her head. "I've never been too good at that."

Oh, how he understood those words. He and Bethany were so very much alike. More than either of them had realized. Both filled with doubts and questions. Both determined to hold tight to life's reins. Because handing them over meant losing control. And losing control was a frightening thing. "But it's not impossible."

She let out a lighthearted huff. "Do you not know me?"

"I know you've done it before." He raised his eyebrow and gave her a nudge with his shoulder. "With me on the dance floor."

She dipped her chin. "This is a little different."

"Not as much as you might think."

"Well, I'm not sure I'll ever be ready to let go."

They were quiet for a while as crickets and cicadas sang their nighttime serenade.

"One thing I've learned about God these last four years? He doesn't often wait until we're ready." If he would have waited until Bethany was ready to dance with him that night at Shorney's Terrace, they never would have danced at all. If God would have waited until Evan was done being angry, Evan never would have come back.

She pulled up a few more stalks of clover and swatted at a mosquito that landed on her ankle. "Did Robin ever tell you I tried to drown myself?"

She asked the question so casually, so quietly, he had to replay it in his head to make sure he'd heard right. When he was sure he had, his skin prickled. "No. Why?"

"That's the million dollar question."

Evan leaned forward.

"I was twelve when I did it. And afterward, everybody in Peaks treated me like a leper. My mother made me go to therapy—she was terrified with what I did." She took a slow breath. "I think because it was the same way my dad took his life."

Her words injected a shot of freezing air inside his skull. Dan's son committed suicide? He always thought Dan's son died from complications after falling from a silo. Not once in their five years together had Dan ever alluded to suicide.

"My mom told everybody it was an accident, but people suspected the truth. I think she thought what I did was God's way of punishing her."

Evan pressed his fingers to his forehead trying to dispel the image of a young girl hurting and ostracized. No wonder she hated Peaks.

"The therapy was useless. I never told anyone why I did it." She set her elbows on her knees, took a deep breath, looked him in the eyes. "You want to know what's crazy?"

He sat very still. Afraid if he moved, he'd ruin the moment.

"I did it because I wanted to go to hell."

She spoke those words to the darkness. They floated from her mouth and hovered in the air like a cloud of electricity, raising the hair on his arms and neck. "Why?"

"Because that's where Fenton said my dad was, and I couldn't stand the thought of him being there alone. Even if I hated what he did, he was still my dad. And I missed him."

Evan's heart cracked. Broke into pieces for the twelve-year-old Bethany. A young girl who was hurting. A young girl who needed grace, not wrath. A message of redemption, not condemnation. A young girl whose family had been torn to shreds by a man who was supposed to share God's mercy but abused his position instead.

"I thought maybe if I joined him, then maybe hell wouldn't be so bad." She looked at her knees. "It didn't work though."

He shuddered. He had no idea where Bethany's father was, but he was most certainly glad Bethany was here—at the fair, next to him. Evan clasped his hands in his lap. Whether to keep himself from going to the hospital and punching a defenseless man in the face, or wrapping his arms around this woman, he wasn't sure. "I'm glad you figured it out."

The lines on her forehead puckered. "What?"

"That Pastor Fenton isn't God."

The corner of her mouth lifted. "I am too."

Thirty-Five

Since Gavin borrowed Evan's car to take Robin home, Bethany had to give Evan a lift to the farm. Exhaustion weighed on her as she watched him disappear into the house. His kitchen light flicked on, then off. His bedroom light shone through the second story window for a few moments before extinguishing. If Evan knew she sat in his driveway for an hour, overlooking her inheritance, contemplating her future, he let her do so in peace.

Velvety blackness shadowed the land, shrouding the farm in a darkened stillness that filled her soul with calm. She looked across the paddock, the pasture beyond, and the spanning rows of corn planted over rolling hills. The humid air and the scent of dewy hay crept into her window, bringing with it a slew of childhood memories.

This farm was a seam, separating her past into a distinct before and after. Her childhood before her father's accident and her childhood after. Getting rid of Dan's land would be like tearing out the seam, selling the good fabric in an attempt to destroy the bad. Did she want to do that? The night filled her car and seeped into her pores, filling her with a strange peace. What was she going to do?

By the time she pulled out of the driveway, the clock on her dashboard read 12:05. The time felt significant somehow. Five minutes into a new day. A new beginning. As she drove the back roads, making her way toward Robin's home, she chipped at the hardened layers deposited on her spirit like lime, searching for herself in all the muck. Over the past ten years, she'd expended so much energy pushing forward, forging ahead, building an impressive façade. Architect. Big city. A woman with goals, money, expensive clothes, and a nice car. But a façade was just that. A façade. A spurious attempt to cover imperfection, masking the worn-out structure hiding beneath.

When she stepped out of her car and walked to Robin's front stoop, she decided to put her skills to use. Real use. It was time to renovate herself—the Bethany behind the façade.

The baby was due in six weeks. Which gave her six weeks to figure out which walls needed tearing down and which walls could stay. Six weeks to rebuild something real.

Someone real.

She creaked open the door, stepped into the foyer, and blinked against the light filtering down the staircase. Was Robin still awake? She twisted the knob and closed the door, trying to silence the catching latch. When she turned around, Robin was there, standing on the stairs, clutching her stomach between her hands, a grimace on her face.

Bethany's pulse hiccuped. "What's wrong?"

Robin concentrated very hard on the bottom step and didn't answer until her face relaxed. "I went to the bathroom because I thought maybe my water broke."

A shock of alarm pulsed through Bethany's limbs. Water either broke or it didn't. What did she mean *maybe*?

"And ever since, I've had a few pains. Like menstrual cramps."

Bethany took three quick steps to the staircase.

"I called the doctor. He said to get to the hospital." Robin's hand trembled as she brought it to her neck, as if attempting to coax out her next words. "It's too early for the baby to come, isn't it? I haven't even packed a bag yet."

Bethany's legs turned shaky. The doctor wanted her to get to the hospital? She took Robin's clammy hand and led her to the door. "I'm sure everything will be okay. Everything will be fine."

She wondered if she was lying.

The child's life flashed through her mind. Seeing that tiny blip of a heartbeat on the screen. The fast-paced whooshing that had filled the doctor's office two weeks later, flooding her soul with joy, excitement, a mysterious longing. She'd watched Robin's stomach grow rounder every day, feeling for herself the tumbles and kicks knocking from within Robin's womb. Bethany tried to swallow. But the muscles in her neck had clenched too tight.

She raced into the kitchen, grabbed Robin's purse, and led her outside to the car. By the time they sat down, Robin's face had screwed up into another grimace. When it was over, she drew in a ragged breath, and looked at Bethany under panic-stricken eyebrows.

"I can't do this, Bethany. Not without Micah."

Bethany stepped through the hospital doors and strode to the front desk. "I'm here to check in Robin Price. She's thirty-four weeks pregnant and in labor."

She glanced over her shoulder. Robin hovered beside the wall, her eyes as wide as her face was white. Bethany looked back at the lady. Tapped her foot. Drummed her fingers against the counter. And checked her urge to jump across the desk and enter Robin's information herself. What in the world was so difficult about typing in a name? What part of *thirty-four weeks* didn't she hear?

The woman looked up, curved her lips into what could only be the same smile she gave every other patient who walked through the doors, and told them to head up to neonatal. Bethany bit back a sarcastic thank you as the woman brought them a wheelchair and Bethany hurried Robin to the elevator. Once inside, Bethany closed her eyes.

Make this turn out okay.

It wasn't eloquent. It wasn't even a request. Bethany's mind uttered the prayer like a demand, like a mother telling her naughty child to stop it, right this instant. When the doors opened, she pushed Robin to the desk. Two nurses sat behind it, both young, both pretty, both bored. The smaller of the two met her at the counter.

"Dr. Hannigan told us to come. She's barely thirty-four weeks pregnant."

The nurse smiled. "He arrived a couple minutes ago." She nodded toward a room, her short curls bobbing like apples. "Why don't you follow me?"

They entered a small room with a bed and a monitor. White and nearly empty. The nurse gave Robin a hospital gown to change in to, left the room, and returned a few minutes later.

"Okay, Robin. My name's Lacy and I'm going to have you lie on the table, so I can check to see what's going on here." She patted Robin's knee.

Bethany sat at the edge of the stiff chair in the corner, tapping her toes against the linoleum floor.

When Lacy finished, she rolled her chair back. "You're dilated to four."

Robin sat up, the blackness of her pupils eating away the pale blue of her eyes. "Isn't this too early? Can the doctor stop it?"

The nurse kept a smile plastered across her face. "Once the water breaks, the doctor doesn't like to stop the progression of labor."

That was it. She didn't elaborate or offer an explanation. Instead, she placed her hand on Robin's forearm and squeezed. "Dr. Hannigan will be here in just a minute."

Lacy snapped the rubber gloves off her wrist as she stood from her chair. She exited the room, leaving Bethany and Robin alone with their fears. Bethany searched for something to say. She pummeled through her repertoire of vocabulary but came back with empty words. Words that wouldn't help. So she kept her mouth closed, her fingers clamped over her thighs, and batted away every negative thought invading her mind. *What if?* after *what if?* flew at her like a possessed pitching machine in a batting cage, but Bethany choked up and kept swinging until the door handle clicked and Dr. Hannigan strode into the room, Lacy behind him.

He sat down in the chair by Robin's bedside as Lacy unhooked something from a machine, drew up Robin's gown, and positioned the device over her exposed skin. As soon as it made contact, that rhythmic whooshing filled the room, pushing a knot of hope into Bethany's throat. She took steadying breaths and forced her mind upon one simple fact.

The baby is fine. The baby is fine. The baby is fine…

Dr. Hannigan studied the monitor. "It looks like you are going to have this little one sooner than we expected."

Bethany wanted to argue. Robin had six more weeks to go. This couldn't be a good thing.

"Have you been having contractions?" he asked.

"Just a few." Her face scrunched up as she said it.

Bethany could tell she was having one now and there was nothing she could do to relieve Robin's pain except wait and watch. And since she didn't want to do that, she hurled her question at Dr. Hannigan. "Isn't this too early?"

"It is premature. Normally we would try to stop it. But since her water broke, we'd risk infection by delaying, and we don't want to do that." The doctor turned to Robin, who no longer twisted her face in agony. "Babies born at thirty-four weeks often do just fine."

Bethany stumbled over his choice of words. *Often*. She knew statistics. *Often* did not mean always. On the flip side of often was rarely. She didn't like the idea of their being even a rare chance of something bad happening to Robin's baby. "What's going to happen?"

"Once the baby is born, we'll have to stabilize him or her. The baby will spend some time in the NICU where we'll check to see how well the lungs are developed, if the baby develops jaundice, that sort of thing."

Underdeveloped lungs? Jaundice? These sounded like frightening things. Serious things. She kept her mouth shut for Robin's sake, who sat white-lipped and trembling in the hospital bed, the monitor releasing that muffled thumping into the air. Bethany wanted to grab a hold of that sound. She wanted to hug it to her chest and make it swear never to stop. But how was it possible to embrace a heartbeat? How was it possible to gain any sort of control over a situation so completely out of her hands?

Robin's face screwed up again. Her breaths came quick. She grasped on to her belly and twisted on the bed. Bethany looked away, her heart beating in tune with the tiny baby's. A frantic pulse demanding attention.

Dr. Hannigan turned to Lacy. "Let's get her into a labor and delivery room. I'm going to visit the NICU. I have a feeling this might go fast."

Lacy looked at Robin and nodded toward the door. "I'm just going to wheel you down the hall. We're going to keep you hooked to the monitor to make sure your baby is doing okay."

Robin gave a feeble nod and scooted out of bed. When she stood, she placed her hand under the swell of her stomach, something Bethany had seen Robin do a hundred times. But this time, Bethany couldn't handle it. She couldn't do this. She was supposed to have six more weeks. Six more weeks until the baby came. Six more weeks to renovate herself. To figure out what she wanted for her future. The baby wasn't ready for this. Bethany wasn't ready for this. And by the look on Robin's face, she wasn't ready for this either.

He doesn't often wait until we're ready.

Evan's words from earlier this evening suddenly took on a whole new meaning.

⚜

After slipping out of the delivery room, Bethany called Evan and told him to meet her in the waiting area. That was where she should go. To the waiting area. So why was she walking down the stairwell, away from neonatal?

She stopped on the second-floor landing, pushed open the heavy door, and stepped into the wide corridor. Up ahead, the reception area was empty. Soft funnels of light reflected off the counter, leaving everything else a muted shade of black or gray. Farther down the hall, a nurse exited a room and walked into another. The silence shouted for attention, commanding the hairs on her arm to stand up straight.

Without seeking permission, Bethany crept down the darkened hall-way—wondering, with each step, what she was doing. She stopped in front of the opened door of room 236. She clasped her hands and pressed them against her abdomen. She should be with Robin, holding her hand, supporting her through her labor. She should not be standing in the entryway of Fenton's hospital room, watching a sleeping man who preached a black-and-white God—where good circumstances meant favor and bad meant punishment.

But what would Fenton say now that he was the one lying in the hospital bed? Now that he was the one suffering? Now that he was the one paralyzed? She wanted to wake him up and ask him. She wanted to demand an answer. Listen to him stammer. Listen to him falter. Listen to him fail. But what good would it do? He probably couldn't even talk.

She eyed the distended veins in Fenton's hands, watched the fragile rise and fall of his chest, and the chords of anger wrapped around her soul loosened their hold, untangling themselves from the destructive knot they'd formed over the accumulating years of her childhood. In the quiet stillness of Pastor Fenton's hospital room, Bethany found herself facing a question. One that demanded an answer. Not in six weeks. But right now.

Which God would she embrace?

She gripped Pastor Fenton's God in one hand—a God who made her mother cower, a God who showed no mercy to a broken man in a wheelchair, a God Bethany spent the last sixteen years ignoring. She examined Robin's God in her other—a God who brought peace when there shouldn't be peace. A God who brought joy when there shouldn't be joy. A God who didn't leave a widowed woman alone in her grief.

Her hands trembled.

Maybe the choice should have been easy. But it wasn't. Not for her.

Robin's God frightened Bethany. Not in the way a cat frightens a mouse or an abusive parent frightens a child. But in the way space and eternity and any unknowable concept frightens a person who doesn't like not knowing. How could she accept this God-without-boundaries and remain who she was? But how could she deny the truth staring her in the face?

Her chest tightened. She stared hard at Fenton—no longer larger than life.

Taking a deep breath, Bethany peeled away one white-knuckled finger at a time. She unclenched her fist. She forced her shaking hand to spread wide. She turned her palm over. And she let go of Fenton's God.

Her eyes closed. She leaned her head against the door, and the angry chords suffocating her spirit for far too long fell loose and floated away.

Thirty-Six

Ice chips cascaded to the bottom of the bucket, spilling over one another in their rush to escape the machine. Evan pulled the bucket away from the lever and turned toward the hall, eager to get back to Robin. He wanted to step in for Micah and be there for her, but he had no idea what to do. This bucket of ice seemed like the only assistance he could offer. While she hadn't requested it, he knew from movies it was a task usually undertaken by the father-to-be, so he pounced on it with mingled relief and enthusiasm.

Where in the world was Bethany?

After her phone call, he'd hopped out of bed, threw on a pair of jeans, a wrinkled T-shirt, and a pair of sandals, and rushed to the hospital. When he reached Robin's room, he'd expected to see Bethany sitting by her side, not a nurse. The sight of Robin, grimacing against whatever invisible pain gripped her womb, caused sweat to bead against his collar. He'd never felt Micah's absence more than he had at that moment.

Evan strode down the hallway, bucket in hand, determined to fill up some of the empty space in that room. Just as he passed the elevators, the door leading to the stairwell swung open. He held up his hand to stop it from slamming in his face and fumbled with the ice just as Bethany emerged from the other side.

"Where have you been?"

"Evan." The relief and gratitude surrounding his name sent warmth throbbing to his fingertips. It clashed against the coolness of the bucket. She pressed her bangs against her forehead with a shaky hand. "I'm so glad you're here. How's she doing? How's the baby?"

"Dr. Hannigan said it's happening fast. Last time they checked, she was dilated to seven. She's really scared." Who was he kidding? "*I'm* really scared."

Bethany's fingers tightened around the strap of her purse. He recognize the determined set of her jaw, only this time she looked nothing like the cold, granite statue he'd compared her to when they first met on Dan's front porch. Admiration swelled inside him. Seven months ago, he'd wanted Bethany to go back to Chicago. To leave Robin and Dan alone. Now, he couldn't imagine supporting Micah's wife without Bethany by his side.

This time, when he reached Robin's room, there was another person inside—an older woman in scrubs. She attended to something at the other side of the room while the young nurse murmured encouraging words to his sister-in-law, who lay curled on her side, a low, pathetic moan escaping from the back of her throat. He strode to her bedside and took solace in the quick-paced tapping of the baby's heart issuing from the machine.

Robin's teeth chattered in tune with her trembling limbs. He set the bucket on the nightstand. "Why is she so cold?"

The nurse readjusted the monitor attached to Robin's belly. "The hormones are making her shake."

At the sound of his voice, Robin uncurled from her ball and searched the room with frantic eyes. "Where's Bethany?"

Bethany stepped around Evan, but before she reached the bed, Robin's mouth screwed up in a painful smile and she buried her face in the pillow. The nurse placed a gentle hand on the curve of Robin's back. "You're doing great. You're doing such a good job. Just keep breathing." But the girl's face was pinched, worried.

The sight made Evan's heart sputter.

"I'm going to get the doctor. I'll be right back," she said.

Robin's face relaxed, but the shaking did not ease. She turned her face deeper in to the pillow and muffled a weak sob. "I can't do this."

Bethany pressed her fingers against Robin's brow and stroked away the tendrils of hair sticking to her forehead. "You get to meet your baby today, Robin. That heartbeat we've been hearing, that tiny person we've seen on the screen? Today you get to hold that little one in your arms."

A lump wedged in Evan's throat.

Robin resurfaced from the pillow, her eyes an imprint of pain he'd never seen before. "I can't do this alone."

"You're not alone," Bethany said. "You have us."

Us. He loved the way that sounded.

"And you have God."

Evan brought his chin back and blinked. Had that really just come from Bethany? Robin drew in a ragged breath. "But God can't hold my hand. He can't hold my baby either."

The lump in Evan's throat doubled. What Robin said was true. God couldn't hold the baby. At least not in the way Micah could have if he were alive.

"You're right," Bethany said.

Evan shot her a look. Now was not the time to say what she was thinking.

"But He brought people into your life who can." Bethany intertwined her fingers with Robin's and squeezed. "We'll hold your hand, Robin. And we'll hold your baby too."

The truth of it crushed his chest. *She's right, God. She's absolutely right.*

But how could Evan hold Robin's hand—or her baby—if he lived in Missouri?

Robin shut her eyes. Quick puffs of air, one after another, squeezed from her lips. Dr. Hannigan rushed into the room, followed by the nurse. Both were frowning.

"Robin, honey," the nurse said, "I'm going to check to see if you're ready to push."

Robin moaned.

Evan felt as if he'd swallowed a hive full of angry bees. What was wrong? What was making the doctor frown? His eyes met Bethany's. She had noticed too.

"Okay, Robin." The nurse looked up from her splayed legs. "You're at a ten. Dr. Hannigan and I are going to need you to push every time you have a contraction."

Robin's head lolled on top of her neck, her limbs trembling against the cotton sheets.

"Robin," Dr. Hannigan said, "your baby's heart rate is lower than we'd like it to be right now. We need to get this little one out quickly."

"The baby's heart?"

Dr. Hannigan didn't hear Robin's faint question. He turned to the older woman in scrubs. "If we don't get the baby out in several pushes, we're going to do an emergency c-section."

But Bethany must have. Because she bent low and tightened her grip on Robin's hand. "Look at me, Robin. Your baby is going to be fine. Just focus on pushing. That's all you need to do right now."

The nurse grabbed a hold of Robin's right leg and motioned for Evan to do the same with her left. "Hold on tight. Let her press against your palm while she pushes."

Blood whooshed past his ears, his throat filled with a dry heat that did not match the temperature in the room. He copied the nurse. And a contraction came. It gripped Robin's body. It wrenched her face. She doubled over in the bed and did exactly what Bethany yelled for her to do.

She pushed.

Robin released Bethany's hand from its vise and fell back onto the bed. Bethany gaped at the monitor. If she could, she would have rent her heart from her chest and shared it with the frantic pulsing of the baby fighting inside Robin's womb.

Dr. Hannigan studied the monitor, tiny frowns etched across every line on his forehead. Bethany's heart stuttered over each one. She wanted to wipe them away. She wanted to reach her hands inside Robin and pull the tiny bundle out to safety. Demand the baby's heart rate to behave. But since she couldn't do that, she found herself pleading, bargaining, and begging a God she'd either ignored or disdained for the majority of her life.

Robin panted in the bed while Bethany held back a scream. Did they just have to sit and wait until another contraction came? Why couldn't she keep pushing?

Robin jerked, then sat up and bent over her splayed legs. Okay. So the wait wasn't long. Pink blotches bloomed on Robin's cheeks and spread to her forehead, until a violent shade of red painted her face and neck. She squeezed Bethany's hand, grinding her knuckles into dust. Bethany ignored the pain and urged her to squeeze harder. Push harder.

Dr. Hannigan looked at the monitor. "Keep pushing, Robin. Push hard. I can see the top of the head. Keep going. That's it."

Bethany's muscles coiled, the air in her chest billowing like flames. Any second now, the doctor would pull out a squalling child. She held her breath. Captured the hot air inside her lungs. Denied it release until she could know for sure the baby was out and alive.

Robin gulped in a loud breath. She let go of Bethany's hand and sunk onto the bed, the redness of her face ebbing away. "I can't do this. I can't..."

Lacy kept one leg in her hand and used the other to squeeze Robin's shoulder. "You're doing it, honey. A couple more good pushes and you'll get to meet your baby."

Bethany looked at the screen. Ever since the doctor said the baby's heart rate was lower than normal, she'd kept her eyes glued to the monitor. And she didn't like what she saw. Why was this happening? Why the decline? She opened her mouth. The pent up air swooshed out in a heated question directed at the doctor. "Is it supposed to be doing that?" she whispered, jerking her head toward the machine.

Dr. Hannigan turned somber eyes in her direction, the answer written on his face. No. No, of course it wasn't supposed to be doing that.

Robin's posture stiffened. She reached for Bethany's hand. Bethany sacrificed it eagerly.

"Okay, Robin," the doctor said. "I need you to push. Push as hard and as long as you can."

Robin bent over, pushing against Lacy and Evan, her entire body tense and trembling.

"The baby's head is crowning, I need you to keep pushing, Robin. Keep pushing for your baby!"

Bethany could not look away from the monitor. Stop! Stop dropping! Get the baby out! Her insides screamed. *Enough, God! No more!* She imagined falling to the ground and pounding her fists against the floor, a twenty-eight-year-old temper-tantrum. She watched Robin's face turn from pink, to red, to purple. Then from purple, to red, to pink.

No! Keep pushing!

Dr. Hannigan must have noticed the change in her posture. He shifted, almost like a jerk, and moved closer. "The head is almost all the way out. Push just a little bit more, Robin. Just a little. We need to get your baby out."

"I can't… I can't do this…" Robin's voice came out weak and breathless, her partially closed eyelids sliding farther down her eyes. "Bethy, I can't do this."

This time Bethany squeezed her hand. "Give it one last push. You have it in you, I know you do." She squeezed harder, shaking strength in to Robin's fingers. "Come on, now. Push!"

Robin screwed up her face one last time. Her body doubled over completely…and she pushed. She pushed until nothing remained of Bethany's hand but a limp rag, squeezed of all its nerves and blood. And just when Bethany thought her hand might sever from its wrist, the pushing stopped. Robin released Bethany's hand and fell back onto the bed.

A momentary silence encapsulated the room. A fraction of nothing but empty space. Bethany's heart stopped. Her lungs stopped. Everything stopped as she strained her ears, reaching out to a sound she knew should be coming. Only nothing came.

Robin lay limp in the bed. The doctor no longer told her to push. The doctor didn't pay any attention to Robin at all. Instead, he and the nurses flocked around a baby Bethany couldn't see. A baby that wasn't crying.

Bethany's heart careened into a fit, palpitating out of control, until a quick movement from the nurse burst through her panic and a sharp cry pierced the air.

A wonderful, glorious, amazing wail.

Bethany's chest collapsed against the sound.

"You have a baby boy. A healthy baby boy."

Dr. Hannigan's words washed over Bethany. Her eyes burned until they pooled and spilled with tears. She turned to Evan, his eyes wide as he watched Lacy work on the crying baby. He ran his hand through messy hair. "Micah's son. Robin, it's Micah's son."

Robin's face crumpled. She covered it with her hands.

Lacy came back with the swaddled infant, wrapped snug and warm inside a blanket with a cap over his head. Robin's tears slid down her cheeks and dripped off her chin, falling onto the precious piece of Micah resting in her arms.

Bethany stood by her side, her body flooding with awe. She devoured every wrinkle, every dimple, every feature on that baby's body, from his scrunched nose to his tiny fingers to the precious point of his chin. She marveled at his design, unable to deny a creator. A master craftsman sharing his masterpiece six weeks early, only to unravel something complete and whole and breathtakingly beautiful. Like a field of wildflowers after the long, harsh months of winter. A gift that symbolized new life. New hope. And new beginnings.

Thirty-Seven

They let Robin hold Caleb Micah Price for two minutes before taking him to the NICU. Although he was breathing on his own and weighed a healthy five pounds, three ounces, they needed to follow procedure.

Bethany sat in the hallway, giving Robin time alone to rest, giving Evan time with his family who had gathered in the waiting room, giving herself time to process her scattered thoughts. She leaned her head against the wall and closed her eyes, an aimless sense of gratitude lifting her spirit.

Watching Robin give birth to Caleb, hearing him come out screaming in all his perfection and innocence, had stroked a piece of her heart she'd only begun to acknowledge. She'd witnessed something profound. Something filled with so much more meaning than the success and recognition she'd chased over the last ten years. The birth of Caleb accomplished in minutes what she thought would take weeks, maybe months, possibly years to achieve. Seeing Caleb's tiny body emerge from her broken friend had blown away her carefully constructed façade. Bethany stood behind the crumbling structure, exposed and naked.

And with the exposure, came a deep ache for something larger than herself. Something powerful enough to hold the broken pieces of her past and the uncertainty of her future. Something that brought forth a healthy baby, despite his plummeting heart rate, despite being six weeks premature. Could Bethany embrace this something—this God of strength and tenderness, this God without boundaries—as her own?

A helpless feeling swooped inside her. Like she was free falling, only she had never agreed to jump out of the plane. She wanted to surrender. She yearned to surrender. But how could she do it without letting go? How could she give God some, without giving Him all?

She squeezed her eyes shut, the deep ache growing inside her—her need to hold on waging war with her longing to let go. She was nothing like Robin. She didn't have a simple faith. She didn't trust easily. She would always wrestle for control. How could a woman like her give her life away?

I'll never be easy, God. You might not even want me.

But the ache swelled and refused to go away. It sat on her chest, demanding attention. Despite her doubts, despite her concerns, an answer bubbled from her soul. She might not be ready. She might not know what she was doing. She might not know the steps to this particular dance. But maybe God didn't need her to know. Maybe that was the point.

She let her head drop, and with hesitancy and coiled muscles, she rolled her tears and her past and her scars and her hopes into a sacrificial offering and presented them to a God she was choosing to trust.

Take it, God. Please take it.

And He did. Not every last drop, but enough to step forward. Maybe for her, this wouldn't be a free fall into faith as much as a steady walk toward it. And maybe that was okay.

"Bethany!"

Evan appeared down the hallway, Gavin and Amanda close behind. Even from her position on the floor, she could see their excitement. Evan motioned for the pair to go in without him. When he reached her, his forehead creased. "Hey."

She tried to respond. She tried to smile or nod or say something appropriate, but her voice was stuck and her eyes welled with tears. Evan slid down the wall and sat beside her. She wanted to cover her cheeks, hide the heat that was sure to be bright red. Why was she always crying in front of this man?

His calloused hand reached over to her lap and took one of hers. "Are you okay?"

She sniffed. Wiped her face with her sleeve. What an understated word. At that moment, she was so much more than okay. She wiped her face again.

"You're kind of a mess," Evan said.

She laughed. "Thanks."

His mouth curved in to a crooked smile. "A beautiful mess, though."

Her breath caught.

He wiped a tear from her cheek with the pad of his thumb and wrapped his fingers around the back of her neck.

Goosebumps marched up her skin. They started at her ankles and raced toward her arms and neck. She didn't want him to move his hand away.

"You were amazing. The way you got Robin through that labor."

She disregarded his praise with a single shake of her head. "It wasn't me who got Robin through her labor."

Evan looked at her, through her, inside her. She wanted to ask him what he saw. What did this exposed, naked Bethany look like?

"Maybe not," he said. "But you sure helped."

"He's perfect, isn't he?"

Evan wiped another tear and let his hand drop away. He leaned against the wall and closed his eyes. "Proof that God is still good."

Bethany examined his profile. "Were you questioning that?"

He shook his head. "No, but I think Robin was." He looked at her. "And then there's you. You've done a bit more than question." Evan brought her hand below his chin and ran his thumb over her knuckles. A ripple of heat tumbled through each finger and somersaulted up her arm. "But you don't question it anymore, do you?"

Her breath came in choppy waves. "Not anymore."

"So what do we do now?" he asked.

"What do you mean?"

"What are you planning to do with the farm? With Robin and the café?"

She took back her hand. "Didn't you hear what I said in the delivery room?"

"But what about your career?"

"That's the beauty of being an architect. You can be one pretty much anywhere." Bethany clasped her hands in her lap. "I never thought I'd say this, but I think I'd like to do more projects like the café." Maybe renovation wasn't so bad after all.

Hope frayed the edges of his face. "You would stay in Peaks for Robin?"

"Not just for her."

"For Caleb?"

Bethany shrugged.

He leaned toward her. "The farm?"

She kept very still. "There's that."

He leaned closer. "Is there something else?"

"You."

"You'd stay for me?"

She nodded. "I finish what I start, remember?"

Evan closed the small gap between them, and like dipping the tip of his toe into a pool to test the waters, he brushed his lips against hers. The gentle touch filled her lungs with a sweet longing. He brought his hand to the small of her back and pressed her closer. Bethany's body ignited. She wrapped her arms around his neck, relishing the minty taste of his lips, the spicy smell of his skin, the hardness of his arms.

She wanted to melt into him. To collapse against his strong body and never pull herself away again. But they were on the hospital floor. And Evan's family was waiting for them inside Robin's room. So when Evan pulled away, she allowed herself to disentangle from his embrace.

"Wow." His husky voice filled with a desire that matched her own.

Bethany nodded. Really. There was nothing else to say.

"I'll have to tell my uncle I won't be renting that land."

"Please do."

Evan stood and pulled her up with him. "C'mon. Let's go see my youngest nephew." He brushed her lips once more with his own. Soft and sweet and much too quick. A natural after-thought to their moment on the floor. It felt comfortable and new and invigorating all at the same time.

She followed him down the hallway. Evan did not let go of her hand when they walked into the room. He held it with a charming possessiveness that made her squeeze his all the tighter. Amanda held baby Caleb in her arms while Gavin did a miniature photo shoot with his camera. Robin watched from the bed, her eyes tired, her mouth smiling, radiating an inner strength born from pain.

And although Bethany still had questions, she couldn't deny what was happening. Somehow, in the middle of Peaks, in the middle of a place she was so desperate to escape, God was making her new. He was bringing her to life.

Slowly and surely.

Like a master architect renovating a worn-out building. One with stubborn mold and crumbling brick and broken windows. The renovation wouldn't happen overnight. It would take time. And through it, she would have to trust. To keep surrendering. As many times at it would take. It might not be an easy path, but it sure was a beautiful one.

Amanda passed the tiny bundle to an awe-struck Evan, and as Bethany gazed at this perfect, new life swaddled in his arms, her heart flooded with joy.

Epilogue

T wo days later, Robin came home. Two days after that, they cele-
brated the arrival of Caleb Micah Price. They gathered around the
small boy. They joined hands. And Evan prayed over him. He prayed for
health. He prayed for love and patience and wisdom and every other single
thing a parent prays for their children. And then he asked God to relay a
message to his brother. That baby Caleb would be well taken care of on this
side of heaven. That he would grow up knowing what a good man his father
was.

Six weeks after Caleb's birth, on Micah's birthday, Bethany and a re-
covering Robin opened the front doors of Willow Tree Café. Drawn in by
curiosity and a complimentary cup of gourmet coffee, the residents of Peaks
gathered to celebrate the grand opening. And Bethany's mother was among
the crowd. She sat alone at one of the tables—sans Pastor Fenton, who had
been moved to a nursing home the week before—sipping on a free mocha.
She didn't talk to anyone. But when Robin sat down at the piano, a hint of
a smile graced Ruth's lips.

When Robin finished, everybody in the café clapped, cooed over Caleb, and congratulated them on such a fine establishment. Bethany deferred
the congratulations to her tired friend and a twinge of worry pinched her
chest. She didn't know how Robin would cope as a single mother. She didn't

know how long it would take for the loneliness in her friend's eyes to fade away. She didn't know if these people would come back when the coffee wasn't free. She only knew that right then, the café was a success, and when Robin looked at her son, she smiled.

Bethany closed her eyes and let the moment wash over her.

Somehow, over the course of building the café, she let the sweat and planning and vision sneak into her soul and take root. Just like the farm when she was a small child. Just like Robin so many years ago. Just like Evan since her return to Peaks. And just like Caleb as soon as she saw his blip of a heartbeat on the ultrasound screen.

She looked down at him—sleeping in his car seat, lips puckered as he nursed in his dreams. This place—the town she'd worked so hard to hate, to ignore, to push aside—had brought her to the girl she used to be before everything fell apart and reconciled her with the woman she'd become since she left. Peaks—in all her attempts to get away—held on tight and refused to let go.

Bethany smiled and leaned in to Evan. He wrapped his arm around her waist and squeezed.

ACKNOWLEDGMENTS

I don't know about you, but this has always been my first stop whenever I buy a new book. Maybe it's because I'm a writer. Maybe it's because I've always dreamed of writing one of my own. Or maybe it's because I know dreams are never reached alone and I long to say thank you.

So thank you. From the bottom of my heart. To everyone who has been a part of this journey. Without all of you, this dream would be nothing but a dream.

Thank you, thank you, thank you…

To Jenny, Grandma Pfau, Holly, and Erin, for being my faithful pre-publication readers. Your belief in my stories carried me through the long waits and all kinds of doubt.

To Ms. Alli Schurr, for answering my random farming questions while waiting for the bus, and Matt and Heidi, for giving me a tour of your farm so I could bring Grandpa Dan's to life.

To everyone at Waterbrook Multnomah, for giving me such an amazing experience as a debut novelist and for the hard work you've put in to this book. You are all amazing!

To Shannon, Jen, and Lissa, for your dedication to this story and for pushing me to make it the best it could be. Even when I wanted to chuck it out the window. I am convinced I have the best editors on the planet.

To Rachelle, for turning my dream into a reality. There's nobody else I'd rather have in my corner. You are truly a dream agent.

To Jeannie and Erica, my amazing critique partners, for seeing something in this project when it was all kinds of ugly.

To Mom, Dad, and Peggy, for listening so attentively to my stories when I was a little girl. It would have been so easy to laugh. But you never did. Even when I read with an accent.

To Melissa and Susan, for not only reading my books but for making this ride so ridiculously fun. I'll never forget how much you screamed and jumped around with me when I told you I was getting published. There aren't words to express how deeply grateful I am for both of you.

To Ryan, for your unending support. To you, it was never *if* I got published, but *when*. God couldn't have given me a more perfect husband.

To my readers, for taking part in Bethany and Evan's story. I hope you return to Peaks to continue Robin's in *Wishing on Willows*. You are the reason I write.

And to Jesus, for taking me on a journey that keeps me so humble, so dependent, so in awe. Who am I that You would give me the desires of my heart? Who am I?